The Three Mystic Heirs

THE ROSE KNIGHT'S CRUCIFIXION #1

Being a Novel of Historical Adventure

and a Romance of Ideas

Strangely Contiguous to

Dumas's *The Three Musketeers*

LAWRENCE ELLSWORTH

A WORD TO THE FORE

The Rose Knight's Crucifixion: A Novel of Historical Adventure and a Romance of Ideas stands on its own, but it's also a parallel novel to Alexandre Dumas's *The Three Musketeers.* It shares certain characters and plot elements with Dumas's classic work, the story of Louis d'Astarac interweaving with that of d'Artagnan, Athos, Porthos, and Aramis.

Here's how it works: *The Three Musketeers* has 67 chapters, and so does *The Rose Knight's Crucifixion,* though the latter is published in two parts, the first 29 chapters as *The Three Mystic Heirs,* and the final 38 in *The Three Monks of Tears.* You could read *Musketeers* and *Crucifixion* separately, simply enjoying the correspondences between the two works, or you could read them interleaved: chapter one of *Musketeers* followed by chapter one of *Crucifixion,* then back to *Musketeers* for chapter two, and so forth. Crazy!

If you do intend to read (or re-read) *The Three Musketeers,* then I recommend my own recent translation of Dumas's most famous novel, published by Pegasus Books of New York and London. It's a sparkling new translation for the contemporary reader, and I think you'd enjoy it.

Table of Contents

CHARACTERS

An **asterisk*** indicates a person recorded in history.

The Vicomte de Fontrailles and Associates

Louis d'Astarac, Vicomte de **Fontrailles***: A young nobleman of Armagnac.

Vidou: His valet.

René des **Cartes***: A scholar.

Jean Reynon, known as **Cocodril**: A rogue.

Gitane: A smuggler.

Beaune: A jailer and inquisitor.

Sobriety **Breedlove**: An English sailor.

Nobility of France

Philippe de **Longvilliers**, *Seigneur de Poincy**: A Commander of the French Priory of the Knights of Malta.

Seigneur **de Bonnefont**: A nobleman of Armagnac.

Isabeau *de Bonnefont*: His daughter.

Éric *de Gimous*: A young nobleman of Armagnac.

Nobility of England

Lucy Percy Hay, Countess of **Carlisle***: A lady of the English Court.

George Villiers, Duke of **Buckingham***: Prime Minister of King Charles I.

Sir Percy **Blakeney**, *also known as "Diogenes"*: Amateur intelligencer for His Grace the Duke.

Enfield: Blakeney's valet.

Balthasar **Gerbier***: The duke's art agent and envoy.

Doctor John **Lambe***: The duke's astrologer and alchemist.

King's Musketeers and Comrades

Aramis: A musketeer, formerly trained as a priest.

Bazin: His valet.

Athos: A noble musketeer.

Porthos: A vainglorious musketeer.

*The Chevalier **d'Artagnan***: A Gascon guardsman, later a musketeer.

Planchet: His lackey.

The Cardinal and His Fidèles

*Armand-Jean du Plessis, Cardinal de **Richelieu***: Prime Minister of King Louis XIII.

*François Leclerc du Tremblay, known as **Father Joseph***: A Capuchin monk, intimate of Richelieu and head of his intelligence service.

*Comte de **Rochefort***: A cavalier, an agent of His Eminence the Cardinal.

*Lady Clarice, Countess Winter, known as **Milady de Winter***: A lady of the French and English Courts, and an agent of His Eminence.

*François d'Ogier, Sieur de **Cavois***: Captain of the Cardinal's Guard.

*Jean de Baradat, Sieur de **Cahusac***: A Cardinal's Guard.

*Claude de **Jussac***: A Cardinal's Guard.

Bernajoux: A Cardinal's Guard.

*Marin **Boisloré***: Agent of Richelieu in England, an officer in the household of Queen Henriette.

The Society of Jesus

*Athanasius **Kircher***: A Jesuit scholar of Mainz, in Germany.

*Jean-Marie Crozat, known as Père **Mikmaq***: A Jesuit priest, recently recalled from the New World.

With the exception of *The Three Mystical Heirs of Christian Rosencreutz*, all published works mentioned in this book are historical.

CHAPTER I
THE THREE MYSTIC HEIRS

René des Cartes picked his way across the shattered laboratory, stepping carefully between the piles of broken glass and crushed crockery. This was the first of Hradčany Castle's series of *wunderkammern,* or wonder-chambers, but as in the art galleries he'd already passed through, this room had been thoroughly looted and vandalized. Everything breakable in the alchemical kitchen had been smashed: alembics, retorts, beakers, and carboys lay in countless fragments between the overturned tables, among drifts of rare earths, dried herbs, and the desiccated organs of exotic animals.

A scream of terror, a woman's scream, drew des Cartes to a window in the thick outer wall of the keep. From the deep embrasure he could see down into a courtyard two stories below where a half-dozen Walloon mercenaries had found the hiding place of one of the deposed queen's chambermaids. Surrounded by laughing soldiers, she reeled shrieking from one side of the circle to the other, then kicked a drunken halberdier between the legs. The man fell, cursing, and the chambermaid dashed through the gap, disappearing into the lower halls. The drunken Walloons tried to follow, blundered into each other, and fell in a heap before the doorway. Des Cartes, sourly pleased that he didn't have to go down to her aid, shook his head and turned away, back into the plundered castle of the King of Bohemia. He had important business within.

The day before had been November 8, 1620, and on the heights of the White Mountain outside Prague, the Protestant forces defending the capital of Bohemia against the invading Catholic army of the Hapsburgs had been utterly defeated in a sudden and decisive battle. Young Lieutenant René des Cartes, attached to the staff of the Comte de Bucquoy of the Catholic army, had watched the battle unfold from the crest of a nearby hill. In less than an hour the army of Frederick V, Elector Palatine and King of Bohemia, the great hope of Protestant Germany, had been shattered and dispersed. The remnants retreated behind the walls of Prague, but by midnight Frederick and the royal family had abandoned the city, taking only what they could carry—and the burghers of Prague, in hopes of clemency, had flung open their gates to the troops of the Holy Roman Emperor.

Des Cartes hadn't been involved in the actual fighting—but then, he hadn't come to Bohemia to fight. Though technically a soldier in the Imperial army, des Cartes's sole reason for being in the Germanies had been to find the mysterious Brotherhood of the Rosicrucians (if they really existed) and learn what they knew (if they really knew anything).

What he had found over the last year and a half of travel had been less a secret society than a loose-knit web of philosophers and unorthodox thinkers, wary men who would not speak all their thoughts or tell all they knew. But what they did say had led des Cartes to reconsider everything he had been taught at the Jesuit college of La Flêche, to question everything he thought he knew about the human mind, body, and soul. After one particularly challenging conversation in Ulm almost exactly a year earlier, a series of vivid dreams in an overheated room had impelled him to a decision: he would devote his life to the study of the mystery of the intellect, the very nature of mind.

What could the mind really know? How did the immaterial soul interact with the material world?

How much of God was there in man? And how close could man approach to God?

His quest for answers had led him to this hill above the ancient city of Prague where squatted the rambling castle of the kings of Bohemia.

Within the great keep, des Cartes stepped gingerly into the next *wunderkammer*, the chamber devoted to astronomy. His dwindling hopes that the looting and destruction had been confined to the outer circles of the castle were dashed: shredded paper was everywhere, and the astronomical tools had been smashed or carried off. The famous suite of instruments hand-built by Tycho Brahe and employed by Kepler to confirm his groundbreaking theories—the nineteen-foot quadrant, the equatorial armillae, the five-foot celestial globe—were in fragments on the Italian tiled floor.

In one corner, snoring loudly and half-covered by a torn map of the heavens, was a sleeping soldier, by the look of him a Pole or Cossack from one of Tilly's mercenary battalions. He had an empty bottle in one hand, but a sword in the other, so des Cartes stepped quietly past him, hand on the hilt of his own sword. Though as a student des Cartes had been so fascinated by the art and science of fencing that he'd written a small treatise on the subject, he had never drawn his weapon in a serious fight and had no intention of starting now if he could avoid it. After the carnage he'd seen in the last two days, he'd lost all personal interest in the applied science of warfare.

Des Cartes cautiously pushed open the heavy oaken door to the next room, and there it was: the final chamber of wonders, the renowned library of King Frederick. And not just of Frederick, but of his predecessor Rudolf II, who'd been a patron of the esoteric, and had played host to such Renaissance luminaries as Giordano Bruno and Doctor John Dee. Like the previous chambers, the library had been vandalized, but at first glance the damage looked no more than superficial. Des Cartes carefully closed the door behind him, wiped his sweating hands on his breeches—*I'm nervous,* he noted to himself, *how interesting*—and got down to work.

Some time later—an hour? Two hours?—a commotion out in the astronomical chamber caused des Cartes to look up distractedly from the book he'd been poring over. From outside there was a thump and a howl of outrage, then a gruff, authoritative, and very French voice said loudly, "Get up, you lazy swine, and return to your company. I mean *now.*" This was followed by the scuffling sound of Polish (or possibly Cossack) groveling.

Heavy footsteps approached across the outer room. Des Cartes quickly but carefully slid his book onto a shelf beneath a pile of maps of Moravia, then grabbed and opened a manuscript copy of William Gilbert's study of magnetism, just as the door to the library thudded open. In stepped an Imperial knight, in full plate armor polished till it shone like silver. He positively *gleamed,* with no evidence whatsoever of besmirching by mud, black gunpowder smoke, horse spit, or blood. He seemed not only to reflect light, but to be the actual source of every ray of light in the room. *Though that's optically absurd,* des Cartes thought. *Nice trick, though. I wonder how it's done.*

The knight strode heavily forward, towering over the scholar. The face beneath the visor was at least ten years older than des Cartes's age of twenty-four, and strikingly handsome, heart-shaped with a hawk-sharp nose, beneath a pair of dark eyes, narrowed now in irritation. "And who, Monsieur," said the knight, "are *you?*"

Des Cartes set aside the manuscript, stood up from his stool, and bowed. "Lieutenant des Cartes, attached to the Comte de Bucquoy, at your service."

"Well, Lieutenant des Cartes, are you aware that whatever you were reading may be heretical, and that this library is now under the interdiction of the Church?"

Des Cartes blinked. "Ah. No, I was not aware of that… Monseigneur." Best to be safe and accord this fellow the title due to higher rank. Now, should he be prudent, and show this officious knight the treasure he'd discovered?

No. Des Cartes assumed an expression of inoffensive deference and said, "Unfortunately, I'm afraid Monseigneur is wasting his time. I've taken a quick survey of the entire library, and haven't found a single volume that's the least bit controversial."

The knight's face fell, and suddenly the warrior of God was a mere disappointed soldier. "Really? Nothing at *all*?"

Best to give him something. "No… however, I believe I *can* show you where they were."

"How's that?"

"Follow me, Monseigneur… what was the name?"

"Your pardon. I am Philippe de Longvilliers, of the Knights of Malta."

Des Cartes had heard of him—a captain on Bucquoy's staff, a rising star of the French Grand Priory of the Knights Hospitaller, or Knights of Malta. He was mainly known as a naval commander, and there had been some speculation among the other officers as to what he was doing on such an inland campaign. He was said to be devout, and to have fallen under the influence of the Society of Jesus. No wonder he was so eager to find the Winter King's "heretical" books: the Jesuits, at the forefront of the Counter-Reformation, would want to see all such works sequestered or destroyed.

"You said you had something to show me?" Longvilliers said impatiently.

Des Cartes led the knight, clanking in his heavy armor, to the rows of shelves at the far end of the library. He indicated two floor-to-ceiling shelves that jutted from the back wall, which was lined with more shelves, all stacked with assorted volumes devoted to botany and horticulture. "Here. What do you see?"

"Nothing," said Longvilliers, baffled. "Nothing but books about plants and such."

"That's all I saw at first. Then I realized that the inner sides of these shelves on the left and right looked somewhat shorter than the outer sides, and that the back wall seemed closer. I measured them, discovered I was right … and then found this."

Des Cartes reached under one of the lower shelves on the back wall, unhooked a latch, and pulled on the shelf front. The entire back wall between the shelves swung open, pivoting toward him on hidden hinges. Behind was a shallow alcove, lined with more bookshelves. Empty bookshelves.

"But there's nothing here!" said Longvilliers.

"Exactly. All of the library's books on esoterica and the occult have been spirited away, probably last night."

"How do you know that's what was on these shelves?"

"Because whoever took them was in such a hurry that he ripped the spine on one book and didn't notice that he'd left this behind." Des Cartes drew a small torn piece of dark leather from his sleeve and handed it to Longvilliers.

"The Three Mystical Heirs of Christian Rosencreutz," the knight read from the gilt letters stamped on the leather. "But that's the book I was particularly told to look for! It's said to reveal the innermost secrets of the Rosicrucians."

Des Cartes nodded grimly. "Maddening, isn't it? *The Three Mystic Heirs,* written by Johannes Andreaeus and printed in a very limited edition last year in Oppenheim by De Bry. The entire print run was thought to have been destroyed when Spinola's Imperial troops sacked the Palatinate—all except the presentation copy given to Frederick, the Elector of Palatine, who'd already left the Palatinate to assume the throne of Bohemia. Now that copy is gone, and who knows where?"

"And why were *you* looking for it, Monsieur?" demanded Longvilliers, suddenly suspicious.

"Oh—for reasons much like yours, no doubt. After all, I'm a good Catholic. And ideas," des Cartes said, "can be dangerous."

"You're right about that," said Longvilliers, "and whoever's taken that book is in mortal peril, body and soul. As he'll learn, when I find him."

He turned with a clink of spurs to survey the books on the remaining shelves, handsome lips pursed in distaste. After a few minutes of pretending to search the rest of the library, the knight declared that there was nothing more to be gained here, and they would leave. Des Cartes followed him to the lower level of the keep as far as the grand audience chamber, where he paused, stooping to tie the laces of his knee-breeches. The knight continued on his way; once he was safely out of sight, des Cartes straightened, listened for a few moments, then slipped back upstairs.

Returning to the library, he drew a slim folio from beneath the maps of Moravia. Before slipping it under his cloak he opened its plain buff board cover for one last glance at the ornate letters on the title page—*The Three Mystical Heirs of Christian Rosencreutz*—and the scrawl beneath it: *author's page proof.*

CHAPTER II
THE BEDCHAMBER OF MONSIEUR
DE FONTRAILLES

Louis d'Astarac, the young Vicomte de Fontrailles, stood in his bedchamber, in front of the small table that he wryly thought of as his "vanity," and regarded himself in the mirror above it, moving slightly to avoid the wavy lines in the imperfect glass. *Could be worse,* he thought. *I suppose. Somehow.*

"Let's not dwell on the imperfections of the flesh," he said aloud. "What is the body, after all? Mere dross. Let's reckon the higher qualities: everyone says those are the things that really matter to a woman.

"*Primus.*" He raised his thumb. "I am the Vicomte de Fontrailles, nobleman of France, lord and master of my own domain, tiny though it may be. Thanks to my vineyards, I'm better off than most of my neighbors.

"*Secundus.*" Beside his thumb he raised his forefinger—but he couldn't quite straighten it: never could. He winced, and continued: "I am a man of culture and refinement. I have studied in Paris, I've been to Court, heard lectures at the Sorbonne and seen a royal ballet at the Louvre. I can compliment a woman's eyes in five languages. I clean my teeth, chew mint, and wash every week.

"*Tertius.*" He started to raise his middle finger, but it was even more crooked than the forefinger. He gave up. "Anyway. I am pure of heart and noble of soul, with an innate goodness and dignity that radiate from within and suffuse my person and personality … well, at least *I* can see it, even if no one else can."

He squinted at the mirror, but his person seemed suffused by no particular radiance, despite his splendid clothes and careful grooming. All were overshadowed by his hunched back, which rose behind him higher than his head. The fine lace and linen of his shirt and hose only emphasized his twisted limbs, and his features were gnomish at best. "Gnomish," he said. "It's better than *monstrous,* say, or *repellent.* 'My darling Isabeau, I know my features are somewhat gnomish, but…' No, forget it." He shook his head, and his brown, carefully-curled hair, which would have been shoulder-length on another man, waved beneath his chin. "The higher qualities, stick to the higher qualities! Keep it elevated!"

There was a knock at the door. Louis said "*Entrez,*" and the door opened to admit the tall, angular form of Lapeyre, his chamberlain, who was also his general factotum and man-of-business.

Lapeyre bowed and said, "We have a visitor, Monseigneur—a man named Monsieur Gerbier. I think he's a foreigner. At any rate, he's certainly not from Armagnac."

Louis reluctantly set aside his thoughts of Isabeau de Bonnefont and focused his attention on Lapeyre. "Gerbier. No, I don't know the name. Did he say what his business was?"

"No, Monseigneur. What shall I tell him?"

"I'll see him, but inform monsieur, with my regrets, that I haven't much time to give him this morning. And send in Vidou to help me finish dressing."

Old Vidou came in, reverently bearing the viscount's best outfit, a doublet, breeches, and half-cloak of dark amber silk, richly embroidered. Fontrailles had last worn it over two years ago, when he'd returned from Paris to assume the viscounty after the sudden deaths from fever of his father and elder brother. It had lain in a chest since then, but Vidou had tenderly pressed out all the creases and restored the garments to their full glory. Vidou wasn't very bright, but Fontrailles prized him because he was dependable, he knew where everything was at all times, and he took far better care of Fontrailles's personal things than he himself would have.

However, Vidou did have a habit of muttering his thoughts under his breath. For Fontrailles, this was amusing at some times, and irritating at others. "We must look our absolute best today, Vidou," he said. "I'm paying a very important call on Mademoiselle de Bonnefont."

"Just setting himself up for a fall, he is," Vidou muttered, helping Fontrailles wriggle the tight-fitting doublet up over the hump on his back. "I prayed to the Good Lord he wouldn't do this. Just wasting my time, as usual."

This was definitely more irritating than amusing. "Quickly, please, Vidou," said Fontrailles. "I haven't got all morning. There's a visitor waiting for me below."

The *grande salle* of the Château de Fontrailles wasn't really all that grand, but Fontrailles was pleased with the way he'd had it renovated, widening the windows to admit more light, laying a parquet floor, and having the stone walls plastered, painted, and papered in warm reds and golds. He thought it compared well with the salons he'd seen in Paris, and he was particularly proud of his cabinet of Italian miniature cameos. His visitor was inspecting them with a connoisseur's eye when Fontrailles entered the hall from the stairwell.

"Monsieur Gerbier? I am the Vicomte de Fontrailles." Louis introduced himself by title rather than by name, for though his name was *who* he was, his title was *what* he was—and as a nobleman that was far more important. "What do you think of my little collection?"

His visitor, a large man dressed in a handsome but travel-stained outfit of green velour, turned toward his host. Louis saw him experience the usual jolt at his physical appearance, though his guest was sufficiently well bred to show it by no more than a slight widening of the eyes and the flicker of an eyebrow. At least he didn't scream and run away, as some children had.

"Ah, Monsieur le Vicomte. How very good of you to see me in this sudden fashion," the man said, in a deep voice with a slight Flemish accent. He bowed. "My name, if you will permit me to introduce myself, is Balthasar Gerbier, and I must say your collection of cameos is impressive indeed. Though not extensive, it reflects both excellent taste and an impressive familiarity with the subject. Who is your art agent, if I may make so bold as to ask?"

Fontrailles smiled, which sent another flicker across Gerbier's face. Fontrailles's smile could be rather alarming. "Having a personal buyer is somewhat beyond my rather humble means," he said. "I perform that function myself."

"Then I redouble my congratulations, for you perform it admirably," Gerbier said pompously. "I speak from experience, as I myself am an art acquisition agent. In fact, it is in that capacity that I have taken the liberty of calling on you."

He didn't look like any art agent Fontrailles had ever met. The man's wardrobe was entirely too fine, and he wore too many jewels—all real, if Louis could trust his eye for such things. A glance out the window into the courtyard showed him an excellent English horse, chestnut in color, with a liveried manservant holding the reins. Another servant stood nearby with a pair of matched riding mules.

It didn't add up. "I'm afraid I don't quite understand, Monsieur Gerbier," Fontrailles said, "and unfortunately, I happen to be pressed for time this morning. How may I help you?"

Gerbier bowed slightly. "Then in the interest of time, I will dispense with the preliminaries and come to the point. I understand that you have assembled a modest collection of miniature automata built by the Rosicrucian mechanist Salomon de Caus. I represent a collector who is interested in buying them—along with any related paraphernalia, such as Rosy Cross pamphlets or volumes. My patron is a collector in the broadest sense of the term."

"Ah," said Fontrailles. He did have a few items of that sort, though it was an interest he no longer pursued. "Might I ask your patron's name?"

"It's probably not in my interest to tell you, since everyone knows how deep his pockets are, but," Gerbier winked at him, "I'll tell you anyway—in strictest confidence, of course."

"But of course."

"I represent His Grace the Duke of Buckingham," Gerbier said.

Well. That explains the horse, and the gems, Louis thought. *But it doesn't explain much else.* He said, "And you came to the far hills of Armagnac, all the way from England to the south of France, just to buy my de Caus clockwork mechanisms?"

"Yes. And related paraphernalia." Gerbier smiled blandly.

This wasn't ringing true. The man must think him some kind of back-country rustic. Unfortunately, Louis didn't have time at the moment to unravel his game, whatever it was. He glanced at the water-clock in the corner and frowned—which was nearly as alarming as his smile—and said, "I'm very sorry, Monsieur Gerbier, but I fear we must continue our conversation at another time. Will tomorrow morning be convenient?"

"As you like, Monsieur le Vicomte," said Gerbier, who didn't seem the least bit put out. "It's my own fault for dropping in unannounced. I'll take a room at that inn in the village, and call upon you first thing tomorrow morning."

"Perfect," Fontrailles said. "Till tomorrow, then."

"Till tomorrow, Monsieur." Gerbier bowed again, and took his leave.

"A satisfactory meeting, Monseigneur?" said Lapeyre, appearing from somewhere.

"Hardly that." Fontrailles shook his head. "It was strange, but I've no time to get to the bottom of it right now. Are the men and the horses ready?"

"Yes, Monseigneur. Everything is prepared."

"I'm sure it is, Lapeyre. I can always count on you. All right, then." Fontrailles took a deep breath. "Wish me luck."

"With all my heart, Monseigneur."

In that spring of 1626 Mademoiselle Isabeau de Bonnefont was twenty years old, the same age as Louis d'Astarac. The Seigneur de Bonnefont and

Louis's father, the elder Vicomte de Fontrailles, had been friends, and their children had grown up playing together in each other's houses, despite the fact that the Fontrailles family were Catholics and the Bonnefonts were Protestants—Huguenots, as they were called in France. As children, Isabeau and Louis had been especially close, and Louis had watched the pretty girl grow into a beautiful woman: petite and lively, flowing hair night-dark, eyes large and deep brown, above a small sharp nose and a broad mouth whose lips were usually curved in a smile. And the mind behind the lovely face had grown sharp and perceptive as well.

Louis's own mind was, if anything, even sharper, but as he matured his hunched back had become more prominent, and he had grown ever more bowed, bent, and stunted. Though he did have one other good friend, a younger boy named Éric de Gimous, it was only into Isabeau's sympathetic ear that Louis had confessed the pains of his condition, physical and otherwise. In the worst times, he had always been able to draw on the knowledge that there was at least one other person who understood.

Isabeau and Louis had been separated when, at age twelve, he'd been sent to Paris to study in the Oratorian seminary to prepare for a life in the Church. Louis had an elder brother, Bertrand, who would inherit the title when his father died, and there was no real place for a second son on the small estate of Fontrailles; Louis would have to make his way elsewhere in the world. His physical deformity ruled out the pursuit of arms, the usual recourse of second sons of the nobility, but the priesthood seemed a natural choice for a boy as bookish and articulate as Louis. So his father had decreed.

Louis didn't share his father's opinion of his prospects; he saw himself more as a diplomat or a courtier than a churchman. It was true that he had passed through a period of intense interest in the Church when he'd thought he might find solace in religion for the burden of his physical defects. For a while, he'd been a virtual shadow to Père Roland, Fontrailles's curate, and had pored over every pious volume in the man's modest library. This had undoubtedly contributed to his father's thinking, though by the time the old viscount had made the decision to send his son to seminary, Louis's religious zeal had faded. However, he would have jumped at any opportunity to go to Paris, which seemed to him the center of the world.

His only regret was leaving behind his friends, Éric and Isabeau. Éric, from another family of Huguenots, was a dark, slim boy who loved poetry. He looked up to Louis because the elder boy knew so many poems by heart and was such a good chess-player, and Éric had been a good friend. But it was Isabeau, merry Isabeau, who had always seemed to know what Louis thought and felt, and it was Isabeau he would miss the most. He wrote to them often, especially to Isabeau—and occasionally, she even wrote back.

In hindsight, it shouldn't have come as a surprise when he received word that his brother Bertrand had begun courting her. Isabeau de Bonnefont was by far the most eligible demoiselle in their part of the province, and both fathers could be counted on to approve the match.

Still, Louis could never quite see his sprightly, quick-witted Isabeau as a mate to the stolid, rather boorish Bertrand. It was an unexpectedly brutal blow when the letter arrived announcing their betrothal. It made Louis realize consciously, for the first time, how deeply he was in love with her.

Then the purple fever had stalked through Armagnac, taking both Louis's father and brother, and everything had changed. Suddenly Louis was the Vicomte de Fontrailles, and Isabeau was no longer his elder brother's fiancée. When he saw, on his return to Armagnac, the woman she'd become, he lost his heart completely. Still, he'd waited a year before he began, tentatively, to court her, and another year before deciding to declare his intentions. But here he was, at last, sending his herald ahead to the gates of the Château de Bonnefont to announce that the Vicomte de Fontrailles had come to pay a formal visit to the seigneur.

Actually, the herald was only Vidou, dressed up in livery that Fontrailles had ordered from Toulouse, and he was beating a drum because he didn't know how to blow a horn. Still, Louis thought, it was not ineffective. He himself was mounted on a fine Spanish stallion that had cost more than he cared to think about, and was followed by six men-at-arms, also mounted— though the last two were on farm-horses. Fontrailles had checked with

Lapeyre: when Bertrand had come to demand Mademoiselle's hand, he'd been accompanied by only four men-at-arms ... and no herald.

They were not unexpected. The Seigneur de Bonnefont, still hale at age fifty, was dressed in the best outfit he could muster, though it dated from the heyday of the previous reign. He welcomed Fontrailles and listened with an appropriately serious expression to the viscount's formal declaration of intent to marry his daughter. De Bonnefont rendered the correct formal acknowledgement, then unbent a little and said, "You're well aware, Viscount, that after the death of my lady wife, I promised Isabeau that she should have the deciding of when and whom to wed." He smiled and said, "She awaits you in the orangery."

Isabeau was alone in the small conservatory, her mother's modern addition to the frowning medieval donjon, sitting in a bower under the potted orange trees that were her special care since her mother's death. She wore the deep red satin dress that Fontrailles knew was her favorite, as it was his. It rustled as she rose to greet him.

He walked carefully up to her, trying to control his breath, and held out his hands; she gave him her own, and he clasped them lightly in his. Her dark amber eyes glistened as he gazed into them, then she looked down with a smile Louis thought almost sad.

"Hello, Louis," she said, in her rich contralto. "I hope you're not going to make a formal speech."

He bowed. "I don't think we need them, do we," he said, "between us?"

"Never," she said.

"You know why I'm here." He released her hands, timidly reached forward with one finger, then lifted her chin gently so he could once again see her eyes.

"I do," she said, with a slight hitch in her voice.

He swallowed, twice. "Then ... will you marry me, Isabeau? Will you be my Vicomtesse de Fontrailles?"

She turned away, looked out across the fields toward the slopes of Mont d'Astarac, Louis's namesake, clad for a few short weeks in its spring coat of green. Her hands twisted slowly over themselves.

Still facing away from him, she said, "Louis … I can't."

He felt the blood drain from his face. "You don't mean that, Isabeau. We're … we're two halves of a pair." He couldn't keep the tremor out of his voice.

"No, Louis. We aren't. Oh, please don't make this terrible!" She turned back to him. Tears coursed down her cheeks.

"But … but, dearest Isabeau … why…?"

"Don't! Don't," she cried. Then, in a whisper: "Don't make me say it, Louis. Please. Please, Louis."

He slumped in on himself, dropped his eyes to the tile floor. He couldn't talk. Where were his wits? His silken doublet suddenly seemed confining, constricting, as if his hunched back wanted to burst out of it. He took a deep breath—another—and then looked up.

"Very well, Isa … Mademoiselle," he said, voice shaking. "I have too high a regard for you to want to cause you any distress. As I think you know well. I thank you for receiving me personally, and deeply regret having placed you in an awkward situation."

"Oh, Louis! Louis!" she sobbed, but he had already turned on his heel. Forcing himself as erect as he could manage, he walked stiffly out the door.

The Seigneur de Bonnefont, expression carefully neutral, was waiting in his entry hall so Louis could formally take his leave—accompanied, Louis saw with irritation, by his old friend Éric de Gimous, emanating sympathy and compassion like a dense perfume. Apparently Éric already knew what Isabeau's answer would be—but much as Louis liked Éric, the last thing he wanted just then was consolation.

After Fontrailles had bowed to de Bonnefont and thanked him for receiving him, Éric, with a devastated look on his slim, mobile face, stepped forward and said softly, "Louis, I'm so sorry. Of course, I've never lost my heart, but I know what Ronsard wrote about 'the enduring pain of aching love.'"

Éric wasn't tall, but Louis still had to look up to meet his gaze. "Well, that certainly makes me feel better," he growled. "Ronsard also wrote 'love in song grows tedious.'"

Éric blinked, shut his mouth, and took a step back. Louis was immediately sorry he'd said it, but he was in no mood to apologize, and simply put his head down and marched out the door.

Vidou, looking crestfallen, and the rest of Fontrailles's entourage were waiting in the courtyard. It seemed *everyone* already knew that Isabeau would refuse him. "Stabs my heart, it does, to see poor Master smote down this way," Vidou muttered. "Not that but he should of known it beforehand."

Vidou, a herald no more, held the stirrup as Fontrailles mounted laboriously into the saddle of his fine Spanish stallion. Louis adjusted the half-cape on his shoulder, took up the reins, and turned his horse toward the gate. "Lead on, Vidou—home to Fontrailles," he said, in control of himself again, at least physically. "When we arrive, set the table in the upper dining room. For one."

CHAPTER III
THE *ANDREAEUS*

Louis d'Astarac awoke slowly. Even before he opened his eyes he knew he was going to have a hangover the size of all Armagnac. Every heartbeat was like a mallet-blow to his head, and it seemed something awful had crawled into his mouth and died there.

The right side of his face was lying on what felt like the top of his writing desk. Gingerly, he opened his left eye, winced at the light, and then winced from the pain of wincing.

It was broad daylight, and a sunbeam, piercing his study window, blazed with malice aforethought on the desktop, right in front of his face. The light glinted from the foot of his wine-goblet and shone viciously from three bright white grains of something-or-other spilled near it.

The sight of the wine-goblet brought back last night's effort to drown himself in the product of his own vineyards—and the reason for it. Isabeau had refused him. Louis closed his eye. There was nothing worth looking at.

Or was there? He tried to think through the pounding, to remember. As he'd drained glass after glass, he'd been cursing his crooked spine and the fate that had made him a hunchbacked monster, certain that if he'd been made like a normal man Isabeau would be his. But he was no more than a distorted parody of a man, and no matter what else he did or became, he would still and always be a monster. Even that pompous ass Gerbier, an art agent who should be trained to view everything with a coldly objective eye, even he had been repelled by the sight of him.

Gerbier. He'd said he'd come to buy Fontrailles's collection of de Caus clockwork automata and other Rosicrucian-type materials. It had brought to mind the Great Paris Rosicrucian Scare, back in '23, when Louis had first gotten interested in the mysterious Brotherhood of the Rosy Cross. One day, during Louis's final year at the Oratorian seminary, Paris had awakened to find placards posted all over the city in prominent places. "We, the deputies of the College of the Brothers of the Rose Cross, are visiting this city, both visibly and invisibly," they read. "Through the Grace of the Most High, towards whom turn the hearts of the Just, all those who wish to enter our Society and Congregation shall be taught our wisdom: the perfect knowledge of how to speak the languages of all countries where we wish to be, how to put aside error and death, to make the visible, invisible, and the invisible, visible."

It had caused a sensation, and a blizzard of pamphlets for and against the Rosicrucians had ensued. The Rosy Cross Brothers were suddenly everywhere in France, and nowhere. The Brotherhood was said to be a society of Protestant natural philosophers that had its origin in the Germanies. However, no one could describe the true extent of the hidden knowledge they possessed or what their real goals were because their membership was secret; no one could point to any actual person and say for certain that here was a Rosicrucian. This did nothing to dampen the public outcry: preachers inveighed against the Rosicrucians' possibly heretical creed, scholars denounced their presumed philosophical discoveries, and politicians decried their potential meddling in France's domestic affairs.

But Louis was thrilled. An underground brotherhood of the wise whose secret knowledge gave them great powers? *Fantastique!* Who could be against that? And presumably a society of scholars who never appeared in public wouldn't be concerned if one of their number was a hunchback. Despite being nominally Catholic, Louis d'Astarac was ready to join such a society instantly and without a second thought—if only he could figure out how. He decided to try to find the truth behind all the noise, the fire behind the smoke.

There *were* certain tracts, originally published anonymously in Germany, which seemed to contain authentic doctrines of the R.C. Brotherhood. The *Famous Fraternity of the Rosy Cross* and its sequel, the *Confession of the Fraternity of the Rosy Cross,* described a secret society of the learned, founded by a half-legendary sage named Christian Rosencreutz. Their wisdom was informed by access to original and authentic Christian doctrine from the time of the foundation of the Church, supported by revealed truth of the "Hermetic Tradition" dating all the way back to ancient Egypt.

According to the tracts, Rosicrucian wisdom combined Christian belief in the intercessionary power of angels with Jewish Cabalistic magic and Egyptian astrology, all of it organized, revealed, and manipulated through the power of advanced mathematics. This was said to be the underpinning of all arts and sciences, which "harmonized" through the power of Number. A person who thoroughly comprehended Rosicrucian mathematics and numerology would theoretically be able to understand the workings of the entire universe, and approach the mind of God.

Young Louis devoured both the *Famous Fraternity* and the *Confession,* fascinated by their hints about a master key to all knowledge. Rosicrucians were supposed to keep their membership in the Brotherhood a secret, adopting the costume and customs of whatever country they lived in. They were to use their secret knowledge only for good—primarily healing, which was always to be done *gratis.* Most importantly, they were to prepare for the day when they would come forth as a body and reveal their great secrets, uniting all religious denominations and revolutionizing human knowledge. This ancient wisdom was quite distinct from all dark witchcraft, false astrology, or alchemical attempts to convert base metals into gold, and the Rosicrucian Brothers were required to renounce all such questionable pursuits.

None of the mathematical or alchemical formulas that were the foundation of Rosicrucian knowledge were spelled out in these anonymous tracts. However, what they could be used for was touched upon, at least allegorically, in a third book, *The Chemical Wedding of Christian Rosencreutz*, by a certain Johann Valentin Andreae. This extended fantasy told of Brother Rosencreutz's attendance at the marriage of a mystical king and queen, personages who also represented alchemical principles. This symbolic wedding heralded a coming new era in human knowledge. It was celebrated for seven days, during which various Rosicrucian sages revealed their powers by performing miracles of "spiritual alchemy," such as creating and restoring life.

Exciting stuff, though Louis had trouble with some of the more convoluted allegories, especially since it was all in German, a language he was still picking up. It posed more questions than it answered, which just whetted young Louis d'Astarac's appetite for more. But how do you track down an invisible brotherhood?

The Chemical Wedding had been published in Oppenheim, and Louis remembered that one of the other students at the seminary hailed from that city on the Rhine. He contrived an apparently casual encounter with the boy, and guardedly opened the subject of the R. C. Brotherhood— guardedly, because he was raising a matter of Protestant heresy in a Catholic seminary. But the Oppenheim boy knew exactly what he meant and referred him, with a certain amount of disdain, to his elder brother, who was a student enrolled across the river at the Sorbonne.

The brother, who was studying medicine, professed at first to have no idea what Louis was talking about. He said he was a good follower of Galen and abominated the errors of Hermetics such as Paracelsus, as well as the discredited medico-astral theories of the spiritual alchemists. His family was of good Catholic stock, he said, driven from Oppenheim by the oppressions of the Protestants.

But Louis knew the notorious weakness of students at the Sorbonne, and after they'd hoisted a few together at the local alehouse, the good follower of Galen opened up and confessed. His family's Protestant oppressors were actually creditors who had foreclosed on his father after a financial scheme had fallen through. This had necessitated an abrupt move to Reims, in France, and a sudden rediscovery of the family's primal Catholic faith. The student had hated leaving Oppenheim, where he'd worked as a printer's devil for the publishing firm of De Bry, but everything had been ruined anyway when Spinola had marched in with his Imperial troops to make the Palatinate safe again for Catholicism.

De Bry had printed the *Chemical Wedding* and a number of other Rosicrucian-type books and pamphlets, some attributed, many anonymous. The student had kept copies of a half-dozen or so of his favorites. Louis may have been rather hideous, but even then he had a nimble tongue, and he managed to flatter the student into pulling these treasured books out from under his bed to show them off. Louis wanted them all – and gradually, over the next few months, he got them, as one-by-one the student sold them to Louis whenever his ready money ran out.

Thus Louis was able to read Robert Fludd's *Compendious Apology for the Fraternity of the Rosy Cross* and Michael Maier's *Atalanta Fugiens,* a gorgeous book of allegorical emblems relating to spiritual alchemy. He had his first encounter with Paracelsist medicine in Oswald Croll's *Basilica Chymica,* and with the magico-mechanical devices of Salomon de Caus in his *Hortus Palatinus.*

Louis had been excited by de Caus's descriptions of his clockwork automata, and had pestered the student until the youth introduced him to another refugee from the Palatinate who claimed to have known de Caus himself. The man wouldn't tell Louis his name, or even emerge completely from the shadows in the tiny *ruelle* where they'd met, but he was in desperate need of money—"For travel expenses," he'd said—so he'd sold Louis four miniature magical clockworks that de Caus had built as models for larger projects. Louis smiled as he remembered how eagerly he'd paid over nearly all of his half-yearly allowance for the automata, and lived on barley and millet for months thereafter.

The automata—an astronomical clock, a tiny roaring lion, a diminutive fountain and a pocket-sized wind organ—had delighted Louis in secret for a year with their miniature whirring activity. Gradually the devices had grown tired, and eventually they stirred not at all. Still, they were proof that the Rosicrucians did have some kind of secrets, and for a time he'd loved them.

The attention span of Paris is eternally short, and soon the Rosicrucian Scare was over, leaving Louis no closer to finding an actual R.C. Brother. He gathered together his last few golden crowns and tried to bribe the Sorbonne medical student into revealing something, anything of use. The student took his money and gave him just one name: that of René des Cartes, an obscure young scholar residing on the Left Bank. "But he'll probably just run you off," the student said, surly to this hunchbacked pest now that he had no more money to spend. "He's not the friendly type."

Friendly he was not; but neither did he run Louis off. He received Monsieur d'Astarac in his small flat in the Latin Quarter with wary politeness, giving the impression that he would gladly dispense with the requirements of courtesy if it were possible for a gentleman to do so. The scholar des Cartes was in his late twenties, ten years older than Fontrailles, with dark stringy hair, deep-set eyes, a rather prominent nose, and a chin that receded behind its black goatee. "I am pleased to make your acquaintance, Monsieur d'Astarac," he said, and if he didn't seem sincerely pleased, neither did he evince the usual distaste at Louis's appearance.

After a few meaningless phrases of introduction des Cartes cut straight to business. "How may I serve you, Monsieur d'Astarac? What has brought you to *me*?"

The scholar was obviously a serious man; Louis decided not to equivocate. "I'm interested in the Brotherhood of the Rosy Cross, Monsieur des Cartes, and you're said to know something about them."

This time the expression on des Cartes's face definitely was distaste. He waved a hand toward the door. "If that's your interest, you may depart now without wasting any more of your time, which I assume is as valuable as mine," he said. "I have had quite enough of people accusing me of being a Rosicrucian just because I spent time studying in Germany. As should be apparent, I cannot be a member of an invisible fraternity when I am obviously quite visible."

"Monsieur des Cartes, I meant no such imputation!" Louis said, alarmed. "I'm just an innocent seeker after knowledge. Much has been said and written about the Rosicrucians; I just want to know the truth."

Des Cartes's face was dark, reticent. "Innocent? Perhaps. Naïve, to be sure," he said, not unkindly. "I tell you in all candor that I have nothing to tell you. And I advise you, sincerely, to adopt another pursuit. Mathematics, perhaps. Or optics."

Louis gave a great sigh, ran crooked fingers through his wavy hair. "Please, Monsieur des Cartes. This is important to me. Isn't there anything you can tell me?"

"No." The scholar's mouth twitched. "But I will give you something. This Rosicrucian business has become such a nuisance that I was going to destroy this item, and I advise you to do the same. But so long as you swear not to say where you got it, I will leave that decision up to you."

Louis swallowed and said, "I promise, of course."

Des Cartes rummaged through a knee-high pile of books in a corner and came up with a slim, buff-covered folio. "Here it is: Andreaeus's *The Three Mystic Heirs*—or part of it, at least."

Louis took the book carefully, gazed at it in wonder. "*The Three Mystic Heirs*? I've never even heard of it."

"*Exactement*," said des Cartes. "Now take it away, Monsieur, and be so kind as not to link my name with the Rosicrucians again."

As quickly as his bowed legs could take him Louis ran back to his lodgings, where he closed and locked his door, took the book to a chair by his single window and opened it. Between the boards he found an unbound folio of the first part of *The Three Mystical Heirs of Christian Rosencreutz,* an apparent sequel to the *Chemical Wedding.* Attributed to "Johannes Andreaeus," it was in Latin rather than German, but it was rife with errors and hand-written corrections—obviously an author's proof of some sort. However, there were no more than two dozen pages: only the preface to the work, not the whole book itself.

The preface promised a book that would reveal the actual formulae behind the secrets of the Rosicrucians, describing a work divided into three long chapters, or "Legacies," each cast in the form of a letter from the aged

Rosencreutz passing on his wisdom to a "grand-nephew" in Bavaria, Bohemia, or Saxony. The First Legacy described the "Rules of Mechanisms," the Second Legacy was devoted to astronomical and astrological matters, and the third described the spells and formulas of Spiritual Alchemy.

For Louis d'Astarac, the most electrifying thing about this preface to *The Three Mystic Heirs* was its reference, in the description of the Third Legacy, to a revolutionary medicine based on sympathies between the macrocosm of the universe and the microcosm of the human body. It promised to describe in the chapter on Spiritual Alchemy practices that could prolong life, defy plagues and cancers, and "straighten the limbs of the deformed."

When Louis read this, he suddenly felt as if he couldn't breathe. He gasped, sat down, and tugged at his collar, then tried to focus his eyes on the page. With the book trembling in his hands, he read it again. There it was: *corrigére membruum deformatus.* "Straighten the limbs of the deformed."

That determined him: he had to find a complete copy of *The Three Mystic Heirs.* He tried every bookseller in Paris, even the stalls of the *bouquinistes* on the Pont Neuf, but in vain; he was told by more than one dealer that no such book had ever been published. He had no more success with inquiries at private libraries, and finally dropped the matter only when another student at the seminary pointed out that his interest in what was, after all, heretical magic, was drawing undesirable attention to him.

There the matter had rested until last night, when the Vicomte de Fontrailles, deep in his cups, mind reeling with confused thoughts of Isabeau de Bonnefont and Balthasar Gerbier, had suddenly remembered that line in Andreaeus's book. He'd dug out the dog-eared folio, found the reference he remembered so well, and wept over it. Then he'd opened another bottle, poured himself a final glass, put his head down on his desk and passed out.

Now his head was hammering so hard that the sound was actually echoing from his door. No, wait—the hammering *came* from his door. From the other side of the panel, his man Vidou cried, "A terrible thing, Monseigneur! Open up! A terrible thing!"

By sheer force of will Fontrailles pried his eyes open and staggered to his feet, clutching at his head to keep it from leaving his shoulders. He pulled the door open and glared at his manservant. "Sacred cat of Italy! What are you blathering about, Vidou? And please, in God's name, hold your voice down."

Vidou swallowed and took a half-step back, and Fontrailles realized he must look even more of a fright than usual. "In the village, Monseigneur," his valet said, "at the inn. They've found a man dead, stabbed—murdered!"

"*Merdieu*! Have they? Was it that Monsieur Gerbier?"

"No, Monseigneur—someone else entirely."

"Very well, Vidou. I suppose I must look into it. Let's go upstairs and see if we can find me a clean shirt."

While Vidou dressed him Fontrailles broke his fast with a few bites of bread—all he could stomach—and tried to straighten out his thoughts. A murdered traveler at the inn! A traveler who was someone other than Gerbier. What were so many travelers doing at the same time in his tiny village, so far from the main roads?

As the local lord, Fontrailles was the closest thing around to a representative of the King's Justice, as there were no magistrates nearer than Tarbes, so he was expected to pay attention to crimes in his domain, especially anything as sensational as the murder of an outlander. By the time he got down to the courtyard his horse was already saddled and ready. The village was just down the hill, but a seigneur never walked when he could ride.

The village of Fontrailles wasn't much more than a crossroads, and nearly everyone in it was employed in either the château or its vineyards, especially since the viscount had begun revitalizing his wine business. Louis's father hadn't had much interest in the winery, preferring to spend his time on horses and hunting. Since assuming the title Fontrailles had changed all that, bringing in a Master Vintner he'd enticed away from the Comte de Peyrac's estate near Toulouse, and building a cooper's shop that was now turning out enough wine-barrels that there was an excess to sell to his neighbors.

The inn, the Auberge of the Fighting Fowl, was right at the crossroads, opposite the church, Fontrailles's new cooper's shop, and the lot where the vendors set up their stalls on market days. It wasn't much of an inn, and derived most of its custom due to the fact that it was exactly a day's travel in either direction from the towns of Tarbes and Mirande. Caubous, the innkeeper, met Fontrailles just inside the gate, moaning piteously and wringing his hands. The hostler held the horse while the viscount dismounted, and then the innkeeper led his lord to the smaller of the inn's two private rooms, the scene of the outrage.

The man was definitely dead. He lay on his back on the bed, eyes protruding, arms flung wide, a carving knife embedded deep in his chest. He was the first murdered man Fontrailles had ever seen, and it took him a few moments to quell his horror and nausea and think about what had to be done. Blood had soaked the blankets and the straw tick mattress. There was another patch of blood on the man's upper lip, but no apparent wound there. He didn't really want to touch the dead man's flesh, so Fontrailles put on his riding gloves before forcing open the corpse's mouth to look within. The dead man didn't seem to have bitten his tongue or the inside of his cheek.

Fontrailles asked, "Did he have a servant?"

"No, Monsieur le Vicomte," said the innkeeper. "He arrived alone. I thought it rather strange."

"His things?"

"His bags are right here, Monseigneur. I haven't touched them!" The man was positively sweating with fear.

Fontrailles poked through the dead man's saddlebags. Travel clothing, nothing more. He opened a pouch and found a few coins, a miniature silhouette of a woman and two children, and three letters. He unfolded the first, revealing four cryptic lines:

Andreaeus

Fontrailles

Armagnac

—Rochefort

Louis felt a sudden chill. His book, his name, his province. What could it mean?

He set it aside and unfolded the next sheet, which was a letter of introduction to His Majesty's Intendant at Toulouse. The third letter authorized the bearer, Monsieur Thomas La Planche, to make official inquiries on behalf of the State. Both were signed "Le Card. de Richelieu."

The hair stood up on the back of Fontrailles's neck. Cardinal Richelieu! This was no ordinary murder. The man hadn't even been robbed. He asked, "Where is Monsieur Gerbier?"

"He left first thing this morning," the innkeeper said, "headed toward Mirande, long before we discovered this ... this terrible thing!"

"Do you recognize this knife?"

"Oh, Monsieur le Vicomte—it's from our kitchen!" The man was nearly prostrate.

"All right, Caubous. Get hold of yourself. I'll talk to the kitchen help first, then the rest of your people."

Nobody had seen or heard anything, nobody knew anything. Of course, they were all terrified, and would barely admit their own names at this point. Fontrailles let it be known that he would be available to listen in private later to anyone who happened to remember anything, and called for his horse.

The innkeeper said, "Does Monseigneur suspect...?"

"Oh, I don't think it was done by any of your people, Caubous. There was blood on the dead man's lip, and it wasn't his own—whoever killed him clapped his hand over his mouth as he did it, and the victim bit him and drew blood. None of your help had a wound on his hand."

"Monseigneur is as wise as a savant!"

Fontrailles snorted. "Enough, Caubous. If any of your people ask for a little time off, let them take it, all right?"

He rode back up to the château, where he summoned his Sergeant and men-at-arms and sent them off after Gerbier, though he had little hope they'd catch him—the Englishman was well-mounted, and by this time had six hours' head-start. Then, trying to think of what else he could do, Fontrailles returned to his study.

Everything there was as he had left it … in other words, a mess. What, one murder in the village, and everyone takes the day off? He would have to speak to Lapeyre about this.

He looked at his wine-goblet, still three-quarters full, and shook his head ruefully. A lot of good getting drunk had done him. He reached to pick up the goblet, and noticed the three little white crumbs at its foot that had caused him such distress in the glare of the morning sunlight. Come to think of it, what were they?

He looked closer. They were irregular, not crystalline, so they weren't any kind of salt. Suddenly suspicious, he peered into the goblet, swirling the wine slightly. There was a white residue of some kind in the bottom of the glass.

A drug—or poison.

He put the goblet down carefully and looked around his study with new eyes. Could some intruder have come in while he lay drunk on his desk? He tried to recall how he'd left everything, to see if anything had been disturbed. There on the desk was a candlestick with a pool of wax that had once been a taper. What else should be there? He thought back: when he'd dropped off, he'd been reading that folio from *The Three Mystic Heirs* that Gerbier had wanted....

But except for the goblet and bottle, his desk was empty. The *Andreaeus* was gone.

CHAPTER IV
THE SHOULDER OF ASTARAC, THE SPLEEN OF VIDOU, AND THE TEETH OF THE COCODRIL

On the third Monday in the month of May 1626, the Loire River town of Meung was in such a state of torpor that it almost seemed to have fallen under a magician's spell. Hot weather had arrived early that year, and it was a struggle even to move in the damp heat. The town guards barely nodded as Fontrailles and Vidou, leading a pair of packhorses and two spares, rode out the east gate onto the road to Orléans.

Fontrailles was happy to put Meung behind him. The innkeeper at the Jolly Miller had complained of being short-handed, having recently lost his hostler, and service had been listless and scanty. Vidou, who was the viscount's valet, had also had to serve as groom to the horses, an indignity that had added one more grievance to his lengthening list.

"Nothing but a pain in the arse, is what it is," Vidou muttered viciously, coughing through the cloud of dust kicked up by a passing ox-drawn wagon. "Travel. A plague on it."

Privately, the Vicomte de Fontrailles agreed with him, though what he said was, "The third day without rain, Vidou! The roads will be nice and firm—we'll have lunch in Orléans, and may make it as far as Bazoches by nightfall. We'll be in Paris before you know it!"

"If my piles don't kill me first," Vidou growled into his beard.

Poor Vidou. I suppose he has reason to be in an ill humor, Louis thought. *It hasn't been an easy trip.*

In truth, Fontrailles had set a killing pace on their ride to the north, pressing on into the lengthening evenings until long after Vidou and their mounts were ready to stop. Bandits and highwaymen made it unsafe to ride after dusk, especially without an armed escort, but more than once they'd pushed on into the darkness, much to Vidou's dismay.

Most of the way they'd had two men-at-arms with them, but in Blois the fools had gotten drunk and fought over a barmaid. Knives had been drawn: one man ended up in the Hôtel de Dieu with a gash in his side, the other in the local prison. Louis had tried to hire replacements, but the pickings in Blois were slim, and he hadn't liked the looks of the ruffians who were available. Maybe he'd have better luck in Orléans.

Fontrailles didn't really want to take the time; he was in a fever to get to Paris. The Duke of Buckingham and Cardinal Richelieu had both sent agents to his tiny fief in the foothills of the Pyrenees, apparently to acquire Fontrailles's partial copy of *The Three Mystic Heirs*—and they'd been willing to kill to get it. If the prime ministers of England and France were that desperate to acquire the secrets of Rosicrucian knowledge, then there must be something to this spiritual alchemy business. In fact, more than just something: it must be the key to great power, or men like Buckingham and Richelieu wouldn't be interested.

If spiritual alchemy really worked, then maybe it *could* prolong life, cure plagues and cancers, and straighten the limbs of the deformed.

And their backs, and shoulders.

Isabeau de Bonnefont had other suitors. She wouldn't keep putting them off forever.

Louis had to hurry.

He'd first left Fontrailles in hopes of actually catching Balthasar Gerbier, the presumed thief of his folio, and murderer of La Planche, the Cardinal's agent. He was starting a day behind Buckingham's man, but he could get lucky: Gerbier might be beset by robbers, or fall ill, or be delayed in any of a half dozen other ways.

Leaving his home had been painful for Fontrailles, in more ways than one. Riding, with his twisted back, was hard for him, and hurt like the devil, even more so at the rapid pace he insisted on. Furthermore, he'd been living for two years among people who were used to having a hunchback in their midst, and who owed him deference as the lord of his domain. On the road, he was once again exposed to the fear and revulsion his deformity inspired in the common folk, who regarded hunchbacks as unlucky, or even unholy. It stabbed him deeper than the pain from his spine.

Fontrailles trailed Gerbier north to the Garonne River, then northwest along the road to Bordeaux, which followed the Garonne toward the Atlantic coast. By the time they reached the gates of Bordeaux, Fontrailles knew they were close behind his quarry—but how were they to find the Englishman in that great, teeming port city?

It was Vidou who provided the break. As they were passing a stable, he suddenly cried, "Monseigneur! Aren't those the mules the Englisher's lackeys were riding?"

"*Merdieu*! I believe you're right. Hey, there! Boy!" Fontrailles called to the stableman who was leading the animals. "There's a half a crown in it if you'll tell me where that matched pair of mules came from."

The stableman gaped at this munificence, and stammered, "But of course, Your Lordship! Monsieur Bingham, the English factor, sold them to us this morning."

"And where would I find Monsieur Bingham?"

"At his warehouse, down on the wharf, Monseigneur."

The warehouse wasn't hard to find, and neither was Mister Bingham, a ruddy-faced merchant who was on the pier with his accounts-clerk inspecting a shipment of bales of dry goods. "Monsieur Bingham?" Fontrailles said, before he'd even dismounted. "I'm the Vicomte de Fontrailles. I beg you to pardon me for introducing myself, but I have an urgent need to find Monsieur Balthasar Gerbier."

Bingham raised his bushy eyebrows. "Gerbier? I'm afraid you've missed him."

"What do you mean, Monsieur?"

For answer, Bingham merely pointed across the water to where an English carrack was tacking out of the harbor into the broad, brown estuary of the Garonne, spreading her sails to catch the wind from the south. "They left an hour ago," Bingham said, "for Portsmouth, in England."

Vidou cursed, but Fontrailles just nodded. This was disappointing, of course, but not unexpected: catching Gerbier had always been a long shot. Fontrailles simply switched to his alternative plan: he would go to Paris and offer his services to Richelieu in the cardinal's presumed hunt for *The Three Mystic Heirs*. He figured he knew as much about the subject as anyone, and far more than most. He could claim that he felt a responsibility toward the cardinal in the matter since Richelieu's man La Planche had been murdered in Fontrailles's domain. Hopefully, whatever the cardinal learned about Rosicrucian spiritual alchemy, Louis d'Astarac would learn as well. And Isabeau might yet be his.

To sweeten the offer, Fontrailles had brought with him his collection of de Caus clockwork devices, which he hoped to present to the cardinal in token of his sincerity and dedication. Packing the miniature mechanisms so they would survive carriage on a packhorse had been the single greatest delay in departing to pursue Gerbier.

But they'd made it safely, men and cargo, all the way north from Bordeaux, through Saintonge, the endless miles of Poitou and the Touraine. Now, if their luck held, they were just three days from Paris. The only thing they needed to worry about today, it seemed, was succumbing to heatstroke.

The road from Meung and the river it followed on the right were both flat and straight. The air was still and heavy; nothing moved but the sun-dazzle on the water and the heated air where it shimmered rising from the surface of the road. Without warning, a brace of partridges erupted from a roadside thicket, thrumming off toward the Loire clucking angrily.

Fontrailles, who'd been almost dozing, came suddenly alert. Partridges didn't break cover like that without good reason.

From the thicket, four or five young men who looked like farmhands came trudging up onto the road, led by an older man wearing the sober clothes and demeanor of a gentleman farmer of the Protestant persuasion. He was armed with an ancient fowling piece, and the others bore the kind of farm implements that could be pressed into service as weapons at need.

If the men were looking for trouble, Fontrailles and Vidou were badly outnumbered; they pulled up while still far enough away to turn and flee if necessary. "Good day to you, Monsieur," Fontrailles called out. "What are you hunting?"

The man harrumphed. "A cocodril," he said.

Fontrailles laughed. "A cocodril! Are we, then, in the Nile delta? I thought that was the Loire over there."

"Monsieur has the right of it," said the farmer, resting his blunderbuss on his shoulder, while the farmhands sat down on the bank in the thicket's narrow shadow. "But, Egypt or no, the Lord has nonetheless sent a cocodril to plague us. Would that my daughter hadn't trusted his smile."

"What happened? Was she bitten?"

"Worse. The reptile promised to marry her, and she believed him. He took advantage of her innocence. When I found out what he'd done, he ran off before I could lay my hands on him. But we'll find him and bring him back."

"Then what? Do you mean to kill him?"

"And violate one of the Commandments? By no means," said the farmer. "Besides, that would be too quick. No, I think I'll make him my son-in-law, then put him to work digging us a new well—a really deep one. Honest labor will drive the devil out of him. He'll be too tired to run off again." He smiled in grim amusement.

Louis continued smiling himself, but couldn't quite repress a shudder. *Would I be so eager to marry Isabeau if this man were her father?* He said, "Best of luck to you, Monsieur, and my congratulations to your daughter on her engagement. Come on, Vidou. We've no time to waste."

"Oh, aye—wouldn't want to be late for our own funerals," Vidou muttered, mopping his brow.

It was an hour later, but the sun had not yet reached its zenith when they heard the baying of a pack of hounds, before the dogs themselves came tumbling out of a grove of poplars onto the road, howling uncertainly and casting about for a scent. They were followed by men, some on horses: a huntsman, a half-dozen beaters and whippers-in, and a man in a priest's cassock, who called out, "Well met, Monsieur! Have you come all the way up the road from Meung?"

"Yes, *mon Père*, we have," said Fontrailles, "and a good day to you! I must say, it's unusual to see a priest riding to hunt, especially in the heat of the day. What are you hunting, cocodrils?"

The priest's face darkened. Louis wished he'd kept his mouth shut, as his jest was apparently badly amiss. "Has the story spread so soon, then?" the priest said through his teeth, the tip of his long nose quivering with anger. "Is this the sort of mockery we're to be subject to henceforth?"

Fontrailles bowed all the way to his saddle. "Your pardon, Father, I beg! I only meant that the day is so hot, one could almost be in Africa, hunting the cocodril. I might as easily have said oliphant, or ostrich." Louis thought, *Ugh! That was lame,* and glanced up to see how the priest was taking it.

He wasn't taking it well, but he appeared determined to salvage what dignity he could. "It's I who must apologize to you, my son," he said slowly, "for allowing my wrath to get the better of me. I've been sorely tried these last two days."

"If there's any way I can be of service in your time of trial...."

"My thanks, Monsieur. Just tell me if, on your ride from Meung, you've seen a man, slim and rather tall, dark of hair and complexion, with a wide face and a toothy mouth. He'd be wearing riding leathers, new boots, and a peaked cap with a feather."

Fontrailles shook his head. "Sorry, Father—we've seen no one of that description."

The priest's nose twitched in annoyance. "Thank you, my son," he said. "If you do, I'd be obliged if you'd send word at once to the rectory in Saint-

Ay. If I'm not there, my niece will receive it."

"You have a niece, then?"

"Indeed." The priest's nose quivered once more with rage. "I have a niece. If only she were a nephew!"

Put my foot wrong again, Louis thought. "Well, we'll be on our way," he said. "Good luck to you in your hunt, Father."

They'd gone no more than half a league farther when there was a rustling in the underbrush at the side of the road, and a voice said, *"Hssst!"*

Vidou jerked back his reins, and his horse shied. "A snake, Monseigneur!"

"No, Vidou," said Fontrailles, "I rather think it's more in the nature of a cocodril."

The underbrush parted and a man stepped out onto the road, a man slim and rather tall, dark of hair and complexion. He had a wide face, and his smile revealed an imposing array of large and unusually sharp teeth. He bowed and doffed his peaked cap, almost sweeping the roadway with its feather.

"Your Lordship is right," the man said, straightening. "Jean Reynon is my name, but I'm known to one and all as Cocodril. I see my fame precedes me."

"Fame may not be quite the *mot juste*," Fontrailles said. "I see you wear a sword. Are you a gentleman, then, and should I call you Monsieur Cocodril?"

The man smiled even more broadly. "I'm always a gentle man with the ladies, good sir, though I wasn't born to the condition. No, I wear a sword because I'm a soldier."

"Captain Cocodril, then? What is your regiment?"

"...A soldier of Fortune, Monseigneur, in the regiment of ramblers."

"And what do you want with me, Cocodril? There are others down the road quite eager for your company."

"Monseigneur is percipient!" The man gestured at Vidou. "I merely wondered why an ornament of the nobility like Your Lordship was traveling with such a scanty entourage...."

Vidou sniffed. "As insolent as he is ugly," he muttered.

Cocodril nodded ironically to the valet. "And as you have an extra horse or two, and goods to protect, I thought Monseigneur might regard with favor a request to place my humble talents at his service."

Fontrailles stroked his bearded chin, considering. A dangerous rogue, no doubt about it—but maybe he could use a dangerous rogue. "What do these humble talents consist of?" he asked.

"I'm tolerably adept with this"—Cocodril gripped his sword-hilt—"and accompaniment by an able bodyguard will demonstrate Your Lordship to be a man of consequence. Moreover, I can cook—being from Marseilles, I make a mean bouillabaisse—I can tend to your horses, and speak for Monseigneur to such base underlings as are beneath Monseigneur's notice."

"References?"

"I was employed most recently as hostler at the Inn of the Jolly Miller in Meung, where I performed all of the functions I mentioned except bodyguard … though there was one occasion, several weeks ago, when I was called upon to help thrash an obstreperous pup of a back-country gentleman. I broke his sword for him."

"And in your spare time, you used your nimble tongue to sweet-talk the daughters of the local gentry into your arms."

Cocodril smiled and bowed again. "Does Monseigneur know of a more pleasant pastime? Besides, one must find some use for one's wits, or they grow dull."

"In my employ, Cocodril, it's a pastime you'll pursue with more prudence in the future. Furthermore, I think for the time being I'll have you send half your pay to the girls you've left behind, to contribute to their dowries."

Cocodril's eyes narrowed, and his grin turned threatening. "I don't think that arrangement will satisfy my financial requirements, Your Lordship. In fact, I am in need of a substantial advance, immediately. And given Monseigneur's rather obvious, ah, *limitations*, I don't think swordplay is among his own humble talents." He tightened his grip on the hilt of his rapier.

Fontrailles casually drew a pistol from his baldric. "You're right, Cocodril, I'm no hand at all with a sword. But I'm a dead shot with a pistol." He ratcheted back the wheellock's spanner. "I urge you to reconsider my offer."

Cocodril dropped his hand from his sword and knelt in the dust of the roadway. "I accept Monseigneur's gracious offer, and hereby swear to him my undying fealty. Allow me to add my humble apologies for any misunderstanding, Monseigneur de…?"

"I am Louis d'Astarac, the Vicomte de Fontrailles. This is Vidou. Mount that last horse, Cocodril. And welcome to my service."

Three days later, they were at the gates of Paris.

The trip had gone much more easily with the addition of Cocodril to their ranks, and even the surly Vidou was somewhat mollified. The tall man was an excellent groom, with a real liking and appreciation for horses, and he did in fact cook a mean bouillabaisse, using bream, shad, and eels from the Loire bought in the fish-market at Orléans, and Provençal spices that came from who knows where. He had a quick wit, a joke for every occasion, and a seemingly limitless supply of really filthy songs that he sang in a decent baritone as they rode along. He was never less than deferential to the viscount, an attitude in which the watchful Fontrailles could detect no shade of irony.

So the days passed quickly, and the morning of the third day found them riding up to the towering gate of Porte Saint-Jacques, the southern entrance to the walled and fortified City of Paris. Louis was excited. Paris! How had he stayed away so long?

There was the usual mob of people, carts, and livestock waiting impatiently to file past the guards and enter the city. As a noble the Vicomte de Fontrailles took precedence over the common herd of farmers, drovers, merchants, and pilgrims, but making their way through the crowd without actually riding over anyone required all their care and attention. At the inner portcullis Fontrailles nodded to the bored archers guarding the gate. Entering the city proper, he steered his horse to a spot out of the main flow of traffic and turned to gather his little entourage about him.

Vidou was close behind, leading the packhorse carrying their main baggage. But Cocodril....

Cocodril was nowhere to be seen.

And neither was the other packhorse—the one that bore the precious collection of automata of Salomon de Caus.

CHAPTER V
THE CARDINAL'S GUARDS AND THE COCODRIL'S TEARS

Cocodril! The damned scoundrel had just been shamming loyalty until he was in a position to make off with something valuable. Forewarned as he was about the man's dubious character, Fontrailles had assumed that he was clever enough to avoid trouble by keeping a close eye on him. But the rascal had slipped the leash, neat as you please, at the first opportunity.

Fontrailles's only chance of catching Cocodril lay in immediate action. The rogue was hampered by having to lead a burdened packhorse, and in two minutes he couldn't have gotten far. Several streets led away from the square inside Porte Saint-Jacques. All were crowded. Which one should he take?

"Is Your Excellency looking for the man who was behind him when he came through the gate?" a young voice said. "The man with the big teeth?"

A street urchin, maybe fourteen years old, was holding Fontrailles's bridle and grinning up at him. Doubtless he was one of the lads who loitered around the gates of Paris, hoping to sell their services as guides to newcomers. "You have sharp eyes," Fontrailles said.

"I'd better have," said the smiling urchin, tossing his head to flip his greasy red-brown bangs out of his eyes, "or I starve!"

"You're hired. Which way did he go?"

"A gold crown if we catch him?"

"Silver."

"Done! Come on! He went this way."

The boy ran down the Rue Saint-Jacques, the main route to the center of the city. Fontrailles and Vidou followed with the horses, pushing as best they could through the crowd, leaving a trail of cursing street vendors, indignant carters, and a washerwoman who spilled her load of clothes and called Fontrailles a "cursed *bossu*"—a hunchback.

Fontrailles grimaced and tried to avoid killing anyone while keeping his eye on the boy. The urchin stopped at the corner of the Rue des Poirées and pointed left, shouting, "There! I see him!" Then he vanished up the narrow side street.

By the time Fontrailles and Vidou reached the Rue des Poirées the urchin was already at its far end, jumping up and down, waving and pointing—again, to the left. The riders splashed through the mucky alley, mercifully less crowded than the main street, and emerged onto the Rue de la Harpe, a major thoroughfare that ran parallel to the Rue Saint-Jacques. On their left loomed the Porte Saint-Michel, another of Paris's fifteen-odd gates. Beneath its crenellated towers the boy stood, shouting and beckoning.

"Cocodril's gone back out of the city," said Fontrailles.

"Never liked him. Never trusted him," growled Vidou. "Made faces at me, he did, when Monseigneur's back was turned."

They passed through the gate and over the drawbridge, hoofbeats echoing hollowly from under the wooden span as the crossed the moat. The boy was waiting on the far side. "He went that way!" he cried, pointing to the right down the road along the moat. "Come on! He'll get away!" The urchin took off running again, ducking between horses and oxen, his bare feet kicking up dust and dung.

From the end of the bridge Fontrailles and his valet could see a considerable distance down the moat road. "I don't see that Cocodril at all," said Vidou.

Fontrailles cursed. "We've been tricked! The boy has led us on a false scent."

"The filthy guttersnipe!" Vidou cried. "Well, I'll see that *he* doesn't get away, at least!" He dug in his spurs and sped off after the boy along the moat road, galloping through a herd of outraged goats.

"Vidou! Stop!" Fontrailles shouted. "Damn it all!" He scooped up the reins of their remaining packhorse and grimly set out after him.

They weaved through the traffic on the moat road, then went left up the broad Rue de Vaugirard. They passed Luxembourg Palace, with its noisy horde of carpenters and masons erecting the queen mother's monument to herself, and the ominous Petit-Luxembourg, current home of Cardinal Richelieu, her erstwhile protégé. By the time they reached the Carmelite convent, the houses were smaller, traffic was much lighter—and the boy had vanished. Beyond were the pastures and fields of the Pré-aux-Clercs, untouched as yet by the building boom of the suburb of Saint-Germain.

Fontrailles rode up and grabbed the bridle of Vidou's horse. "Vidou, if you ever charge off again without orders, I'll send you back to Armagnac to pull weeds in the vineyards."

Vidou hung his head. "Monseigneur is right. I ought to be thrashed. I was just so angry at Cocodril, that grinning pig of a dog."

"All right. We've wasted enough time chasing this hare. Let's ... what is that infernal din?"

All the bells of the Carmelite convent were ringing at once in a patternless cacophony. A series of joyous cries and whoops followed as the gates of the convent banged open and four cavaliers, one of them enormous, marched out arm in arm. The youngest and scruffiest shouted the loudest of all and held four swords on high like a captured enemy banner. They marched triumphantly away toward the city, a parade unto themselves, collecting a rowdy crowd of followers out of sheer high spirits.

"Help! Oh, help, Messieurs," cried a distraught nun, in the white habit of the Carmes-Deschaux. She ran up to Fontrailles, whose dress marked him as a gentleman, despite his shape. "A massacre! Such blood. They brought them inside, and what are we to do?"

"Hold the horses, Vidou," Fontrailles said. "Show me, Sister."

A few bells still tolled randomly in the belfry as Fontrailles followed the sister through the gates. Four men in red tabards were sitting on the steps of the chapel, where some of the more level-headed nuns were binding their wounds. A fifth lay at their feet, dead. All the men's scabbards were empty of swords.

"Your pardon for the intrusion, Messieurs," said Fontrailles, "but can I be of any assistance?"

"Name of a name! You arrive a little too late for the show, Monsieur," said a tall man with a shock of white hair whose thigh was being bandaged. "Ten minutes ago is when we needed assistance."

"Enough, Biscarat," wheezed a compact, muscular man of about thirty, who had obviously suffered a serious wound through the body. "Thank you, young man. We are guards of Monsieur le Cardinal, and have just suffered a misfortune at the hands of a gang of those assassins who call themselves King's Musketeers. I am Ensign de Jussac, and these," he indicated his wounded comrades, "are Cahusac, Laduite, and Biscarat."

"Louis d'Astarac, Vicomte de Fontrailles, at your service. I have three horses outside the gate and can carry three of you to a surgeon's, or wherever you like. I'm afraid one of you will have to walk."

"I can walk," said Biscarat.

"On a wounded leg?" Jussac said. "Everyone admires your courage, Biscarat, but your wound is bad enough without aggravating it." He coughed, which appeared to hurt.

"It's nothing!" Biscarat said. "The Petit-Luxembourg isn't far."

"We are not going to shame His Eminence by being seen carried into his hôtel, wounded and defeated. La Houdinière's townhouse is close by; we'll have Monsieur le Vicomte take us there. Now, who walks?"

The man the ensign had called Cahusac raised his hand and pointed at himself, gargling. He was wounded in the throat and couldn't speak.

"What about Truchet?" Biscarat said, indicating the dead man.

"We'll send for him," Jussac said. "Very well, Cahusac, lead the way. I think...." But he closed his mouth, then his eyes, and suddenly slumped, unconscious.

With the help of Vidou and the nuns, Fontrailles got the wounded Cardinal's Guards mounted or bound onto the horses. Then Cahusac, occasionally pausing to spit blood, led them to a house on the Rue de Seine, just outside the city walls and not far from the river. Once within, a great fuss was made over the wounded guardsmen by the members of the household. La Houdinière, another officer in the Cardinal's Guard, insisted that Jussac be placed in his own bed.

Jussac, once settled in the high, canopied bed, awoke long enough to exchange a few words with La Houdinière. Then he turned to Fontrailles and said, "I owe you my thanks, and the thanks of Monsieur le Cardinal. Have you newly arrived in Paris, Monsieur le Vicomte? I don't recollect having seen you before, and...."

And my appearance is rather memorable, Fontrailles mentally finished for him. "In fact, I have just arrived, Monsieur de Jussac, with the intention of offering my services to His Eminence, your master."

"I shall be delighted to recommend you to him," Jussac rasped, "once I'm back on my legs." Then he fainted once again.

"He's lost a lot of blood," said La Houdinière, a slim and wiry man with the leathery look of an old soldier. "I'll have to watch that charlatan of a surgeon to make sure he doesn't bleed him further."

Fontrailles said, "I saw the musketeers who did this, marching away from the convent. Who were they?"

"Jussac said it was the so-called Three Inseparables: Athos, Porthos, and Aramis, plague take them." La Houdinière glowered. "Along with some young devil of a Gascon named d'Artagnan. It was this d'Artagnan who wounded Jussac—a lucky blow that'll likely be the making of his reputation."

Fontrailles took his leave and made his way down to the kitchen door, where he found Vidou scrubbing blood from his saddle. "Half a day pissed away," the valet muttered. "We'll never catch that Cocodril now."

"Half a day invested in a manner that will get me a personal introduction to the cardinal!" said Fontrailles, clapping his lackey on the back. "Cheer up, Vidou! You're like a perpetual rainy day."

"And what do we do now, Monseigneur?"

"I've been corresponding for several years with a scholar here named des Cartes. We should find a welcome with him."

Monsieur des Cartes lived in modest lodgings in the Latin Quarter near the Sorbonne, but his manservant told Fontrailles that monsieur was not at home, and regrettably he could not say when he would return. Fontrailles gave the man his name and said he would come back the next day.

"Where do we go now, Monseigneur?" Vidou asked in the street outside des Cartes's house. "We'll be needing a place to stay, and to have us some dinner."

"Your luck is in, Vidou! I have the answer to both those quandaries," said a familiar voice. "Assuming Monseigneur approves, of course."

It was Cocodril—behaving, to their astonishment, as if nothing whatever had happened. He sketched a bow to Fontrailles, put his cap back on his head at a jaunty angle and smiled expectantly.

Vidou exploded. "Quick, Monseigneur! Hold him while I get the Watch!"

Cocodril looked puzzled. "The Watch? Whatever for? I've just been looking for suitable lodgings for Monsieur le Vicomte, and I believe I've found something that he'll find satisfactory. Indeed, I've already engaged it, on a trial basis, and I've bespoken a dinner from the tavern next door."

Fontrailles scowled. He had an impressive scowl. "Cocodril, you're a rogue and a liar. I must confess my first impulse just now was to draw a pistol and blow your brains out, but that would have been unforgivably crude, especially on a friend's doorstep. Besides, I see that you've returned to us without the packhorse carrying the automata, which ensures that I won't pistol you out of hand. So where is it?"

"But how have I offended, Monseigneur? I lost sight of you in the crowd when we entered the city, but, being a man of industry and initiative, I immediately went to work on your behalf. I asked myself, what will my master need? Lodgings, of course! And I've found them."

"The packhorse?"

"Waiting for us there, safe and sound! It would have been irresponsible to drag your precious collection through the streets while looking for you."

"And certainly less safe for you, once you found us. In fact, how *did* you find us?"

"Yesterday Monseigneur mentioned his intention of calling on his friend, the scholar des Cartes. I asked some students at the Sorbonne and they directed me here."

"Huh. If you haven't any conscience, at least you have wits. Take us to these lodgings. But first, give the address to des Cartes's manservant so he'll know where to find us."

The lodgings were, in fact, more than satisfactory: the third floor of a house in the Place Dauphine, the new triangular plaza at the foot of the Île de la Cité, the island in the Seine that was the heart of Paris. The Place Dauphine was adjacent to the Pont Neuf, King Henri IV's broad bridge that crossed the base of the island and served as both open-air market and carnival. A noisy place, the Pont Neuf, but only a few paces away, inside the Place, it was relatively quiet.

Cocodril showed them through the three-room apartment he'd found as if conducting royalty through a palace. The rooms were clean and decently furnished. Most important, in one corner was Fontrailles's collection of automata, still in their dusty travel cases.

Fontrailles considered Cocodril, who stood proudly in the center of the room, hands on his hips, light glinting from his preposterous grin. "Vidou, go see that the horses are properly stabled," Fontrailles said.

"But Cocodril here's the groom," Vidou complained.

"Do as I say. I need to have a private word with Monsieur le Cocodril."

Vidou went out, grumbling. Cocodril maintained his smile, but, possibly suspecting what was coming, drew himself up to his full height. Muscular and vigorous, he towered over the stunted Vicomte de Fontrailles. Louis had seen him wielding his knife while preparing their meals and knew the man was fast. He'd have to be careful.

"It was a good plan, Jean-Reynon-known-as-Cocodril," Fontrailles said. "Hiring the street urchin to lead us a merry chase was brilliant. I assume things began to go wrong when you got to the Pont Neuf and found that a collection of miniature clockwork devices is not easy to dispose of quickly and profitably. So you decided your best bet was to continue to play the part of the loyal servant, confident that you could charm me with your agile tongue or awe me with your physical prowess."

Cocodril's grin became, if possible, even broader. "But not at all! Monseigneur's poor opinion of this humble servant is based on a series of regrettable misapprehensions. Everything is as I have represented it, I assure you, on my honor!" He took a step closer to Fontrailles.

"I suppose it's fortunate for me that you didn't dig deeper into my collection," Fontrailles said, looking up at him, "or you would have found the gold."

"Gold?" Cocodril's eyes flickered toward the stack of cases in the corner, and in that instant Fontrailles drew his pistol and fired it off in his face. As intended, the bullet buried itself in a ceiling-joist, but Cocodril reeled back, hands in front of his eyes, blinded. Louis reversed the pistol in his hand and clouted Cocodril over the head with the butt. The man fell to the floor, stunned and whimpering.

Fontrailles dropped the pistol, pulled Cocodril's own dagger from his belt, knelt and held the point to the man's throat. "Don't move," Fontrailles said, though his own hands were shaking. "Now let's continue our little talk."

Cocodril ground his fists into his eyes and wept. "You've blinded me!"

"It won't last. And neither will you if you think to take advantage of me again. You're clever, Cocodril, but you're not wise. If it's money you want, you'll do far better by serving me than by trying to cross me."

Cocodril blinked, squeezed his eyes shut, then opened them again. "I can see!"

"Then you can see where I'm holding your knife. And you can see what's in my other hand." He reached into a pocket and pulled out a clinking handful of coins. "Here's the gold, Cocodril. It's your bonus for finding this place. It is, as you said, quite satisfactory."

Feet pounded up the stairs outside, and there was a banging on the door. "Monsieur de Fontrailles! What's going on in there?"

It was the voice of his new landlady. Fontrailles went to the door and opened it, revealing Madame Chasserel, who lived downstairs, and her big manservant Pomarg, who held a nasty-looking bludgeon. "My apologies, Madame," Fontrailles said, bowing, and trying to control his ragged breath. "I was just disciplining my footman."

Madame Chasserel, a trim, solid fifty-year-old wearing widow's weeds, peered past Fontrailles to where Cocodril, face blackened and mustache in tatters, was just clambering to his feet. "Ah," she said. "Good. One can't be too strict with the help, I always say."

"I don't anticipate any more trouble," Fontrailles said. In fact, he was elated. Despite Cocodril's skills and size, he'd put the bigger man in his place!

Madame Chasserel pursed her lips. "It's just as well. I like you, despite your unlucky looks, and I'd hate to have to turn you out."

"I'm obliged to Madame for her candor."

"By the way, there's a note just came around for you. Pomarg?"

Pomarg, now rather embarrassed by the bludgeon, leaned it against the wall and drew an envelope from his sleeve. "A runner just brought it," he said timidly, with a dip of the head.

Fontrailles took it near a window and opened it in the light of the waning day. As he'd expected, it was from René des Cartes:

My dear Fontrailles,

My apologies for having missed you earlier today. Unfortunately, there are good reasons why I should not be at home to visitors at present. I must warn you … but these are matters that cannot be committed to paper.

Be so kind as to meet me tonight, at ten o'clock, on the bridge over the moat outside the Porte de Nesle. There I will explain what I can.

It would be prudent to destroy this note. And believe me, my friend, this is a time for prudence.

Your obedient servant,

R. C.

CHAPTER VI
HIS MAJESTY KING LOUIS LE PETIT

"Isabeau, my love! My bride!"

Smiling mischievously, Isabeau de Bonnefont de Fontrailles curtseyed to her new husband, then placed her hands on her shoulders and slid her wedding dress down. In an instant, she stood naked before him, revealing at last the slender form he'd imagined so many times. At first her hands modestly hid the soft furred place between her legs, but then she raised them and held out her arms to him. "Are you ready, Louis?" she asked softly.

He was ready. He stood, and looked down at her—for his legs no longer bowed, and his back was straight. He stood tall, erect, and masterful: as straight and erect as his cock, which jutted from his loins like an iron shaft. It yearned to be within Isabeau, his smiling Isabeau. She laid back on his bed, spread her perfect legs, and beckoned to him.

That, of course, was when he awoke. That was when he always awoke. For he couldn't quite imagine what it would really be like to make love to Isabeau. Louis d'Astarac lay tangled in sweaty linen and bedclothes, and groaned.

Not that he'd never lain with a woman, for of course he had. Like all but the most devout students at the Oratorian seminary, he'd spent time in the brothels of Paris, and pursued serving-maids and tavern girls. But unlike his more comely friends at the school, he'd never caught any of the girls he'd pursued, and had never slept with a woman he hadn't had to pay for.

And maybe that was why the dream of making love to Isabeau was always incomplete: because he'd never slept with a woman whose love was freely given to him. It must, somehow, be different—better, in some way he couldn't yet grasp.

Though his cock seemed to have no trouble imagining it. It was still rock-hard, thrusting up against the bedclothes: *The only part of me that's really straight,* he thought. Privately, Louis referred to his member as Louis-le-Petit—or, when it was as commanding as it was at present, His Majesty Little King Louis.

From an early age he'd always had a powerful interest in girls and sex, dating back, ironically, to right about the time when it became clear that most girls found him repulsive. Unable to participate in elder brother Bertrand's rough boyish games, and unwelcome, moreover, the lonely young hunchback had tried a few times to join the activities of the girls. He'd been turned away with barely-concealed scorn, even by his younger sister, Hélène. Only Isabeau de Bonnefont had seen past the twisted appearance of the stunted boy from the neighboring viscounty, enjoying his quick wits and mordant sense of humor. And in return he had conceived an affection for the pretty little demoiselle that verged on worship.

Someone scratched at the door of his bedchamber—Vidou, of course. Cocodril, whose manners were more modern and less deferential, would have knocked. Fontrailles threw off the bedclothes and called, "Come in, Vidou. Let's get some windows open; this place is an oven."

Vidou entered, bearing washbasin, razor, and towel. "Monseigneur slept well?"

Fontrailles snorted. "*Merdieu!* To tell the truth, I'm not sure I know what 'sleeping well' means. With this back of mine it hurts no matter how I lie on the bed. And now, damn it all," he snapped, "I've barely gotten up, and already I've broken my first rule of conduct!"

Never, ever complain about it! To be hunchbacked is weakness enough.

"Huh!" Vidou muttered. "He's got a right hard-on this morning, he does."

Startled, Fontrailles glanced down at his nightshirt to see if he was showing, then realized that Vidou just meant he was in an ill humor. He smiled wryly at himself and shrugged asymmetrically. "*Bien,* Vidou. Shave me well—mind the shape of the Royale!—and then lay out my second-best city ensemble. I'm calling at the house of a *Grand* this morning."

As Vidou did up the twenty-seven buttons on the front of his pourpoint, Fontrailles cursed inwardly at the fashion that dictated tight, form-fitting doublets for the gentry. The stiff jacket forced him painfully erect, and brought back all too vividly the memories of his father's attempts to correct his condition.

Though only one son, the eldest, could inherit his title, the old viscount had welcomed the birth of a second. Mortality rates were high, and it was as well for a noble family to have a cadet behind the firstborn. But as young Louis grew it became clear that he suffered from a deformity that made him more of a liability than an asset. The viscount ordered him to stand erect, to sit only in straight-backed chairs, to sleep on a board, but as time passed young Louis's back grew only more curved, his legs and arms more bandied and bent.

Their neighbor, the Seigneur de Bonnefont, had in his youth been to school in Bordeaux for a year, and was proud of his education. It was he who introduced the viscount to the works of the great physician Ambroise Paré, one of which described curvature of the spine and proposed methods to correct it. There was a drawing of an iron "corselet" that could be locked around a patient, with bands of metal like an outer skeleton. It was fitted with screws so that gradually, over time, it could be tightened. Thus would the crooked be straightened.

The viscount gave the drawing to his ironmonger and ordered that the corselet be made. The smith looked at the picture and scratched his head. Then he shrugged his massive shoulders, called for a dozen barrel-hoops, and got down to work. A week later, the thing was finished—and almost before it was fully cooled, eight-year-old Louis d'Astarac was forced into its iron embrace and locked inside.

It hurt him, and he screamed. He screamed for a long time. It was disturbing for the household, so he was locked in the root cellar until his screams finally dwindled to sobs. He sobbed for days. The thing was heavy, and it never stopped hurting him—but after a week of the iron corselet, he was almost used to the pain and the weight.

Then they tightened it.

One week later, they tightened it again. And so on, every week, for an agonizing year. Then one day the viscount told the ironmonger to remove his device and called for his younger son so he could inspect the results.

Louis did his best. "See, father!" he said, trying to stand tall. "I'm straight now, like Bertrand! It worked, father!"

But it hadn't worked. If anything, the boy was more stunted, his back more crooked than ever. Louis saw the lines of disappointment form on his father's face and cried, "No, father! Please! *Don't put me back in the cage!*"

His father, who was not a heartless man, shook his head, and Louis never saw the corselet again. But every time he buttoned on a form-fitting doublet he felt those metal ribs once more tightening around his body, and for a moment he was once again a boy encased in an iron cage.

"Cocodril!" Fontrailles called, as Vidou fastened the final button. "Are you here?"

"But yes, Monseigneur!" The tall man ducked as he entered Fontrailles's bedchamber, all grinning servility. The black of the powder-burn had been scrubbed from his face and his mustache looked almost normal again. "How may I serve? I am at your disposal, body and soul."

"Indeed. Run down to the Pont and find someone who can tell you how to get to the hôtel of the Duc de La Trémouille. We're calling on him this morning—or rather, on one of his men."

"I obey instantly!"

Fontrailles intended to follow up on something des Cartes had told him at their meeting the night before. It was one of the few useful pieces of information he'd been able to get from the scholar.

Last night he and Cocodril had left their new lodgings for the appointment with des Cartes at half past nine. They were well armed, for the streets of Paris were dangerous at night. The peddlers and mountebanks who lined the bridges and embankments in daylight gave way after dark to gangs of thieves and cutthroats.

They crossed the Pont Neuf to the Left Bank and turned right along the quay, past the walls of the grand new Hôtel de Nevers. Ahead the looming black mass of the medieval Tour de Nesle squatted on the riverbank. Round and topped with crenellations, it looked like a rook from a chessboard, until one got close enough to see the broken chimney that rose from one side of its pinnacle, the ragged laundry drying on makeshift scaffolding, the pockmarks where bricks were missing from its walls.

The Tour de Nesle anchored the west end of the Left Bank's city wall to the river. Just inside the tower was a fortified gate, the Porte de Nesle: it opened onto a humpback stone bridge that spanned the moat, which was stinking, shallow, and muddy here where it trickled into the Seine. Even this late at night the Porte de Nesle was open to traffic, for the city had burst the bounds of the western wall and a new *faubourg*, a suburb, was building around the old Abbey of Saint-Germain.

Fontrailles reached the center of the moat bridge as the bells of Paris began to toll ten. The man he assumed must be des Cartes was waiting for him, cloaked and hooded. As he approached, the man turned toward him, and in the shadows of the hood Fontrailles recognized the features of the scholar. Des Cartes nodded in response to Fontrailles's polite bow, then glanced at Cocodril. "Wait back at the gate, Cocodril," Fontrailles said, "but keep an eye on us." Cocodril saluted gravely and strolled back toward the Porte de Nesle.

"Monsieur Louis d'Astarac, now Vicomte de Fontrailles? I am René des Cartes; welcome back to Paris." The man looked around, saw no one closer than Cocodril, and pushed back his hood. His eyes were more deep set than Louis remembered, and lines were beginning to appear around his mouth. Despite his words, his expression showed no warmth; in correspondence he'd always taken a serious tone, so Louis decided he'd better keep his remarks sober and to the point, lest he be dismissed by this somber man as a frivolous youth.

"First of all, Monsieur," Fontrailles said, "permit me to thank you for taking the time to meet with me. If precautions such as these are necessary then my visit must be an imposition."

Des Cartes shrugged. "The letter you sent me from Bordeaux, Monsieur de Fontrailles, is in part responsible for the necessity of these precautions. I received it only two days ago—you must have made a fast trip to nearly keep up with the post-horses." He looked intently at Fontrailles.

He's testing me. Louis had written to des Cartes before leaving Bordeaux, describing the incidents at Fontrailles, his intention of coming to Paris, and asking what the scholar knew, if anything, about the history of *The Three Mystic Heirs*. Louis thought, *Why should that make des Cartes so wary?*

"We did travel fast, but not *that* fast," Fontrailles said. "You say the letter only arrived two days ago? You think it was delayed, read by someone else?"

Des Cartes nodded. "I think it very probable."

"When you received it, was it still sealed?"

"Yes—but I have no faith in such things as seals. What one man can do, another can undo. The same applies to codes and ciphers. There are some matters it is simply not safe to refer to in writing. One such matter is the … work you named in your letter."

"The *Andreaeus*?"

Des Cartes nodded again. "Precisely."

"Whom do you suspect of intercepting your mail?"

"Spies of the Cardinal … or perhaps the Jesuits."

"The *Jesuits*?"

"Yes. I've known that the Society of Jesus was keenly interested in that work since at least the Battle of White Mountain—and they've known the same of me. The Rosicrucian secrets are a challenge to Catholic orthodoxy, so naturally the Jesuits want to suppress them. The same cannot be said of His Eminence, cardinal though he may be."

"Nor of the Duke of Buckingham, it seems. Do you know this agent of

Buckingham's, this Balthasar Gerbier?"

"He is in Paris."

Fontrailles's jaw dropped. "He can't be! He took ship from Bordeaux for England!"

Des Cartes shook his head. "No. He is here; he called at my house, an hour before you did, along with a woman, Buckingham's agent in Paris." A smile touched the corners of his mouth. "I was not at home to Monsieur Gerbier, either."

"But how could he have gotten here so quickly from … oh. I see. He was never on that English ship at all."

"No doubt he learned that you were pursuing him and arranged a little piece of theater to throw you off." Des Cartes turned and leaned on the parapet of the bridge, gazing across the river at the royal palace of the Louvre. "These are experienced men, and they play a deep game," he said. "It's why I came to warn you personally. I've enjoyed our correspondence over the last two years, Monsieur de Fontrailles. You possess a keen mind, with an ability to think clearly that is all too rare, especially in the French nobility. But you are young, and you do not know these people." He looked back at Fontrailles, eyes glinting like flints. "Get out of this while you still can. It's what I intend to do."

"Monsieur, I thank you for your good wishes. But I must have that book."

Des Cartes sighed. "I felt that way once myself. It seemed to me that Rosicrucian thought might offer the answers I couldn't find in orthodox philosophy."

"So the Rosicrucians really exist, then?"

"Oh, they do … or they did. I met some of them during my travels in Germany: Brügi, Faulhaber, and others whose famous names would surprise you. They found their philosophical home in the Palatinate, but when the troops of the Holy Roman Emperor marched in they brought the Inquisition with them. The Rosicrucians scattered or went into hiding."

"But their wisdom, their secrets," Fontrailles asked eagerly. "Could they really do the things they claimed they could?"

"As to that, I cannot say," des Cartes replied. "Personally, I saw no miracles done."

"But I see that you doubt."

"I doubt everything I've never seen, and much that I have," des Cartes said, "all but the existence of God."

"You would not advise me, then," Fontrailles said, "to trust in the wisdom of the Rosicrucians?"

"That you must decide for yourself," des Cartes said. "You have a capable mind: use it. As for me, I have thought a great deal in the last ten years, thought about thought itself, and I no longer believe in the syncretic methodology of the Rosicrucians. They reach too far, try to embrace too much, to envelop and incorporate all knowledge. Their mathematics are too complex and too self-referential. I think the truth is simpler, more elegant."

"So you don't believe in spiritual alchemy? There must be *some* overarching principle that unifies faith and science, or the universe makes no sense."

Des Cartes pursed his lips. "You may be right—but I don't believe the answer is in the Christian cabbalism of the Rosicrucians. They ask *how*. I think the real question is *why*."

Fontrailles laughed briefly, without mirth. "*How* will do very nicely for me, if you please. I need tools. I need instrumentality. I'll leave the pursuit of truth to those more qualified, such as yourself, Monsieur des Cartes."

"What is this so-desperate need, Monsieur de Fontrailles?"

Fontrailles spread his arms. "Look at me! I'm a mockery of a man. I want to be who I ought to be."

To his surprise, des Cartes did look at him, considered him from head to toe, as if seeing him for the first time. "Your physical form is far from optimal, it's true, but you appear healthy, and you don't seem to be missing anything. The important thing is that your mind is strong and sharp. The body is just a mechanism, after all."

"You're serious, aren't you?" Fontrailles sighed. "If I could think as you do, I suppose it would be a consolation. But I've heard a different story every day of my life."

"You are, as I remarked, still young. Fortunately, you are intelligent, and when somewhat older you will see things differently. Though you may not have the opportunity to get much older if you do not drop your search for this dangerous book."

"No. I must have it," Fontrailles said. "Monsieur des Cartes: do you know where it is?"

"I do not. I can tell you that one copy survived the sack of Prague and was kept thereafter by someone in the entourage of the Winter King. Frederick's mechanist, Salomon de Caus, might know where it is...."

"De Caus! He's alive?"

"I cannot be sure. He was alive six months ago when he came to Paris. He sent a note stating his intention to call upon me, but he never came. He disappeared."

"Did you try to find him?"

"No. I want no part of this affair, though it continues to be thrust upon me." Des Cartes frowned. "I advise you to leave well enough alone ... but if you cannot, the lawyer Albert Quinot may know what's become of Salomon de Caus. He's a Huguenot from Lorraine, and used to be de Caus's man of affairs. He's now a notary in the household of the Duc de La Trémouille."

"Thank you, Monsieur. That gives me a thread to follow. And yourself? What will you do?"

"The powers contending for this book have begun to kill people. I would prefer not to be one of the casualties. My father is King's Magistrate in Nantes; I should be safe in his house until this affair plays itself out."

"God protect you, Monsieur des Cartes. I'll certainly do everything in my power to keep your name out of these matters."

Des Cartes smiled, a trifle sardonically. "Then may your powers be the equal of your intentions, Monsieur de Fontrailles." He drew his hood over his head and Fontrailles knew the interview was over.

So the next morning Fontrailles and Cocodril set off to try to speak with Albert Quinot, who might know something about the whereabouts of the great Rosicrucian mechanist Salomon de Caus, a man who might himself be able to point them toward King Frederick's copy of *The Three Mystic Heirs*. It was definite progress. "It's hard to believe I've been in Paris only twenty-four hours or so," Louis said to himself.

"Pardon, Monseigneur?" said Cocodril. They were crossing the Pont Neuf toward the Left Bank, retracing their steps of the night before.

"Nothing. So where is the Hôtel de La Trémouille?"

"Near Luxembourg Palace in the Faubourg Saint-Germain, on the corner of the Rue de Vaugirard and the moat road, Your Lordship."

"Indeed. We must have passed it yesterday when we were chasing your hired street urchin."

Cocodril grinned. "I have no idea what Monseigneur is talking about. We should go straight ahead, I believe, up the Rue Dauphine."

"I know my way around Paris, Cocodril. I studied here as a youth."

"Monseigneur was fortunate. I spent my youth shoveling shit," Cocodril said. "Begging your pardon, Lordship."

The Hôtel de La Trémouille was an imposing mansion within a walled enclosure, almost a fortress. Most of the newer mansions of the nobility in Paris had a more open and expansive plan, with tall, many-paned windows right on the street. But the Duc de La Trémouille was one of the leading Huguenot noblemen in the north of France, and when Huguenots in Paris drew up plans for their houses they remembered the Saint Bartholomew's Day Massacre of 1572, when virtually every Protestant in the capital had been butchered.

If Fontrailles had been calling on the master of the house he would have ridden his best horse. However, since he just wanted to talk to one of the household functionaries, he thought he would be less conspicuous afoot, so he passed by the mansion's great iron-bound carriage-gate and knocked on the man-sized door to its side. As he waited, he could hear the *thwack* of balls from the tennis courts across the street and the cheers of the spectators when a point was scored.

The door was opened by a dour-looking gatekeeper. He peered suspiciously at the ill-matched pair on his doorstep, but admitted that Albert Quinot was within and the viscount might speak to him, if it pleased the viscount. "There's a shipment of goods needs receiving, so he should be at the tradesmen's entrance," the gatekeeper said. "Across the forecourt and through that portico."

At the tradesmen's entrance they did find a man quarreling over a bill of lading with a transport factor, but he turned out to be the notary's assistant. Quinot, the man said irritably, had found more urgent business to attend to that morning. If Monseigneur really wanted to talk to him, the assistant added with a touch of malice, Quinot could be found in his chamber on the second floor, above the library.

Fontrailles returned to the forecourt and stopped short: there appeared to be some sort of commotion at the mansion's main gate. The doors opened briefly to admit three men in the red tabards of the Cardinal's Guard, before being slammed shut and barred in the face of other men who appeared to be pursuing them. There were angry cries from the street outside, and the gatekeeper shouted "To arms! The hôtel is under attack!" The Cardinal's Guards all had their swords out, and one of them appeared badly wounded.

Sober-garbed Protestants bearing an assortment of weapons poured from various parts of the hôtel into the forecourt, where the guardsmen were trying to organize a sortie into the street outside. "This is damned inconvenient," Fontrailles said. "Everywhere I go I run into Cardinal's Guards who've had the stuffing beaten out of them. Cocodril, get up on that wall and see if you can figure out what's really going on."

Cocodril gave him a snappy salute. "Where will you be, Monseigneur?"

Angry shouts of "Burn the hôtel!" came from outside in the street.

"Watch yourself, Cocodril," said Fontrailles. "As for me, I'm going to try to find Master Quinot while this place is still standing."

CHAPTER VII
IN THE HOUSEHOLD OF THE HUGENOTS

To reach Albert Quinot's room in the Hôtel de La Trémouille, Fontrailles had to make his way up a staircase thronged with armed Huguenots going down. It was like trying to swim upstream against the spring flood, but by the time he reached the first landing the flow had diminished considerably. Even a *Grand* like La Trémouille could have only so many retainers.

The second floor was a warren of small rooms used as residence by the staff and had a much lower ceiling than the soaring ground and first floors. Fontrailles was far enough now from the uproar at the gates of the hôtel that he could hear only the occasional distant shout. Following the directions of the notary's assistant he soon found the chamber assigned to Quinot. The door was slightly ajar. Fontrailles, intent on his quest, didn't hesitate: he pushed it open and stepped within.

It was a small chamber, and the furnishings consisted of no more than an armoire, a small table, a chair, and a bed. Lying on the bed was Isabeau de Bonnefont.

Louis's eyes almost burst from his head. "Isabeau!" he cried. "You, here?"

The woman slid lithely from the bed and stood up, and Louis realized several things. First, this was not Isabeau de Bonnefont, though she had the same dark hair, large brown eyes and wide, smiling mouth. Second, she was completely nude. Third, she was stunningly gorgeous in a way that made his pretty Isabeau seem almost plain, though this woman was five or six years older than the Demoiselle de Bonnefont.

Louis gaped. She was tall, with generous hips, and silky brown hair both above and below. Her breasts were full, with thick, dark nipples. She showed no inclination to cover them, or her sex; instead she put her hands on her hips and laughed aloud. "Close your mouth, Monsieur, lest you drool on your shoes!" She put her hand over her own mouth and said, "Oh, pardon. That was rude, wasn't it? And we haven't even been introduced."

This kicked Louis out of his paralysis by enabling him to fall, gratefully, into the routine of etiquette. He bowed—which was difficult, because it meant he had to take his eyes momentarily off her. "Louis d'Astarac, Vicomte de Fontrailles, at your service, Mademoiselle."

"Madame, as it happens: Comtesse Camille de Bois-Tracy. You may kiss my hand." She held out her right hand expectantly. He walked toward her and took it. What else could he do?

As he bent over her hand, his face, as she had doubtless intended, was within a few inches of her loins. Beneath her glossy thatch he could clearly see the coral of her lower lips. He smelled the warm scent of sex. Louis-le-Petit stirred and stiffened in his breeches.

He straightened, face burning with what was certainly a visible blush. He only hoped his erection was hidden by the flaring hem of his doublet. The woman's face was lit by silent amusement—obviously she wasn't about to help him out, so he cleared his throat and said, "Madame is, um, alone?"

This was so patently inadequate that he blushed anew. What an idiot he was, to allow himself to be so nonplused by a mere naked woman!

She smiled, but at least she didn't laugh, so she wasn't completely heartless. "I wasn't alone," she said, "but my companion went rushing out when all the shouting began. What's going on, Monsieur? I'm not used to having men leave me like that."

Happy to have a question he could answer, Fontrailles said, "There's some sort of scuffle at the gates of the hôtel. The Cardinal's Guard is involved; one of them seemed quite badly wounded."

"God's balls! The Cardinal's Guard? Why didn't you say so before, instead of standing there gaping like a farm boy? Here, help me on with this."

The woman—*no, the lady*, Louis corrected himself: *she's a countess*—turned and began gathering underthings from the foot of the bed, and in a moment Fontrailles was amazed to find himself helping her into them. A tiny galvanic shock ran through him every time his fingertips touched her flesh, but she was through playing with him and appeared not to notice. After the linens came the outer layers, which he obediently laced, tied, and buttoned wherever she indicated, until she was fully clad in a high-waisted court dress of deep violet silk that emphasized her astounding figure. She hid her finery under a long, hooded cloak, and said, "A thousand thanks. You are armed, Monsieur de Fontrailles; would you oblige a lady by escorting her from the premises?"

"Of course, Madame. This way," he said, though there was only one way out. *I'm an idiot.*

In the corridor they met Cocodril, whose face split in a monstrous grin when he saw Camille de Bois-Tracy. "Has Monseigneur found what he was looking for?" he said happily.

"Shut up, Cocodril, and fall in behind," Fontrailles said. "We are escorting madame from the premises."

Cocodril leered as the lady passed him. "I shall always be happy to walk behind madame."

The lady smiled back—and then her hand shot out, grabbed Cocodril by the collar and jerked him off balance. "Mind your tongue, *canaille*," she said, still smiling, "or I'll have it out." She straightened her arm and Cocodril, shocked, was slammed against the corridor wall.

Cocodril looked more abashed than Fontrailles had ever seen him. The viscount glared at his servant, to make sure that madame knew that he, too, disapproved of Cocodril's behavior. But before he could say anything she raised her hand to forestall him. "Later," she said. "Now we need to get out of here."

Fontrailles nodded, turned, and hurried toward the staircase, the countess right behind him in a flurry of rustling silk. Cocodril followed, shaking his head in rueful astonishment.

They went down one flight, to the first floor, where Fontrailles led them into a long gallery. Below, on the ground floor, the staircase opened directly into the forecourt, which Louis wanted to avoid since the lady seemed allergic to Cardinal's Guards. The gallery ran across the rear of the forecourt, so as they passed the windows they could see La Trémouille's excited retainers below, manning the street wall and hurling insults at some unseen enemy beyond. The handful of red-clad cardinal's men stood out distinctly among the dark-clothed Huguenots.

Fontrailles gestured out the window and said, "What's that all about, Cocodril?"

Cocodril shrugged. "Some quarrel with a gang of King's Musketeers and Royal Guards, as far as I could tell. Once I could see it was just a street brawl, I came to find you."

"Well done. We go down here, Madame la Comtesse." Fontrailles indicated another staircase at the end of the gallery. At its foot they came out into the portico that led to the tradesmen's entrance. "This way," he said, and they left the commotion behind them.

They exited by the hôtel's trade gate onto the Rue de Condé, which was unguarded, everyone having run to the main gate on the Rue de Vaugirard. In the street the countess paused and donned a silk domino mask that matched her dress. "Thank you, Monsieur le Vicomte," she said, pulling up her hood to further conceal her features. "I will need no further escort. Besides," she smiled slightly, "I believe you'll want to go back and have a private interview with Monsieur Quinot. No?"

It was a dismissal. She turned and sashayed off toward the Porte Saint-Germain. Fontrailles and Cocodril watched her go, fascinated, neither daring to make a move to hinder her.

"Monsieur le Vicomte," Cocodril said, "that was… She was…."

Fontrailles nodded. "Yes, she certainly was, Cocodril. She had us heeling like hounds. Rather embarrassing. Fortunately," he added, "we're not likely to cross paths with Madame de Bois-Tracy again."

Fontrailles did indeed desire a private interview with the notary Albert Quinot, especially after finding a naked countess in his room, but Monsieur Quinot was nowhere to be found.

The attack on the mansion's front entrance was over: the besiegers had been frustrated by the hôtel's walls and stout gates and, evidently unwilling to follow through on their threat to fire the place, had declared victory and disbanded. The defenders, proud of having made one brief but ineffective sortie for the honor of the house of La Trémouille, still clustered in the forecourt, discussing the incident excitedly. A few authority figures moved among them, breaking up the chattering groups and sending the retainers back to their work.

The badly wounded guardsman, a famous duelist named Bernajoux, had been carried into the mansion, where he was confidently expected to die of his wounds. The other Cardinal's Guards had slipped out after their opponents had departed.

No one could tell Fontrailles with exactitude where he could find Albert Quinot. He'd been among the men who had sallied out the gate on the sortie against the besiegers, but nobody had seen him since. Exasperated, Fontrailles checked the notary's office, his room—still empty—and returned to the tradesmen's gate. No Quinot. And his inquiries were starting to draw questions that he preferred not to answer.

"Let's go home, Cocodril, while we can," said Fontrailles, on the receiving end of a suspicious look from the gatekeeper. "We'll try again later after this place has returned to normal."

On the Rue de Condé they turned toward the gates of Paris. "May I tell Monseigneur of an amusing coincidence?" Cocodril said.

Louis, who'd been thinking of the nude form of Camille de Bois-Tracy, shook his head to rid himself of the persistent image. "What coincidence would that be, Cocodril?"

"I recognized the leader of that rabble of musketeers and guards outside the hôtel. It was that provincial lad I had the honor to thrash and disarm in my last week of employment at the Inn of the Jolly Miller."

"Indeed? That's curious. Do you remember his name?"

"He styled himself the Chevalier d'Artagnan, Monseigneur."

"D'Artagnan? That's the same lad who wounded Ensign de Jussac in that brawl yesterday."

"He's a fractious youth, Monseigneur, and disrespectful of his elders."

"Didn't like him, eh? He sounds like a dangerous thug. Well, I doubt if a boy who makes a practice of assassinating His Eminence's Guards will have a very long career in this town."

Louis returned to contemplating Madame de Bois-Tracy. *I must think about something other than her anatomy,* he thought. *Use your wits, "farm boy"! What was a woman like that doing in an obscure notary's bedroom?*

Well: if he had a good reason to interrogate Albert Quinot, he had to assume that others would have the same motive: finding Salomon de Caus. Though the lady's method of eliciting that information obviously varied from his own, he thought wryly.

What was it des Cartes had said about Gerbier's visit to him? *"He called at my house, an hour before you did, along with a woman, Buckingham's agent in Paris."*

Buckingham's agent. No wonder she wasn't eager to meet the Cardinal's Guard.

And no wonder she hadn't been surprised to see him, and failed to register the usual distaste for his deformities. Gerbier had doubtless described the Vicomte de Fontrailles to her. She knew who he was the moment she saw him.

Vidou was waiting nervously for the viscount in the Place Dauphine, outside the house where they'd taken lodgings. "Don't go in, Monseigneur! There's a man waiting for you upstairs, a man who says he comes from the cardinal. I'm sure he's here to arrest you!"

"Indeed? From the cardinal!" Fontrailles rubbed his chin. Apparently he hadn't kept a sufficiently low profile since he'd arrived in Paris. "Did he name himself, Vidou?"

"He said he was Monsieur de Cavois, Monseigneur. I said I didn't know when you would return, if ever, but he insisted on waiting."

"I see."

Cocodril loosened his knife in its sheath. "Shall we go deal with him, Monseigneur? I'm not afraid of His Eminence's Guards if they're such pincushions that a provincial like that d'Artagnan can poke holes in them."

"No, Cocodril. If Richelieu wants me, he's certain to get me. Go check on the horses and see about dinner. Vidou, come with me. Let's see what Monsieur de Cavois wants."

As they entered his chambers, Cavois, a blond, thickset man in thigh-high boots and the now-familiar red tabard of the Cardinal's Guard, was standing at the window overlooking the Place. He must have seen them arrive, but he'd waited for Fontrailles to come up rather than rushing down to arrest him. Either his visit was a friendly one or he was confident that his man had no chance of escape.

"Monsieur de Cavois? I am the Vicomte de Fontrailles," Louis said, assuming a haughty demeanor and using what he hoped was an impressive tone of authority. "You asked for me, I believe?"

"I did, Monsieur," Cavois said, bowing but showing no evidence of awe. "I have the honor to represent His Eminence the Cardinal, who requests the favor of an interview."

"When, Monsieur de Cavois?"

"Immediately, if it please Your Lordship," Cavois's tone clearly indicated that whether it pleased His Lordship was entirely irrelevant.

Fontrailles gave a curt nod. "I would be honored to attend upon His Eminence." *As if I had a choice. I need time to think.* "Would Monsieur oblige by waiting while I attire myself in garments suitable to such an august interview?"

"What Monsieur is wearing will do just fine," Cavois said firmly.

"Very well. I'll just send for my footman."

"I will attend upon Monsieur," Cavois said. "Let's go."

"You're right. Let's go," Fontrailles said, as brightly as he could. "Vidou, tell Cocodril that the great cardinal has favored me with an interview. Don't wait up."

CHAPTER VIII
A COURT CONSPIRACY

Monsieur de Cavois, Captain of the Cardinal's Guard, led Fontrailles out the gates of Paris and into the Faubourg Saint-Germain, where Richelieu was roosting while his new Palais Cardinal was being built, much nearer the Louvre—and the king. *Saint-Germain again!* Louis thought. *I spend more time in this suburb than in the city proper.*

Cavois didn't bother to shorten his stride to match that of Fontrailles, so Louis had to hustle to keep up with him. It was probably, he reflected, a deliberate humiliation. It was said His Eminence liked to keep the nobility of France firmly in its place: subservient to the crown, and to the crown's chief servant, the cardinal.

They passed behind the blocky Church of Saint-Sulpice and turned up dusty Rue Garancière, which led directly to Richelieu's lair, known by its new name of the Petit-Luxembourg. For a hundred years the tall, grim, rambling mansion had been called the Hôtel Luxembourg, until Marie de Médicis appropriated its name for the grand palace she was constructing on the adjacent property. The massive central pavilion of the Petit-Luxembourg, six stories of dark stone capped with a tall, steep slate roof and towering chimneys, loomed ominously at the end of Rue Garancière, and Louis almost shuddered as they approached. Everyone knew that sometimes people summoned by the cardinal didn't return, and were next heard of as being in the Bastille or the dungeons of Vincennes—if they were heard of at all.

There were a great many red-clad guardsmen in and around the Petit-Luxembourg. Armand-Jean du Plessis, Cardinal de Richelieu, had been prime minister to King Louis XIII for less than two years, and the reins of absolute power were not yet firmly in his grip. He had many enemies—more every day—and assassination was a political tool that had been used to remove royal favorites before. So His Eminence was guarded as well as any man in Paris, except, perhaps, the king himself. Fontrailles was conducted through at least four layers of security before they reached the cardinal's inner sanctum, and he assumed there were probably more that he didn't see.

At last Cavois and Fontrailles were passed into Cardinal Richelieu's study, a tall, narrow room paneled in dark wood and floored with dark carpets. The walls were ornamented with maps; a suit of Spanish jousting armor stood disapprovingly in one corner. A glow emanated from two lamps burning on the broad desk at the far end of the room. More light filtered in through the tall, curtained windows behind the desk, through which also came the dim but incessant noise of hammering from the Luxembourg. The only sound from within the room was the scratching of a pen in the hand of the Prime Minister of France, who sat behind the desk in a tall chair, facing an irregular wall of stacks of paper.

Richelieu was not alone: behind him, in the shadows, stood a still gray figure in the coarse woolen robe of a Capuchin monk, face invisible beneath its hood. This could be none other than Father Joseph, the head of Richelieu's intelligence service, and one of the most feared men in France.

"Capitaine de Cavois et Monsieur le Vicomte de Fontrailles," the audiencer announced, before leaving the room and closing the tall, heavy door behind him. Richelieu wrote for a few seconds more on the document before him, then signed it with a flourish, put down his quill, and looked up.

Cardinal Richelieu was a slender, almost slight man, but even sitting behind a desk he radiated an aura of barely-restrained power. It was his eyes, mainly, Louis thought: he had the eyes of an eagle, piercing, far-seeing, the eyes of a creature of unlimited will, and no mercy for its prey. Louis felt those eyes look into him and measure him, while the mind behind them summed him up and filed him in his proper place.

The cardinal flicked a finger, beckoning them. The heavy carpet deadened their footsteps as they approached. Louis swallowed several times. The palms of his hands were sweating, and he quelled an impulse to wipe them on his breeches. He stopped when Cavois did, and they both bowed to the floor.

"You are malformed, Monsieur de Fontrailles," Richelieu said, in a rich brown voice with metal in it. Louis couldn't quite keep from wincing at the remark, and he was certain the cardinal noticed it. "That must be an unfortunate burden to you and your family," Richelieu continued. "Yet you are said to be a clever young man, a correspondent of scholars, and you were educated by the Oratorians here in Paris."

He paused, and Louis guessed he was supposed to say something. "Your Eminence is well informed," he temporized.

This was so obvious that Richelieu didn't deign to acknowledge it. "A clever young man," he repeated, "and yet I wonder if you are not too clever for your own good. You study dangerous heresies and meddle in matters outside your competence." Richelieu's eyes bored into him. "It might be wiser, Monsieur le Vicomte, to stick to your vineyards in future, and attend to the responsibilities to which you are obliged by your heritage."

He was being given a chance to back out, alive. It was tempting—but there was still Isabeau. "I would have been more than content to do as Your Eminence suggests," Fontrailles said carefully, "had I not felt a far greater responsibility thrust upon me. I could not regard as a coincidence the murder in my *vicomté* of one of Your Eminence's accredited men, at the same time that I was paid a visit by an emissary of the Duke of Buckingham. As an added outrage, something was stolen from me that should more properly have been put into Your Eminence's wise custody." He took a deep breath. "If I had not been preoccupied with my provincial concerns, perhaps both of these misfortunes could have been prevented. I felt it my responsibility to the crown, and to Your Eminence, to atone and amend."

"And that is the reason you have come to Paris?"

"It is, Monseigneur."

Richelieu stared at him for a long, uncomfortable moment, then flicked another finger and said, "Thank you, Monsieur de Cavois." The officer bowed and took his leave. The cardinal waited until the door was closed again, and then said, "Monsieur de Fontrailles, you possessed a copy of *The Three Mystic Heirs* that you had obtained from the dilettante scholar René des Cartes. You have allowed it to fall into the hands of our enemies, the English. That was unforgivably careless. It is important that you tell me what you can remember of its contents."

Louis's eyes widened. So much for keeping des Cartes's name out of the affair. And it seemed it was true what they said, that the cardinal knew everything. Or, almost everything. "It… was an incomplete copy, Monseigneur, nothing more than an author's proof of the preface. I'm sure I could paraphrase it most accurately, should Your Eminence so desire, but I'm afraid the results would be disappointing. It included none of the prescriptive formulae it said were in the later chapters."

Richelieu registered this, and almost smiled. "That is both good news and bad news," he said, "though perhaps more good than bad. It means that the English do not yet possess what may turn out to be a powerful weapon."

"And it explains why Balthasar Gerbier came to Paris instead of taking ship for England," Louis said, risking a throw for broke. "He hadn't yet gotten what he'd come for."

"Quite so, Monsieur de Fontrailles. So you are, in fact, a clever young man." Richelieu inclined his head slightly. "Are you clever enough to have discovered what has become of Salomon de Caus?"

"Not … yet, Monseigneur." *There doesn't seem much point in being circumspect with this man,* Louis thought. *All right, to the devil with it.* "I had hoped to learn his whereabouts from the notary Albert Quinot, his former man of business, but he's disappeared."

"Not entirely. He's in the next room," said Richelieu, with a surprising touch of smugness. So the man *was* human, after all.

Louis nodded, as if to acknowledge a superior move in chess. "*Eh bien.* Your men must have seen an opportunity to spirit Quinot away during the street brawl. I imagine they didn't plan the disturbance, but took advantage of it once it occurred."

"More or less," said Richelieu. The cowled figure of Father Joseph leaned forward and whispered something. The cardinal pursed his lips, and then said, "Yesterday, Monsieur de Fontrailles, you were on the scene of the mêlée in which my man Jussac was badly wounded. This morning, just as you arrived at the Hôtel de La Trémouille, there was a distracting disturbance in the street outside. Both incidents involved the musketeers Athos, Porthos, and Aramis, and the Gascon youth d'Artagnan. Please explain the connection."

"There is none, Monseigneur. It was sheer coincidence."

"Indeed." Richelieu steepled his hands and gazed at him over his fingertips. "But you said, Monsieur, that you do not believe in coincidence. Neither do I."

Uh oh. Fontrailles felt cold sweat at his brow. *Change the subject, fast.* He said, "Eminence, an agent of the Duke of Buckingham was also in the Hôtel de La Trémouille at that time."

"Was he?"

"She, Monseigneur. I encountered her in Quinot's room." For some reason, Louis found himself reluctant to continue. The Cardinal raised an eyebrow and he knew he had no choice. "She named herself the Comtesse de Bois-Tracy," he said, unaccountably angry with himself.

"Bois-Tracy," Richelieu said musingly. The cowled figure leaned forward and whispered again in his ear. "Ah, yes. The countess is an accomplice of Madame de Chevreuse, who is herself an intimate of Buckingham's. La Bois-Tracy has recently insinuated herself into the social circle of my niece, Madame de Combalet. Interesting."

Richelieu sat back in his tall chair and considered for a minute, then leaned forward, once more steepling his fingers. "Last month there was an attempt on my life," he said. "It wasn't the first, but it was well planned, and could have succeeded. In the wake of that assault, His Majesty authorized me to augment my own guard, the members of which have been selected for their martial prowess. However, recent events, including these damnable brawls with the King's Musketeers, have exposed the flaw in choosing my men solely for their ability to fight."

The cardinal paused again, seemed to come to some sort of decision, and continued. "Monsieur de Fontrailles, I am in need of men with brains in their heads. Relying on duelists like Bernajoux to perform political missions such as detaining the notary Quinot has been a mistake. These regrettable street fights have left a number of vacancies in my guard, and I am minded to fill them by creating a unit dedicated to the investigation of clandestine activities." Richelieu leaned forward, a hawk considering a rodent. "You have stated, Monsieur de Fontrailles, that you feel a responsibility to the crown, and to me. Will you discharge this responsibility by accepting a command position in the Political Squad of the Cardinal's Guard?"

Father Joseph leaned forward and hissed an objection into the cardinal's ear, of which "heretic" was the only word Louis could make out. *The spook in the cowl doesn't much like me,* Louis thought. *It's mutual.*

Richelieu smiled a little, but shook his head. "No, my friend. Jussac gives him a good character; we will see what this young man is made of." He turned back to Fontrailles. "Monsieur le Vicomte? What do you say to my proposal?"

I'll have a much better chance of putting my hands on The Three Mystic Heirs *if I'm working for Richelieu rather than against him,* Louis thought. He said slowly, "You do me too much honor, Monseigneur—but I accept, with gratitude."

Richelieu nodded. "Good. Now, attend. Father Joseph has reminded me that you have not always been wise in your choice of associates, and that you have shown a disturbing tendency for unauthorized personal investigations. Henceforth you will curb this tendency and devote your energies to what problems I assign you." He picked up a quill, dipped it in ink, wrote a few lines on a fresh piece of paper, and handed it across the desk to Fontrailles. "You are now an ensign in the Cardinal's Guard. You will report directly to Capitaine de Cavois, but may receive assignments from Father Joseph here, from my aide the Comte de Rochefort, or even from myself. You will recruit your own assistants, but Cavois will lend you aid as needed until you are able to do so. Choose men who are subtle, but loyal and fearless."

Fontrailles tried, with a fair amount of success, to keep the paper from shaking in his hand, though his palms were still sweating. He was awash in both fear and exultation. "Your Eminence wastes little time," he said.

Richelieu nodded curtly. "We have no time to waste. France is surrounded by enemies, while the State is corroded from within by corruption and rebellion. Eternal vigilance is the price of order."

He's made that speech before, Louis thought. "Shall I assume that my first assignment will be to track down and seize for Your Eminence the Winter King's copy of *The Three Mystic Heirs*?" He wasn't entirely able to keep the eagerness out of his voice.

The cardinal nodded and said, "You are, as you have pointed out, obligated to do so."

"Then I should probably start by speaking to Albert Quinot."

"Quinot has already been subjected to rigorous questioning, and we are convinced he knows nothing. Isn't that so, Father Joseph?"

The cowl nodded.

"I leave it to you to devise another line of pursuit. As for us...." Richelieu indicated one of the tallest stacks of paper on the desk before him. "We have more urgent business to attend to. I have reliable reports that a dangerous conspiracy is afoot among the disaffected nobility. This plot must be crushed. As soon as I have all the facts I need, I will persuade His Majesty to move against the plotters, which will require a strike into Brittany. In the meantime, this affair of the Rosicrucian book is in your hands."

Stand up straight, Louis thought. *Show your zeal.* "You may rely on me, Your Eminence!"

"Perhaps so. One can hope." He glanced at the tall Flemish clock that stood in the corner opposite the suit of armor and tapped his finger impatiently. "In any event, Monsieur Ensign, that is all the time I can spare for you today; I must see the king about this matter of the brawl outside La Trémouille's house. I will send Rochefort to acquaint you with what little we know of this Rosicrucian business."

He stood, and once more Fontrailles felt those eagle eyes bore into him. "Just remember, Monsieur de Fontrailles," the cardinal said, "that now you belong to me."

CHAPTER IX
D'ASTARAC TAKES A JOB

Walking away from the Petit-Luxembourg after his interview with Richelieu, Louis's knees trembled with reaction, but he was buoyed by a growing elation. He, Louis d'Astarac, an obscure young man from the minor nobility, had crossed verbal swords with the greatest mind in Europe—and lo! His head was still on his shoulders! He'd wriggled out of Father Joseph's imputed connection with Richelieu's enemies, the King's Musketeers; his assistance to Jussac and his men had paid off; and he hadn't even needed to offer the cardinal his collection of Rosicrucian clockwork automata—which in retrospect seemed like a rather naïve idea. Had he really thought he could bribe Richelieu, a man who could take whatever he wanted?

He *was* strangely annoyed with himself for having betrayed the name of the Comtesse de Bois-Tracy—but why shouldn't he have? After all, he didn't owe her anything. She was an agent of their enemies, and she'd manipulated him mercilessly.

But, death of God, what a body she had! And a brain, too—not unlike Isabeau. Weirdly enough, she even looked rather like Isabeau, at least in her face. Otherwise, of course, Camille de Bois-Tracy was taller … and had a fuller figure ... and her thighs....

Enough!

Predictably, Vidou wasn't as happy about the interview with the cardinal as his master. "Like enough he's put his foot in it for good this time," the valet muttered, as he pulled off Fontrailles's boots.

Cocodril, on the other hand, was thrilled. "The Cardinal's Guard! Now we're getting up in the world—and they *need* some new blood, some vigor and vinegar, the way they've been getting manhandled by the King's Musketeers." He twirled the end of his mustache. "I daresay I'll look rather well, swaggering around in one of those red tabards."

"I daresay you would, if I were going to bring you into the guards with me," Fontrailles said, "but I'm not. His Eminence the Cardinal has enjoined me to recruit men of subtlety, and that lets you out. You, Cocodril, will continue in your capacity of footman and *gen d'armes*."

"What? Oh, Monseigneur, that hurts! That strikes to the quick! Why, at need I can be as subtle as a solicitor, as sly as the fox! Just try me, Monsieur le Vicomte—you won't be sorry."

"That will do, Cocodril. I need you more where you are."

"Monseigneur will regret it," Cocodril said sulkily, "if he runs up against that young brute d'Artagnan without my sword at his side."

"I'm going to command the Political Squad, Cocodril—I have no intention of crossing swords with anyone. However, as a noble officer in the service of His Eminence, it would be unbecoming for me to lack personal retainers. So shut up and retain."

The next day dawned even hotter than the day before, so after Vidou brought in his breakfast the new ensign donned his lightest chemise and trunk hose, then sat at the table that served him as a desk to ponder how to proceed. His best chance, Louis thought, was to continue to try to find Salomon de Caus, who had a direct connection to the book. According to des Cartes, the Rosicrucian mechanist had been in Paris as recently as six months before. If de Caus had made contact with des Cartes, Louis reasoned that he might have communicated with other scholars as well. He opened his writing box, took out paper, pen, and ink, and began a series of letters to send to his network of philosophical correspondents inquiring discreetly after Salomon de Caus.

Though he had promised to try to keep des Cartes out of this affair, he also sent a note around to his residence to ask for another meeting. He was unsurprised to receive a reply informing him that Monsieur des Cartes had already left for Nantes for an indefinite visit.

By that time the afternoon heat was at its zenith and Fontrailles was perspiring so freely that he gave up on writing. He leaned out of the open window in his bedchamber above the Quai des Orfèvres and looked down at the Seine, hoping to catch a breeze. Watching the river part sullenly around the piers of the Pont Neuf, Louis remembered a day in Armagnac the previous June when he and Isabeau had sat by the bank of a stream and listened as it found its way around and over the rocks. The brook, which divided the Fontrailles domain from the fields of the Bonnefonts, would dry up entirely by mid-August, but in June there was still enough water between its banks and green grass on its verge to make reclining beside it pleasant on a hot afternoon.

Isabeau's chaperone, an elderly woman who'd been her nurse when she was a child, was sitting far enough away that she and Louis could converse without being overheard, but in truth they had been speaking of nothing consequential: the weather, this year's prospects for the vineyards, correspondence with distant friends and acquaintances. Isabeau was wearing white, a light Spanish summer dress, Madrid being closer to Armagnac than Paris, and was far more comfortable than Louis in his heavy hunting leathers. Somehow whenever he saw Isabeau he always seemed to be embarrassingly overdressed or underdressed. He drew a handerchief from his sleeve and mopped at his brow. "I'm having a devil of a time getting letters through to Wilhelm Schickard in Germany," he said. "The religious wars, you know."

"It's terrible," Isabeau replied, tossing her dark hair out of her amber eyes. "On Sunday our minister was urging us to make contributions for the defense of the Protestants of Lower Saxony. Do you ever worry that the religious wars will return to France? Our families would be on opposite sides."

"Oh, I think we're too reasonable here in Armagnac to fly at each others' throats over such trivia as infant versus adult baptism," he said, not at all sure he believed it. "We may be Catholic on my side of the stream, but I've asked our curate to avoid anti-Protestant rhetoric."

"What if I asked you to join the Reformed church?" she said. "Would you do it—for me?"

There was mischief in her eye, but he answered her seriously. "If I did, all my people would feel obliged to convert as well, or court trouble by defying me. *Cuius regio, eius religio,* you know. And they've already been through it twice: in the middle of the last century, when my family converted to the new religion alongside the families Bonnefont, Gimous, and Castelnau, and then when my father reconverted to Catholicism so he could be appointed Sénéchal of Armagnac by the king. I don't think I could do that to them again."

"I see," she said, gazing pointedly off into the distance. "And I thought you had a higher regard for me than that." She couldn't quite conceal her smile. "And what about your soul? It's eternal torment for you Papists, you know. Our minister says so."

"If I was sure I had a soul, I'd entrust it to no one but you," he said, trying for a merry tone to disguise the fact that he meant it. "But to turn Huguenot? How would I explain it to my friends in Paris?"

"Paris!" Her eyes were suddenly alight. "Are you going back there?"

"I have to, at some point," he said. "I'm climbing the walls from boredom in my tiny château. There are so many *books* in Paris, Isabeau— and people who've actually read them! One can *talk* with such people."

"Louis," she said, sitting up, "teach me what you've learned from these books. I want to talk about them, too—with you."

He nearly returned a derisive remark at the idea that a woman should read about, or discuss, natural philosophy. But he stopped himself, because this wasn't just a woman—this was *Isabeau.* "All right," he said, heart pounding for some reason he couldn't name, "I will."

"You'll have to help me with the Latin," she said.

"I'd be *delighted* to help you with the Latin."

"And if there is any calculating involved, I can return the favor."

Louis made a face and she laughed. Though he picked up new languages easily he had never had any facility with numbers, a skill that came naturally to Isabeau—she had even helped sometimes, when they were children, by doing his arithmetic assignments for him. Now her father allowed her to handle all the accounts for the Seigneury of Bonnefont, and Louis suspected she could even teach his man Lapeyre a thing or two in that regard.

"All right, then: that's settled," Isabeau said. She stood, raised her hands above her head and stretched, the south breeze molding the fabric of her dress against her slim curves, causing Louis's heart to skip two or three beats. "I'd better be getting back; it's time for mother's medicine, and I need to make sure our cook isn't too drunk to make Papa's dinner."

He stood, but didn't stretch. Why draw attention to his deformity? He said, "Your new cook is a drunkard?"

"Yes, but he's such a good cook that we forgive him."

"So you can forgive a man his liabilities if he can make up for it in other ways?" he said, trying to keep his voice light. "There's hope for me yet!"

"Of course there is, *chéri*. But, Louis," she teased, "we already *have* a cook."

After sundown Paris cooled to a tolerable level, so Fontrailles was decently dressed when Vidou entered, muttering glumly, to announce a visitor: the Comte de Rochefort. Louis hastily buttoned his collar and told Vidou to show him in.

The cardinal's foremost intelligence agent was a haughty cavalier in his early forties, tall, dark-haired and dark-complected, with a slight scar on his temple as of a bullet-wound. He was dressed simply but impeccably in modish doublet and breeches of violet.

Fontrailles welcomed him in and they sat at a table in the largest room of the apartment, the one with the view of the Place Dauphine. Vidou brought glasses and wine. Rochefort eyed the Vicomte de Fontrailles with unconcealed skepticism, and spoke with a hint of severity. "I'm told you're to be the cardinal's man for looking into plots involving possible devilment and sorcery," he said. "Better you than me, Monsieur, is all I have to say. I'd rather deal with things I can understand."

"Indeed?" Fontrailles said, striving for nonchalance despite the aura of grim danger that hung about the Comte de Rochefort like a dark cloak. "And what's your area of expertise, then?"

Rochefort smiled tightly, which drew down the scar at his temple. "Spies, assassins, and poisoners," he said. "In other words, the common run of humanity—folk with nothing uncanny about them. So I've no complaints about passing off this Rosicrucian business to you."

"What can you tell me?"

"Precious little. Most of what I can tell you is what we *don't* know. We don't really know if a full copy of *The Three Mystic Heirs* still exists. In fact, for all we know there might be more than one. We hadn't known, for example, that the copy you owned was only partial."

"I wanted to ask about that," Fontrailles said. "The man you sent after it, who was murdered—was his family provided for?"

Rochefort was plainly surprised by the question. "But of course! What do you take us for, Monsieur? We may be spies and assassins, but we are not *animals*."

"No, no, certainly not. Sorry," Fontrailles said.

"Don't do that."

"Don't do what?"

"Apologize. You're a *cardinal's* man now. We don't," Rochefort said stiffly, "apologize."

"No. Right. Sor ... I mean," Fontrailles shrugged and sighed, "there's a lot to learn."

"*Vraiment*. Now, Monsieur, we know that the Duke of Buckingham is aware of this book and is also after it, and there may be others as well. Buckingham is a notable patron of alchemists and astrologers, and is even reputed to employ black magicians, so you may find your investigations opposed by sorcery. However, I assume you have experience with such things, or you would not have been given this assignment."

"Naturally," Fontrailles said. "But … suppose I didn't?"

Rochefort's mustache twitched with amusement. "Then I imagine I'd better give you this item that Father Joseph sent for you." From a large pouch at this belt he drew forth a wooden box about the size of one of his long, strong hands and placed it on the table. It was a beautiful thing, with intricate mother-of-pearl inlay, and looked like an oversized watch box. Rochefort flipped up a small latch, opened it, and lifted out a wooden figure of a long-legged, long-necked bird, with splayed feet, a spherical body, and a smaller spherical head at the end of its neck. The head sported round staring eyes, a beak like a pointed dowel, and a curious cylindrical hat.

Rochefort stood it carefully on the table with one hand while holding its head erect with the other. "What it is?" Fontrailles asked.

"I am informed that it is a Thaumaturgical Ostrich," Rochefort said drily, "and that in the presence of magic or a magician its head will bob regularly up and down." He released the head and it fell slowly forward, the body rotating at the hips; it bounced once, then came to rest with its beak pointed straight down at the table. "No sorcerers here," Rochefort said. "Assuming it works."

Fontrailles picked it up and inspected it closely. Its appearance was … ludicrous. "Wherever did this come from?"

"According to Father Joseph, it's quite ancient and valuable; this is the only one of its kind to survive the sack of Constantinople." Rochefort produced a sheet of paper. "You'll have to sign a receipt for it."

"You must be kidding."

"Father Joseph doesn't jest," Rochefort said, "and I'm not known for my sense of humor either."

"I've *so* much to learn." Fontrailles signed the receipt. "Any other help you can give me?"

"Not at present. This conspiracy of the *Grands* is requiring all our resources. It's a dangerous plot this time, with real power behind it. Everyone useful will be going with the cardinal to Brittany."

Ignoring the implied slight, Fontrailles asked, "And what will you be doing, Rochefort?"

The count's brows twitched at Fontrailles's familiarity in using his name without a title. "I, *Monsieur*, have been given a covert assignment in Brussels. I'm to infiltrate that hive of Spaniards to learn who is really pulling the strings of this conspiracy." His mouth twisted slightly. "It was Father Joseph's idea. One doesn't question the ideas of Father Joseph."

Louis couldn't quite imagine the haughty Rochefort infiltrating anywhere, but perhaps there were depths to the man he wasn't yet aware of. "I'll take that as a word to the wise, and try to avoid crossing the Capuchin," he said. "Any other advice for a new officer in the Cardinal's Guard?"

"Well," Rochefort said, looking down his nose, "if you are to join a guard of gallant cavaliers, Monsieur, you might endeavor to look the part. A man of the sword in service to cardinal and crown should display a certain style, carry himself with a touch of dash. Look to it, Monsieur."

Fontrailles was surprised, and rather stung. "But what's wrong with this doublet and breeches? I paid fifteen crowns for this outfit in Bordeaux."

Rochefort wrinkled his nose. "That much?"

Early the next morning Fontrailles, with Vidou at his heels, went to the Rue de la Pourpointerie. "What are we doing here, Monseigneur?" Vidou asked. "These shops look expensive."

"Apparently, Vidou, if we are to be an officer in a guard of sword-slinging cavaliers, we must look the part. We must wear the slashed doublet, the lace collar, the broad hat, and the high boots. Vidou, we must swagger."

"Well, I'm not wearing no lacy underthings, me," Vidou muttered. "No, not even if he says I have to."

A gaudy cavalier, with a broad hat on his head and embroidered half-cloak draped carelessly over one shoulder, issued with a flourish from the bright red door of a couturière across the street. "That one," Fontrailles said. "We'll go in there."

Two hours later, the Vicomte de Fontrailles stepped in front of a mirror, garbed *à la mode* in the full ensemble of a fashionable cavalier. "Well,

Monsieur, what do you think?" asked the clothier, visibly nervous. "Is this what Monsieur had in mind?"

Louis gawped at the appalling vision reflected in the mirror. The slashed doublet gaped absurdly on his crooked torso. The lace at his wrists hung almost to his knees. He peered out from beneath the broad brim of a hat that his hunched back kept bumping down over his eyes. "I look … I look like an ape dressed up for a costume party," he said.

The haberdasher winced. "The more extreme fashions of the day are simply not suited to everyone, Monsieur," he said. "Perhaps something a bit more conservative…."

Louis shook his head stubbornly, which made his hat's tall ostrich feather waggle back and forth. "No, curse it. Hell's fish! Why try to pretend I'm not a short, ugly hunchback? If they want a cavalier, I'll give them one." He turned to the clothier. "I want *more* lace," he said. "I want the boots *higher*—up to here! And I want a *bigger* hat! Only pin the brim up in front, so I can see where I'm going."

"Is … is Monsieur sure that's what he wants?"

"They're going to laugh at me anyway, Monsieur le Couturier. I may as well have a laugh back at them. When can you have it ready?"

CHAPTER X
A SEVENTEETH-CENTURY LETTER BOMB

Though Ensign de Fontrailles was now a member of the Cardinal's Guard, it was more in the capacity of intelligencer than swashbuckler. He wasn't expected to join in mounting guard around the Petit-Luxembourg or escorting the cardinal around Paris—which suited the other guardsmen just fine. In fact, with the exception of Jussac, the cavaliers of the Garde Cardinale were not best pleased to have the eccentric Vicomte de Fontrailles installed as one of their officers—especially once they saw his new wardrobe. Whether the other guards recognized Fontrailles's outlandish get-up as a mockery of their own sartorial excess was questionable. However, they certainly found the idea of a hunchbacked guardsman absurd, and their barely-concealed contempt stung Louis more than he cared to admit.

The lack of esteem was mutual; Louis thought the Cardinal's Guard the biggest bunch of mallet-heads he'd ever had the misfortune to meet. Boastful boys who refused to grow up, their only interests were fighting, gambling, screwing, and clothing. Worst of all, they were shockingly good at all these pursuits, whereas Fontrailles was a conspicuous failure—as they continually reminded him in not-so-subtle ways. They'd ask, "Up for a little rapier sparring this morning, Ensign de Fontrailles?" or "We missed you at the roistering last night, Ensign de Fontrailles—were you with your mistress again?"

Louis briefly considered calling out one of these preening ruffians to a meeting involving pistols at dawn, on the assumption that the cavaliers of the guard would take him more seriously if he put a ball through one of their number. It was a seductive idea, but Louis reminded himself that he wasn't out to make a career in the Cardinal's Guard, just use his position to get his hands on *The Three Mystic Heirs*. Besides, the challenged party had the choice of weapons; his opponent would probably pick swords over pistols, and that would be the end of Louis d'Astarac.

Was it so these swaggering bullies would no longer look down on him as a subhuman monster that he was so determined to find a cure for his deformity? To be able to dance, ride, and fence, and moreover, to be able to look these louts in the eye? *No,* he told himself. No: it was for Isabeau.

So he set aside his rankling at the other Guards' disdain and got down to the work of finding the lost Rosicrucian book. Which still meant finding someone who'd seen Salomon de Caus.

He sent out more letters. The answer, when it came, was from near at hand. The monastery of the Brotherhood of the Minims was near the Place Royale, in the quarter of Paris called the Marais; the superior of the monastery, Marin Mersenne, also happened to be a first-class mathematician who maintained an active correspondence with natural philosophers throughout Christendom ... including, he reported, Salomon de Caus.

Mersenne invited Fontrailles to an austere dinner in his study at the monastery, a cell as full of books and papers as it was empty of furnishings and ornamentation. "Dinner" turned out to be a ragout of parsnips, not exactly Louis's favorite dish. *These Minims live up to their name,* he thought. But Mersenne was quite voluble for a monk, and told Fontrailles that he had not only heard from Salomon de Caus, he'd had a visit from him.

"You did?" Fontrailles, who'd been raising his goblet of watered wine to his lips, placed it back on the table untasted. "When was this, if I may ask?"

"Last winter," said Mersenne, a man with a long, narrow, but mobile face that could lighten or darken suddenly, smiling or glaring with surprising intensity. "I don't recall the date exactly, but it was during Advent. He looked unwell, as if suffering from a long illness, and his speech was rambling, almost incoherent."

"Had you known him before?"

Mersenne, spooning up the last of his parsnips, shook his tonsured head. "Only by reputation. I'd read his *Raisons des Forces Mouvantes*, which, though it wallows in the deplorable spiritual errors of the Rosicrucians, nonetheless represents a true advance in our understanding of mechanics. I'd written to commend him on it, so when he arrived in Paris he called on me to ask my advice."

"What about?"

"His former patron, Frederick of Palatine, had fallen on hard times, and de Caus was looking for a new one. One must have funds to be an engineer, of course—so much more expensive than mathematics. De Caus was thinking of approaching Richelieu and wanted to know the best way to go about it." Mersenne paused, eying Fontrailles's virtually untouched bowl of parsnips, then sighed and continued. "I advised him first to take a prolonged rest to restore his health, and second, if he wanted to interest the cardinal, to emphasize the practical, even military applications of his work. He didn't care for this; he was on the verge, he said, of rediscovering some of the ancient principles governing the interplay of fluids and vapors and needed support for pure research. He raved on for some time about pulmonary and circulatory hydraulics. Poor fellow," he concluded, "I haven't heard from or seen him since," and then sighed again, though whether about de Caus's condition or Fontrailles's unfinished parsnips Louis couldn't tell.

"Do you know where he was staying, or who else he was planning to see?" Fontrailles asked.

"I do not; he was quite wary of answering direct questions," said Mersenne. "However, shortly after our meeting he sent me a coded letter, with a preface in plainscript saying that if I needed to see him again his whereabouts could be found in the code."

"Really?" said Louis. This *was* news. "And did you decode it?"

"I started to, as it was a *mathematical* puzzle, you see, and thus somewhat intriguing, but when I realized the problem employed Rosicrucian tropes and allusions I set it aside. The whole thing just seemed like more maunderings of a disordered mind; and after all, I had no real reason for further contact with Monsieur de Caus."

"Did you keep this letter?"

"I keep *everything*. I'm sure it's filed in last year's correspondence." Mersenne turned to a nearby shelf and shuffled through a stack of paper. "And here it is!" he said with satisfaction.

"May ... may I see it?" Fontrailles asked.

"If it interests you," Mersenne said. He handed the letter across the table; Fontrailles took it, then carefully slid his bowl of parsnips toward the mathematician. "Really? Oh, but I've had enough," Mersenne said, before picking up his spoon. "Of course, it would be a sin to let it go to waste."

While Mersenne slurped, Louis read: "My dear Monsieur Mersenne; Should you need to find me, there is a Puzzle in this Parabola." There followed a curious little story told from the viewpoint of a man walking in an allegorical wood: typical Rosicrucian imagery, involving red and white rosebushes, a cave, and a talking lion who introduced the narrator to two marvelous beasts, then challenged him to guess their names.

This appeared to be the puzzle: "The first wondrous creature, pure White in Color, smiled at my Curiosity, and replied, 'My name contains two and seventy, and yet hath only seven letters; the third is one-third of the second, and the fourth is three more than the first.' The second creature, who was more Russet and Hairy, said, 'My name is yet greater, for it contains an hundred, ten and eight in letters no more than nine; the first and fourth are equal, while the fifth and eighth combined are the ninth.' At first I greatly Wondered at this, then shortly Reckoned it Out."

The letter was signed, "S.C." Fontrailles asked, "Might I copy out this puzzle?"

"Oh, certainly," Mersenne said. "Mind the heresy, though."

That evening Louis wrestled with the puzzle for two hours, but it was no use: he'd never had much of a mathematical mind, and didn't even know where to start to solve the thing. *"Merdieu!"* he cried, throwing his goose quill across the room. "I'll never figure this out without help. But Mersenne's afraid of sacrilegious contamination, so he won't solve it for me; and while des Cartes could probably do it in his head, I promised to leave him out of this." He brightened. "I know: I'll send it to Isabeau. She probably won't get it either, but at least she'll know I'm thinking about her. And I haven't written her yet this week."

The next day he called on Capitaine de Cavois to inquire if there was such a thing as a King's Mathematician to whom Fontrailles could apply for help, but Cavois had no time for puzzles. "Name of a name!" he snarled at his ensign. "The guard leaves tonight for Nantes with the king, and you dare bedevil me with such rubbish? Save it until we return!"

"But that could be weeks!" Fontrailles sputtered.

"Months, even."

"But this is the cardinal's business!"

Cavois gestured at the paperwork piled on his desk. *"Everything* is the cardinal's business, lad. You'll have to wait your turn."

"Are you taking all the guards with you? What if I run into trouble and need an extra hand?"

Cavois scowled, then said, "Bernajoux is staying behind—you can have him."

"Bernajoux, the duelist?" Fontrailles asked. "Isn't he still recovering from those wounds that guardsman gave him?"

Cavois shrugged. "It's the best I can do. Now get out of here, or I'll put you to work writing requisition letters."

Two days later, because there were, as always, delays, king and Court departed for the western provinces, and Fontrailles was left to his own devices. *And so far,* he thought, *my devices seem distinctly inadequate.*

He spent several days on the Left Bank at the Sorbonne, on the theory that a philosophical engineer might long for the company of his peers, but though many of the professors and students had heard of Salomon de Caus, none had seen him. "I need to think more like an intelligencer," Louis told himself. "I wish Rochefort were here—then at least I could ask a spy how one goes about spying things out. The only other spy I've met was the Comtesse de Bois-Tracy. Come to think of it, she was looking for de Caus, too; if he's to be found, she's probably already found him. Maybe I should be looking for *her*."

It was, at least, an idea—and while the countess was not exactly a public figure in Paris, she was a memorable enough presence that eventually Fontrailles was able to pick up her trail. After a week he had located her place of address, and had determined that madame was, like everyone else, Out of Town.

And so the long hot Paris summer wore on: nobody had seen de Caus; nobody had heard from him; nobody had any idea where he was.

Once a week Fontrailles checked in on his theoretical subordinate, Bernajoux, who was recovering rather well considering how badly he'd been perforated by the young d'Artagnan. Fontrailles was returning one evening from visiting Bernajoux when he was met at the door by Vidou. "Letter for you, Monsieur," he said.

"Who's it from, Vidou?" Fontrailles removed his oversized hat and mopped the sweat from his brow with the lace of his cuff. "Another natural philosopher telling me he knows nothing about the whereabouts of Salomon de Caus?"

"No, Monsieur—it's from Mademoiselle de Bonnefont."

"Isabeau! Why didn't you say so? Give it here!"

"Bad news, most likely," Vidou muttered, as Fontrailles cracked the wax seal and unfolded the stiff paper of the letter.

My Dear Louis,

I received your most recent letter, the one with the little puzzle in it. It was wonderful to hear from you, as always. Rest assured that every time I bow down to the good God, you are in my prayers.

As for the puzzle, it did take a few minutes to work it out, but eventually I got it.

The letters of the animals' names were referred to as numbers, so I assumed it was probably a simple alphabetic number-letter substitution, but at first I miscounted because I didn't realize that two pairs of letters, "I" & "J" and "U" & "V," were each being counted as one. After that, it was quite simple.

The first beast is a Licorne–

L 11

I 9

C 3

O   14

R 17

N   13

E   5

–Which adds up to 72, of course; and the second beast is a–

M   12

A   1

R 17

M   12

O   14

U   20

S 18

E   5

T 19

...Adding up to 118, as you see. Are there streets of those names in Paris? And do they intersect?

There is little news here in Armagnac. The warm summer has ensured that we shall have a good harvest from the vines. Your sister Hèléne has written from Estang: she is well, and sends her love. I am being courted by Éric de Gimous, and he has told my father that he intends to ask for my hand in marriage.

I may accept him.

Take care, and may God watch over you,

Isabeau de BONNEFONT

CHAPTER XI
THE PLOTS ENTWINE

At the corner of the Rue des Marmousets and the Rue de la Licorne, behind the stately church of Sainte-Madeleine de la Cité, which the Bishop of Paris called his own, stood a tall old medieval house that jutted farther out over the street with every story, as though it was leaning away from the house of God that bulked up to its rear. Behind it, far beyond Sainte-Madeleine, the sun was setting, and the few lights in the dark narrow streets of the Île de la Cité were already being lit.

On the corner of the Rue de la Licorne, in the ancient tavern with the sign of the unicorn that had given the street its name, two men hunched over a bottle of wine and considered the old house on the opposite corner. "Are you sure you're up to this?" asked Ensign de Fontrailles. "The doctor said you should have another two full weeks of rest."

"Doctors—pfah!" Bernajoux spat through his extravagant black mustache. "That doctor has killed more people with his decoctions than I have with my sword. Besides, didn't you say this wizard you're looking for isn't at home?"

"That's what the concierge told me," Fontrailles replied, taking a sip of the wine and wrinkling his nose in disgust. It was thin and acidic, an offense to every vintner in France. How had this tavern stayed open for centuries serving such plonk? He put the glass down and the letter from Isabeau crinkled inside his doublet. *And there,* he thought, *is the true source of my dismal mood.* He grimaced and said, "The concierge told me they hadn't seen Monsieur de Caus in months, but were afraid to enter his room because of his 'unchancy fanglements.' Then she made the sign against *fascinatio*—the evil eye."

Bernajoux drained his glass with every sign of satisfaction and poured himself another. "So you suspect this wizard's inner sanctum might be guarded by some sort of hell-born monstrosity, and you brought me along to spill its guts? Wise move, *mon Officier.* After half the summer in bed, I'd like an opportunity to flex my wrist."

"I doubt there will be any need for swordplay," Fontrailles said. "Anyway, de Caus is more of an engineer than a wizard."

"Oh? Then this woman, this concierge, is she young and pretty? You need me to romance her as a diversion while you trespass within?"

"No, the concierge is away, visiting relatives—and in any case she's a toothless crone who smells like burnt garlic. Probably not your type."

"Ha! Not unless she were wealthy. But see here, *mon Officier....*" This time there was definitely some sarcasm in the way Bernajoux said it. "...If you've got a problem that can't be solved with a kiss or a thrust, why bring me along? I'm no spy—nor worse, a scholar."

"Oh, I won't ask you to do anything *ungentlemanly,*" Fontrailles said. "To be candid, I intend to break into de Caus's room, and I don't want any interference from his neighbors. If anyone objects, it will be your job to bristle that impressive mustache and look stern."

"That I can do," Bernajoux poured the last of the wine into his glass. "This won't take long, will it? I have a mistress or two eagerly awaiting me."

"Really? I thought everyone had left town but us."

"Not everyone." Bernajoux twirled his mustache. "Just a great many husbands."

As usual with older houses in the city, the stair to the upper floors had its own, unlocked, side entrance. Inside it was as black as the inside of a mine, so Fontrailles paused to light the dark-lantern he'd brought along. With the light escaping its narrow shutter they were able to see their way up the venerable staircase, which made querulous complaints at every step.

"De Caus's room is at the top," Fontrailles said. "Is there light enough for you?"

"You have a light?" Bernajoux said. "I can't see anything past that gigantic hat of yours. Speaking of which, I'd been meaning to ask, *mon Officier*, why you wear such a thing. Did you lose a wager?"

"I have my reasons."

"No doubt. I once knew a man who wore all his dead wife's gold teeth on a chain around his neck; he said the same thing."

Louis didn't even attempt to reply to this, just concentrated on not tripping over the irregular risers of the decrepit stairs. There were two doors at every landing, but none of them opened as they passed, and they encountered no one before reaching the door at the top.

"Doesn't look like the entrance to a wizard's room," Bernajoux said. "I thought such places always bore dire warnings in ancient scripts."

"God knows what you've been reading, Bernajoux...."

"Read? Me?"

"...But I suppose I'd better check the door for magical traps." Fontrailles took the lantern in his left hand and pulled the inlaid box containing the Thaumaturgical Ostrich from a belt pouch. Though he was trying to assume an air of confident experience, his hands were shaking, and as he opened the latch he bobbled the box; the bird flipped out and tumbled to the floor, where it broke into three pieces.

Fontrailles groaned; the ostrich's head, with its ridiculous cylindrical hat, twitched once and stopped. "I hope that wasn't valuable," Bernajoux said.

"It is—was—a magic-detector." Fontrailles placed the pieces carefully back in the inlaid box. "It was supposed to bob up and down in the presence of magic ... or a magician."

"Ah," said Bernajoux. "And you've broken it. So how will we learn if baleful magic awaits behind the door?"

"The usual way, I suppose," Fontrailles said. "We'll just open the door and find out."

"You know," Bernajoux said, "sometimes these houses have back stairs or some other way out. Perhaps I should post myself at the rear in case your wizard tries to escape."

"But what if he conjures up a hell-born monstrosity? You're not afraid of magic, are you, Bernajoux?"

The guardsman bristled. "Monsieur! The imputation is offensive, and I insist you withdraw it at once!"

"All right, Bernajoux: consider it withdrawn," Fontrailles said. "I just want to make sure we're doing the right thing."

"You're the officer here—I'm sure *you* know best," Bernajoux huffed. He spun on the heels of his tall cavalry boots and stalked off down the stair.

"These cavaliers are so *touchy*," Fontrailles muttered, before turning his lantern back on the door. It did not, in fact, look any different from the other six doors they had passed on the way up. *But this is the door to the sanctum of a Rosicrucian mechanist*, Louis thought. *Could he have set some kind of trap?*

He leaned forward to look at the lock, and the broad brim of his hat bumped against the panel; he backed away in alarm. "Confounded nuisance." Removing the oversized hat, Fontrailles hung it from an empty sconce on the wall behind him. Then he knelt next to the door, as low as he could, reached up and gingerly lifted the wrought-iron handle. It rose halfway and stopped: the door was locked.

But so had been the pantry of the Château de Fontrailles when the old viscount's sergeant-at-arms had shown young Louis, with a wink, how to open it by slipping a slender blade between the door and the jamb to lift the latch within. Remembering that lesson, the young viscount had come prepared this evening with just such a blade. Now, crouching to the side of the doorway and making himself as small as possible, he pushed the knife into the gap beside the door and slid it up past the handle until it made contact with a bar within. Then he pried up with the knife with one hand while he jerked on the handle with the other.

The door popped open and swung wide. Instantly a green flash burst from inside the room, blinding Louis and disorienting him. He heard a thunk from before him, a whir above his head and a crash from behind. He threw his back against the wall and blinked rapidly to clear his vision while fumbling for the lantern. The shutter, cranked wide, sent a shaft of light that leapt up the wall across from the door, showing him his puckered hat, driven deep into the plaster by a still-quivering crossbow bolt. *"Merdieu,"* Louis breathed.

He pivoted the lantern and looked carefully through the open doorway. Standing just inside was a four-foot bronze statue of Cupid, whose traditional bow and tiny darts had been replaced by a murderous heavy crossbow, now discharged, its string still faintly thrumming. A small green flame, the last remnant of the blinding flare, played amid the curls atop Cupid's head, and glistened from the wire that looped to the lock. As Fontrailles watched it flickered and went out.

He got shakily to his feet and entered the room, stepping carefully around the bronze Cupid, surveying the chamber with the beam from his lantern. The light illuminated a shelf near the door, and Fontrailles said, "I'll be a duck's *derrière.*" For there in a row stood no fewer than nine Thaumaturgical Ostriches. As he watched, the bird second from the left creaked, then swiveled slowly, head dropping until its beak tapped the shelf.

Fontrailles shook his head, then turned the lantern on the rest of the room. There was a narrow unmade bed, a workbench covered with all manner of tools and intricate devices, and a writing desk at the back wall beneath a shuttered window. Dust coated every surface; the place seemed quite abandoned.

Eagerly, Fontrailles crossed the room to the desk, set down the lantern, and proceeded to search through the papers of Salomon de Caus, erstwhile mechanist to the Elector Palatine.

Almost at once he found a thick octavo journal of numbered pages crammed with sketches, diagrams, and coded text. "Could this be the man's personal workbook?" he said in wonder. He flipped quickly through it, noting that some of the sketches included Rosicrucian and alchemical symbology, then moved over in front of the lamp so he could better make out the inky scrawls. His hip bumped against a waist-high wooden box that stood next to the desk, and a small, rather musical chiming noise sounded from within. Intrigued, he placed the book back on the desk and turned to look at the box.

It was three-foot cube, a large inlaid wooden box with a latch on the top edge nearest him, the metal silver-plated and engraved with cabalistic symbols. A box such as this, Louis thought, must contain something very important. He watched with almost clinical detachment as his hand reached for the silver latch. *Am I really going to do this?* he thought.

Apparently so; his fingers curled under the edge of the latch, lifted it and flipped it open. The top leapt up as if spring-loaded and flew away from him as all four sides of the box dropped at once, revealing a crouching, demonic ape that immediately began clashing a pair of shrill gongs right in front of Louis's face. Its yellow eyes stared, its teeth were bared in a hideous grin; Louis shrieked and backed away from it.

Almost at once the shuttered window over the desk burst inward as Bernajoux crashed into the room, boots-first. In a single motion of ineffable grace he slid across the desk, landed on his feet before the ape-demon, drew his rapier and lunged, plunging the blade between the clashing gongs and deep into the horror's chest. There was a discordant sound of snapping wires and uncoiling springs, and then the thing was quiet.

"Ha! If that's not a hell-born monstrosity, I don't know what would be," Bernajoux said, placing a boot on the thing's still-grinning face and wrenching his rapier free. The ape-demon fell back with a rattle and clang, the tassel waving on its red Turkish hat.

Fontrailles shut his gaping mouth, then managed to say, "I think it's more of an 'unchancy fanglement.'" He took a deep breath. "How ... how did you get here?"

"I climbed a convenient buttress on the back wall of the church," Bernajoux said, inordinately pleased with himself. "When I heard you cry out, it was an easy leap to the eaves to swing in through the window."

"Blue heavens, Bernajoux! What are you like when you're not recovering from a wound? I suppose I should thank you."

"That would be courteous," Bernajoux said pleasantly. "Are the papers on the desk important? Because they've caught fire."

Fontrailles spun to see that his lantern, knocked over by Bernajoux's sudden entrance, had started a little blaze on the desktop. A dark powder that had spilled from an upended bottle began to ignite and throw colored sparks. *"Mon Dieu!"* Fontrailles cried. "De Caus's papers! Help me put it out!"

With the aid of a blanket torn from the bed they finally managed to smother the blaze, though Louis thought that Bernajoux seemed more interested in making merry quips than in extinguishing the fire. In the darkness after the last flame was stamped out Louis found his battered lantern, re-lit it, and took stock of the damage: most of the loose papers turned to ashes, and the octavo notebook charred and partly burnt away. "A thousand devils!" Fontrailles cursed. "What rotten luck."

"Is it a spell book?" Bernajoux asked. "Do you suppose it contains any recipes for love potions?"

Fontrailles just glared, which seemed to affect the guardsman not at all. "Tell you what," Fontrailles said. "Why don't you go out on the landing and keep watch. If anything else needs to be annihilated, obliterated, or otherwise destroyed, I'll call you."

"Mais oui, mon Officier!" Bernajoux saluted with a click of his spurred heels, turned and sauntered from the room. Louis thought he heard a faint chuckle as he went.

Fontrailles pocketed the blackened notebook and proceeded to search the rest of the room, sneezing occasionally from the dust he raised. There were a number of curious items on the workbench, some of which Louis couldn't identify, but he found nothing that indicated where the mysterious mechanist had disappeared to. The number of half-finished projects on hand certainly seemed to indicate that the occupant hadn't planned a prolonged absence.

He checked the desk for hidden compartments, but found none. Baffled, he shrugged and turned to go, then stopped and drew the inlaid box once more from his belt pouch. He removed the broken pieces of his

Thaumaturgical Ostrich and put them on the shelf next to the row of similar birds, then selected one of the intact ostriches, placed it carefully in his box, and took his leave.

On the landing Bernajoux was inspecting his boots for scuff marks when Fontrailles rejoined him. "Did you find what you were after, *mon Officier?*" he asked brightly.

"Probably not." Fontrailles looked ruefully at his hat, driven deep into the wall. He said, "I'll never wear *that* again."

"Indeed?" said Bernajoux. "Then the affair wasn't a total loss."

The next morning Fontrailles quickly determined that the contents of the charred notebook were encoded using the simple substitution cipher Isabeau had described in her letter. He spent all morning decoding the first three pages, which dated from Heidelberg in the summer of 1616, ten years earlier. These were less than enlightening, as they addressed nothing but de Caus's plans for the great Palatine garden and his business affairs, which were somewhat tangled—apparently he had not yet been prosperous enough at that time to hire Albert Quinot to handle such things for him.

Fontrailles was interrupted when Vidou brought in his dinner, along with the news that the king's business in Brittany was at an end and the Court would soon be returning to Paris. "Are you sure?" Fontrailles asked. "It might be just another rumor."

"Nay, Monsieur, some of the royal advance riders are in town already."

"Sacred cat! I'd better hurry—I have to have some results before the cardinal returns." *And before Isabeau marries Éric,* he appended mentally.

"Slim chance o' that," Vidou muttered as he shuffled from the room, "sittin' up here all day working them puzzle books."

Fontrailles began skipping ahead in the notebook, decoding short passages and hoping to strike something interesting. Notes about ideas for automata, entries about avoiding creditors, frustration with the shortsightedness of his patron—but nothing about *The Three Mystic Heirs.*

The pages seemed to be growing dim. Fontrailles glanced at the window and saw that the light was fading, the last rays of the late summer sun glinting from the spire of the Grands Augustins across the river. He'd been hunched over his table all day and was stiff, cramped, and ink-stained. It was high time for a walk to stretch his limbs and order his thoughts.

The Place Dauphine was in shadow, and the slapstick comedy troupe that performed on the platform at the south end had already packed up its props and costumes and retired for the day. Fontrailles strolled out onto the Pont Neuf and watched the bustle as daytime Paris hustled to get home before the long shadows of night brought out the predators.

A tug on his sleeve jarred him out of his brown study. "Monsieur de Fontrailles?"

Louis turned and saw a nondescript man of about middle height, dressed in clothes that were worn and none too clean, looking like any of a thousand other citizens of Paris on the great bridge that evening. On closer inspection, there was something indefinably menacing about this particular man—maybe it was the way he glowered at Fontrailles through his right eye (the left was covered by a patch), or maybe it was the hilts of assorted weapons that showed through the opening in his cloak.

Fontrailles instinctively glanced over his shoulder—difficult, for a hunchback, and it sent a sharp pain down his spine—to see if the man had a confederate sneaking up behind him. It didn't seem so. "What do you want?" Fontrailles said. "And how do you know my name?"

"You have an appointment, Monsieur," the one-eyed man said.

"An appointment? I don't know about any appointment. Who with?"

The man leaned forward and hissed, "*With the Capuchin.*"

"With Father Joseph? Ah, well—as long as *he* knows about it, that's good enough for me. Lead on."

"It's tomorrow morning, nine of the clock," the man said from the side of his mouth. "Rue Garancière. Don't be late." He turned and began to walk away.

"Wait! Rue Garancière? Which house?"

"Don't worry about that—we'll see *you*," the one-eyed man said. Then he melted into the crowd and was gone.

Oh, excellent, Louis thought. *An appointment with the cardinal's personal spook.*

And what results do I have to show him?

He hurried back to his lodgings, sat down again with the notebook and turned to the very last page. The writing was eccentric, blurred in places, and the edges of the page were charred; it took Louis over an hour to decode it. Completed, he had the following entry:

14 April 1626

Followed today by a black robe. Trapped me in an alley and threatened me with some sort of hand axe. Said I knew what they wanted, and I had only twenty-four hours to give it to them.

Said his name was Mìkmaq. Said they knew where I lived.

Said if I didn't give it to them, they'd put me in Bicêtre, and then I'd be sorry.

It's time to go.

This was mostly gibberish, but there was one reference Louis could understand: *Bicêtre*. The Paris asylum for the mad. He shuddered; he'd been to the place, on a charity visit while in seminary, and it was horrific, a fortified prison where the insane were punished for their madness.

If de Caus was indeed in Bicêtre, Louis knew he couldn't get him out on his own. He could call on the cardinal for help, of course, but then de Caus would end up in the custody of Richelieu, and there were no guarantees that the cardinal would share whatever he learned from him with the Ensign of his Political Squad.

Louis heard muttering behind him and realized that Vidou was in the room, dusting his little collection of the once-magical automata of Salomon de Caus that stood on the mantel. It was one of those sultry evenings that sometimes come in early September as if in denial of autumn, and while Vidou turned to open the window, Louis pondered the model clockworks, hoping for inspiration. A fountain, a wind organ, a rampant lion, an astronomical clock: beautiful things all, of intricate construction, testimony to the Rosicrucian mechanist's craft and esthetic. What could they tell him about the problem of their maker?

Inspiration eluded him. Louis took down the fountain, the wind organ, and the clock, and set them on the table. He was almost dizzy with fatigue. Last of all he set the eighteen-inch brass lion next to them, sat down in his chair and peered into its dark eyes. He said, "Speak to me, O Lion."

The lion opened its mouth and emitted a tinny roar.

He blinked, the room spinning. Beyond the lion, the wind organ on the table began gaily tooting the Elector Frederick's wedding march, while the astronomical clock commenced ticking away, tiny cycles and epicycles slowly rotating. The little fountain, its miniature hydraulics seeking vainly for fluid to pump and whirl, rasped and whined.

Louis, his eyes almost leaping from his face, scooted his chair back until it hit the wall beneath the window. What the hell was happening?

He was so spooked by the seemingly animated automata that he almost missed the thump as a heavy object hit the floor to his left. He glanced down, then stared: a metal sphere, smoking and studded with spikes, hissed on the floorboards, still quivering from its sudden arrival.

Louis had never seen one before, but he knew what it was: a petard.

He was about to be blown to bits.

De Caus's notebook was still in his hand. He swiped the book at the petard, vaguely hoping to bat it back out through the window through which it had obviously come, but he succeeded only in hitting it hard enough to embed one of its spikes into the cover. Result: he was holding the book, and stuck onto the book was the smoking petard. The sparking fuse was almost burnt down to its entry-hole.

He threw both book and petard out the window. The bomb exploded, and Fontrailles was thrown back into the room amid diamonds of shattered glass.

The next thing Louis knew Vidou was helping him to his feet as Cocodril leaned out over the blackened window sill. "Somebody running along the quay," Cocodril said. "Shite! He's gone around the corner. We'll never catch him now."

Fontrailles coughed, shook his head, and said, "Don't worry: once he realizes I'm still alive, he'll probably be back for another visit."

"Ah, but now *I* shall be on my guard!" Cocodril said, striking a stalwart pose. "If he returns, I'll see that he regrets it!"

"No doubt."

"But what do we do now, Monsieur?" Vidou asked.

"Well, Vidou," the viscount said, "I suggest you see about getting us a new window."

With an attempted assassination behind him and an interview with Father Joseph ahead of him, Louis d'Astarac spent a sleepless night. The next morning, not entirely at his best, found him in dusty Rue Garancière, near Richelieu's lair of the Petit-Luxembourg, just as the bells of Saint-Sulpice tolled nine. The one-eyed bruiser materialized from a crowd of passersby, tapped Fontrailles on the shoulder, and led him to an unprepossessing house a half-block from the end of the street. Once inside, his guide introduced him into a dim and chilly rear chamber furnished only by a long table and a couple of chairs. The walls were spotted with mildew and the hearth looked as if it hadn't had a fire in it for a century, at least. "Wait here, Monsieur," One-Eye said, before withdrawing.

Fontrailles sat down, only to start immediately back to his feet as an inner door opened to admit a compact figure, cloaked and cowled in a coarse fibrous robe that made Louis itch just to look at it. Father Joseph walked to the middle of the room, bare feet slapping gently on the rough, cold floor. He nodded to Fontrailles, sat down in the second chair, and pushed back his peaked cowl.

Fontrailles bowed respectfully, waited for a second nod from the Capuchin, then sat as well. Father Joseph's back wasn't humped, but otherwise he was nearly as ugly as Fontrailles. He had a prominent, rather bulbous nose and protruding eyes beneath a tall forehead like carved granite, across which a single black, bristling eyebrow crawled from temple to temple. More black bristles sprouted from his chin, cheeks, and upper lip, forming a spiny ruff that repelled the edges of his collar and cowl, which probably spared him some serious abrasion, as the wool looked stiff enough to turn a blade.

Further consideration of Father Joseph's remarkable appearance was interrupted when the gargoyle opened its mouth and whispered, "Welcome, my son, and may God in his infinite mercy bless you with wisdom and humility. Thank you for being so kind as to call upon me today."

"Well, of course, Father. Anything to oblige." Fontrailles leaned forward so as not to miss a word. This whispering business was more alarming than shouting would have been. "How may I serve?"

"Our master, His Eminence the cardinal, has recently tasked you with the recovery of a certain heretical work, which I shall not name," hissed Joseph, his eyes protruding so far that Louis half expected to see them emerge from their sockets on stalks. "Whether the prescriptions expounded in the said work may be employed without danger to the immortal soul of the employer is as yet unresolved. What matters is that its possession be denied to our enemies—if only because even the souls of heretics should be sheltered from sin, as they may someday be redeemed."

Louis felt his own eyes starting to protrude. "My thought exactly," he said.

"In that case," the spook whispered, "please report your progress in this blessed work."

Fontrailles had expected that Joseph would get around to business eventually and had already been mentally marshaling his excuses. "Well, the search must, of course, begin here in Paris, and as the Court spent all summer in Brittany and has only just returned to the capital, progress has necessarily been rather limited."

"But there *has* been some?" Joseph interrupted quietly.

"But naturally! I am about to make arrangements to hire several experienced agents, and am closing in on Salomon de Caus, who is suspected of having been in possession of King Frederick's copy of the work-that-shall-not-be-named."

"Hmm. I have reviewed your case, and it occurred to me to wonder why you had taken such a personal interest in a book of such dangerous ideas. What would you do with the work, if you had it?"

For a moment, Louis missed it—then he realized that it actually hadn't crossed Father Joseph's mind that he might want to use the book himself to cure his deformity. In this, at least, the Capuchin had something in common with the scholar des Cartes, in that neither really perceived him as malformed: des Cartes cared only about Fontrailles's mind, and Joseph was interested only in his soul.

In any event, this time he had an answer for Joseph's question. "As I explained to His Eminence," he said smoothly, "after my partial copy of the Nameless Work was stolen from my château, I realized its value to the State and assumed personal responsibility for its recovery."

Father Joseph smiled, which made the bristles around his mouth writhe as if they had a life of their own. "Such devotion is rarely found outside the monastic orders, and is to be commended when it appears," he whispered. "The feelings of betrayal," he continued, in a voice so low that Louis had to strain to hear it, "are commensurately greater on those regrettable occasions when such devotion is found to be counterfeit. Indeed, when the betrayed visits harsh penalties upon the betrayer, it is hard to condemn such punishment, no matter how severe. Am I understood?"

"Monseigneur speaks with utmost clarity," Fontrailles said. "Are there any specific instructions for me?"

"There are. The Duke of Buckingham is in Paris."

"The English prime minister! It's been kept very quiet."

"It is not a state visit. The duke is here in secret, come to pursue an illicit relationship with ... a French lady of high rank. However, we also suspect that he has come in hopes of acquiring the book which you have been assigned to recover." The black eyebrow rippled. "We learned this from a traitor within our own organization, whom we discovered and then induced to talk. Among the things he told us is that he had informed Buckingham's people that you were our agent in the quest for the book. So be wary, my son: the duke may send agents of his own to put you out of the way."

"*Ohé*," Fontrailles said. "I believe he already has. Last night, I was ... set upon."

"And?"

"The attack was, uh, *foiled*, Father." *There*, Louis thought. *That sounds appropriately hardbitten and intelligencer-like.*

The cowl nodded. "It is well. If, in your investigations, you encounter Buckingham or any of his agents, you are to report it without delay. Do you understand, my son?"

"I do!"

"One other matter. The recent conspiracy against His Majesty was put down thanks to the blessed endeavors of His Eminence the cardinal—but due to a blunder on the part of one of our own agents, a principal plotter in the scheme was allowed to escape. The offending agent has been … admonished, and the conspirator has been tracked here to Paris. A few of us have returned in advance of the Court, but we are short-handed, so you may be called upon to assist in this malefactor's apprehension."

"Only too happy, Father," Fontrailles said, though he was anything but.

"Then be on your way, and may God go with you and bless your endeavors." Without further ado the Capuchin stood and flat-footed out of the room.

Outside the door Fontrailles found the one-eyed bruiser, who conducted him to the street. "Make no mistakes," the man said. "I'll be watching you."

This seemed to Louis entirely gratuitous. Must *everyone* threaten him? "*Merdieu!*" he burst out. "What are you menacing me for? We're both servants of His Eminence! Furthermore, I am a nobleman of France and will not be spoken to in this manner. You may in time be ordered to stick a knife between my ribs, but you can at least show me proper respect while you do it!"

To Louis's gratification the bruiser actually seemed somewhat abashed. "I'm just doing my job, Monsieur le Vicomte," he said defensively. "I don't mean anything by it."

"Well," Fontrailles sniffed, with towering hauteur, "all *right,* then."

CHAPTER XII
LUCY HAY, THE COUNTESS OF CARLISLE

The Vicomte de Fontrailles counted doors again, pretending he wanted to make sure he got it right, but really he was just procrastinating. "Rue de Vaugirard," he said, "between Fossoyeurs and Férou, second door on the right, under the sycamore tree." There were only three houses on the block, and only one sycamore tree, so there was really no way to mistake which house belonged to Aramis the musketeer—but still Louis hesitated. The Petit-Luxembourg was only a few hundred paces down the road, and the whole neighborhood was a hive of Cardinalists. Could he risk being seen paying a call on a King's Musketeer?

He glanced up and down the street, in a manner he hoped was more nonchalant than furtive, and didn't see anyone he recognized. Which meant nothing, of course—anyone detailed to spy on him would be bound to be a stranger.

His humped back tingled as if he was being watched, and he spun suddenly around. No one. Enough dithering: on with it!

When word had come two days before that Ensign de Fontrailles was summoned to assist in apprehending the escaped mastermind of the late conspiracy Louis had cursed feelingly, then sent Vidou for his weapons and Cocodril for his horse. Less than thirty minutes later he had reported for duty at the Petit Arsenal next to the Bastille. He was wearing his red Cardinal's Guard tabard for the first time since he'd been invested, and feeling faintly ridiculous as he surveyed the collection of veterans he was expected to augment: hard-faced Cardinal's Guards, jaunty Royal Guardsmen, even a few haughty King's Musketeers. The Comte de Rochefort was in command of the makeshift detachment, and when Fontrailles arrived—Rochefort's glare told him he was the last to appear—Rochefort mounted his tall black horse and led them out.

Instructions were passed back from Rochefort as they rode out the Neuilly road. The unnamed conspirator had been tracked to a small town on the outskirts of Paris, where he'd been trapped inside the local church. He might be alone, or he might have confederates; the detachment was to surround the church and enter it simultaneously from all sides.

Fontrailles, hampered by his deformity, was a poor rider, and he ate the others' dust the entire way. When he arrived at the town's central square the cordon around the church was already in place, and he hurried to join a group of three musketeers about to enter the south transept.

After a brief glance of surprise the musketeers decided not to notice him, and Louis decided to return the favor. When the signal came to enter the church he followed them through the side door, then kept as far from them as he could as they fanned out to search. Thus he was alone when he noticed the small door behind a pillar in the north wall, and the musketeers' snub doubtless contributed to his decision to investigate it on his own.

The door opened on a short stairway leading to a crypt beneath the transept, and as Fontrailles entered he heard a sound from below. Foregoing his sword, he drew two pistols, cocked them, and went down to single-handedly catch the fugitive conspirator. That would show them!

No one was more surprised than Louis when, upon cornering his quarry with shaking pistols, he found that he knew him. The rebel leader was none other than the Chevalier d'Herblay, once Fontrailles's closest friend when they had both been in seminary as youths.

And Fontrailles had found that he just wasn't Cardinal's Guard enough to arrest an old friend. He'd warned d'Herblay that the church was surrounded, but his friend had simply smiled, donned the tabard of a King's Musketeer, and slipped out to join his would-be captors—who asked him why he'd taken so long to catch up with them, and called him "Aramis." Aramis, one of the famous Three Inseparables, the heroes of the musketeers.

So instead of single-handedly capturing the most wanted man in France, Fontrailles had helped him evade justice. The detachment had returned to Paris empty-handed, and Fontrailles had returned to face the fact that, if de Caus was being held in Bicêtre, he still had no chance of getting him out without assistance. Which brought him to his current reluctant situation in front of the house of Aramis the Musketeer.

It was a modest house, as befit a musketeer residing in a hive of Cardinalists. "I'd gird my loins, if only I knew what that meant," Louis said to himself. "Look on the bright side: he might not be at home." Finally he forced himself to knock. He hadn't even finished rapping before the door opened beneath his fist, revealing a plump, mild-looking, soberly-dressed fellow who looked at him inquiringly.

Louis, being nervous, made the mistake of smiling, and the plump fellow's eyes widened in alarm. Before the man could slam the door Fontrailles blurted, "Monsieur Aramis? I mean, is this the residence of Monsieur Aramis? And is he at home to visitors?"

"D'Astarac!" came a voice from inside. "Come in, *mon ami*, come in. Bazin, some wine for the Vicomte de Fontrailles, if you please."

It was Aramis, Fontrailles's old friend the Chevalier d'Herblay, smiling amiably. A strikingly handsome young man, slight and supple, Aramis was the picture of cavalier elegance in an outfit subtly embroidered black-on-black, highlighted by white lace and silver piping. He showed no evidence of the anxiety one would expect to see in a fugitive from justice. "We expected you somewhat earlier, I'm afraid, and now I haven't much time," he said, in a voice as sophisticated and elegant as his costume. "A pressing social engagement. Still, since it's you, I suppose I'll just have to arrive somewhat fashionably late.'"

"What do you mean, you expected me?" Fontrailles took the seat Aramis offered him at a table in the kitchen, beside where a rear window opened onto a tiny garden. "I didn't send ahead to say I was coming."

"Quite so," said Aramis, sitting across from him. "But you have a lackey called Cocodril, do you not?"

"Yes...."

"And you sent him around to make discreet inquiries to find out where I lodged, did you not? Ah, thank you, Bazin. Here's a little sauterne I picked up in Lorraine, d'Astarac; I think you'll like it." Aramis smiled.

"All right, I get your meaning," Fontrailles said. "Cocodril wasn't discreet enough, I suppose. Devil take it! I thought he'd be less conspicuous than if *I* went around asking such questions."

"No doubt, my dear d'Astarac, no doubt. But whatever other qualities your Cocodril may have, he does not have the makings of an intelligencer."

"And that's my problem! I *need* intelligencers, dependable men with brains in their heads. But the only people I know in Paris are scholars, or, God help me, artists!"

"That *is* a problem. And so you came to me, presumably because I've already been involved in at least one conspiracy, and can be expected to be acquainted with conspirators."

Fontrailles winced. "I wouldn't have put it so bluntly, d'Herblay ... but, yes."

"Please try to get into the habit of calling me 'Aramis,' *mon ami*. It would be awkward if I was connected with the missing Chevalier d'Herblay."

"Sorry."

"Think nothing of it. Anyway, I believe I can help you. When a big conspiracy collapses, as ours did, it does put a lot of fellows out of work, some of whom are more-or-less reliable."

"A thousand thanks ... Aramis."

"Just reassure me on one little point, d'Astarac." The musketeer leaned forward, and Fontrailles saw a glint in his eye that reminded him of a shining swordpoint. "You've accepted a commission in the Cardinal's

Guard—God knows why, but I'm sure you have your reasons. That means you owe your allegiance to Cardinal Richelieu, who, if he only knew it, would love to have my head on the block. So I'd be obliged if you'd state that you're not planning to use these men in a way that would endanger me, my friends, or the interests of Their Majesties the King and Queen."

"Not at all, my dear Aramis! You see, I've been assigned to locate...."

Aramis held up a hand. "That's enough, d'Astarac. Don't tell me anything I don't need to know. I think I can find you three good men. Will tomorrow evening be soon enough?"

"That would be splendid. Thank you, my friend. To your health!" Fontrailles sipped the sauterne. "Say, this is good. I don't suppose the grapes they make this from would do well in Armagnac, more's the pity."

"Perhaps not," Aramis said, "but from what I remember of your own wine, you have nothing to be ashamed of. Send a few bottles around and I'll feel more than compensated."

"With pleasure!"

"*Ahem,* Monsieur." It was Bazin.

"Quite right, my friend," said Aramis. "D'Astarac, I really must be on my way. I'll meet you tomorrow night, but not here. Do you know the Posset-Cup tavern, near Saint-Sulpice?"

"I'll find it."

"*Au revoir,* then. Bazin, my cloak."

As Fontrailles made his way back toward the city proper, he mentally reviewed his encounter with Aramis and found his performance somewhat less than satisfactory. *Am I really that feckless, or is d'Herblay just appallingly competent?*

On the other hand, his friend's recent plot against the Cardinal *had* been an utter failure. Maybe he shouldn't expect too much from these men d'Herblay had promised to bring him.

"Monsieur de Fontrailles," Aramis said, in the Posset-Cup the next evening, "allow me to present Gitane, Beaune, and Parrott."

"A thousand thanks, Monsieur Aramis," said Fontrailles. "You said they were all experienced men, and I must say, they do seem to have a certain … *air* about them."

The air the men had about them was causing the other patrons of the Posset-Cup, a respectable neighborhood tavern, to look at them sideways and edge toward the door.

"I knew you'd be pleased," Aramis said. "Let me fill you in on their backgrounds. This is Gitane."

A dark-faced fellow with a patch over his right eye and a scar trailing down his right cheek took a step forward and removed his hat respectfully. *Why do all these spies wear eye patches?* Louis thought. *I swear they do it just to look sinister.*

"Gitane is a shipping expert," Aramis said, "specializing in the evasion of governmental inspections and imposts."

"You mean he's a smuggler," Fontrailles said.

"Perhaps so, *mon ami*, but there's no need to insult the man."

"He doesn't look insulted. Are you insulted, Gitane?"

The man's dark face split in a jagged grin. "Not the least bit, Monseigneur."

"Good," Fontrailles said. "Well, I think I can use a thick-skinned shipping expert. And who's this? Beaune, you said?"

"Quite so." Aramis beckoned forward a fair-haired, burly brute with hands the size of roast hens but a mild and amiable expression. "Beaune was an interrogator for the Duc de Vendôme," Aramis said, "Before the Duc was…."

"…Taken away to be interrogated, after the recent conspiracy," said Fontrailles. "What else can you do besides persuade people to talk, Beaune?"

The big man smiled shyly and opened one immense fist to display a half-dozen slim slivers of metal. "With these, I can open just about any kind of lock you like, Monseigneur," he said, in a surprisingly high voice. "I had lots of time to practice, on manacles, and cell doors, and suchlike."

"Improving yourself in your spare time; I like that. Shows real initiative," Fontrailles said. "And you—Parrott, was it? What kind of name is that?"

"English, may it please your lordship," said the third man, stepping forward. He was another big man, though not nearly as outsized as Beaune, and would have been handsome but for a great purple birthmark that sprawled across the left side of his face. He said, "My mother was French. She never liked England, and brought me back to France when I was fifteen. That's where I learned my trade."

He had a slight accent, but his French was relatively refined: perhaps he was a by-blow of some English aristocrat, brought up in a noble household. "And what *is* your trade, Mister Parrott?" Fontrailles asked.

"Parrott has a talent for replicating useful correspondence or official documents," Aramis said, "thus obviating needless bureaucratic oversight."

"Monsieur Aramis means I'm a forger," Parrott said. "I'm also a good man at following people without letting on I'm doing it."

"Splendid," Fontrailles said. "Very well, lads, you're engaged. I hereby induct you into the Political Squad of the Cardinal's Guard."

"Will we be wearing them red floppy cloaks with the crosses on 'em?" asked Gitane.

"No, I rather think plain attire is more apt for our purposes," Fontrailles said. "Now let's sit down, have a round of drinks, and work out the details."

"I can't thank you enough, Aramis. I mean it," Fontrailles said, as the two friends walked slowly up the dark Rue des Fossoyeurs. It had been a long day, and Louis's back was burning with fatigue. "Now I can do without relying on swashbucklers like Bernajoux, who are more trouble than they're worth. Present company excepted, of course."

"'A friend loves at all times, and a brother is born for adversity,' saith the Lord. But save your thanks, d'Astarac, until the day is done," Aramis said. "I have one more surprise for you back at my lodgings."

"Another sauterne?"

"Even better."

"Very well. I'll trust in your impeccable taste."

In a very few moments they were at Aramis's door, where a smiling

Bazin ushered them in. "Ah, all the comforts of home," Aramis said. "A crackling fire on the hearth, a pleasant divan before it, and on the divan, a beautiful lady."

"*Bon soir,* my dear Aramis," the lady said. "And to you, Monsieur le Vicomte."

It was the Comtesse Camille de Bois-Tracy.

Of course.

Louis had thought about her virtually every day since their encounter in the Hôtel de La Trémouille. He'd found his romantic daydreams about Isabeau frequently turned into fantasies about Camille de Bois-Tracy. This had happened so often that it was almost anticlimactic for Louis to encounter the subject of his erotic musings in the flesh.

Fontrailles bowed, making his best effort to conceal the pain of doing so. "How pleasant to see you again, Madame," he said, and then turned to Aramis. "And how do you come to know the countess, *mon ami?*"

Aramis smiled his slightly crooked smile. "One can't dabble for long in conspiracies in this city without making the acquaintance of Madame de Bois-Tracy. She's always plotting one thing or another. It's a hobby she pursues with some passion. Isn't that so, Countess?"

"You are always so charming, Aramis," the lady said, rising. Louis gulped. Relaxing in front of the fire she'd loosened her bodice, and the results were striking. She smiled at Louis, which made him a little dizzy, and said, "I'm surprised you never mentioned before that Monsieur de Fontrailles was one of your friends."

"Everyone has their secrets—as Madame knows all too well," Aramis said.

"How amusing you are," the countess said.

"As droll as the day is long," said Fontrailles. "Aramis, don't be coy about Madame de Bois-Tracy's secrets. I know perfectly well that she's an agent of the Duke of Buckingham, and I'm sure she knows I know it. And as the duke is in Paris even now, I'm sure she has urgent business to attend to—as do I, for that matter. So why have you brought us together? Besides the obvious goal of amusing yourself, that is."

"Because I rather think you're both in pursuit of the same thing," Aramis said, "and I hate to see my friends at cross-purposes."

"Nonsense, Aramis."

"You're driveling, darling."

"Am I?" said Aramis. "I don't think so. I think you're both trying to locate a certain gentleman named Salomon de Caus, because you hope he might lead you to a lost book titled *The Three Mystic Heirs.*"

"I *must* hang up my cloak," Fontrailles said.

"I'll pour us some wine," the countess said.

"Go ahead, fuss about while you compose your faces," said Aramis. "I promise not to look till you're done."

"Aramis, *chéri,* sometimes I could just kick you," the lady said.

"In this case, Aramis," said Fontrailles, "Madame de Bois-Tracy and I are in complete agreement."

"Then you really should call her by her real name," Aramis said. "Allow me to introduce you properly."

"*Aramis...*" the countess hissed in warning.

"Louis d'Astarac, Vicomte de Fontrailles," Aramis said, cheerfully ignoring her, "I present to you Milady Lucy Hay, Countess of Carlisle."

"Son of a *bitch!*" said Milady Lucy Hay, Countess of Carlisle, in English. Then, reverting to French: "How did you learn that, you wretch?"

"'Open rebuke is better than secret love.' It wasn't that difficult, my dear, once I realized you were actually an Englishwoman. You really must watch your accent. I assumed a lady of your nobility and obvious charms would hardly be unknown at the English court. I described you to some friends from across the Channel, and they were unanimous in their identification."

"Aramis, you are insufferable!"

"Sometimes, sometimes. No one's perfect, after all. Bazin, be so kind as to finish pouring the wine. I think we're all ready for a drink."

"Madame, I must apologize for my friend's behavior," Fontrailles said stiffly. "I'm sure neither of us realized we were coming here this evening just so Monsieur Aramis could be amused at our expense."

"Oh, come, d'Astarac—it's not like you to be so self-righteous," Aramis said. "Here, drink this and unbend a little. Appearances to the contrary, I didn't bring you two together just for a little joke. I really think you'd be better off joining forces."

Louis *did* need a drink. He swallowed the wine. "What makes you think our goals are the same?" he said.

"Oh, various things I've heard each of you say, and other things I've heard whispered around. One puts two and two together. Or in this case, I hope, one and one— for I'm quite fond of you both, and would hate to see you cutting each other's throats."

"But I'm after ... *the item* ... for Buckingham," the countess said, "and he wants it for Richelieu."

"True," said Aramis, "but I know both of you, and blind loyalty to ministers of state isn't in your natures. I'm quite sure you both have your own reasons for pursuit of, ah, *the item*, and can probably find some basis for compromise if you get it."

"Even if that were true," Fontrailles said, "how could we help each other? I'm no closer to finding *the item* than when I first met madame, here, some months ago—and I imagine she hasn't done any better, or she wouldn't be here now." He slurred the last phrase a bit. The wine seemed to be getting to him more quickly than usual, which was probably a measure of how tired he was.

"That's where I think I can be of material help to you both," Aramis said. "You see ... I believe I know where you can find Monsieur Salomon de Caus." The musketeer smiled rather smugly and looked from Fontrailles to the countess, savoring the moment.

"Well!" said Fontrailles, trying to take this in. He felt confused, somehow. Was de Caus not in Bicêtre after all? How had Aramis found him?

"Well, well, well," said the countess. "Why haven't you told me this before?"

"As I explained: you and d'Astarac are both friends of mine," Aramis said. "I couldn't tell just you, Madame."

"You might as well," the countess said. "There's no point in telling the viscount, here."

"What?" said Louis, through a thickening haze.

"Why is that?" said Aramis.

"Because," said the countess, "I've poisoned his wine."

CHAPTER XIII
MONSIEUR DE CAUS

For Louis d'Astarac the next few hours were delirium, an unending nightmare of being dragged behind a galloping horse down a dark, muddy road, punctuated by kicks to the stomach, vomiting, and violent diarrhea. The poison seemed to have struck him blind, but he still had the power of hearing — though what he heard was curiously confused, the sound sometimes painfully loud, sometimes dwindling as if disappearing into the distance. He definitely heard glass clinking, and the voices of Aramis and Lady Carlisle, and from this he developed the impression that his friend and his poisoner were taking their ease, drinking and chatting, while he writhed blindly on the floor in his death-agony.

Gradually his sensory impressions sorted themselves out, and the fires in his gut began to bank somewhat. A ruddy, rotating blur appeared out of the dark, which he eventually realized was the slow return of his eyesight. Distinct, intelligible phrases began to emerge from the hiss and welter:

"...Dry heaves at last, thank God!"

"...Clean this clyster, Bazin."

"...He looks better naked than I would have expected."

This last remark, in the voice of the Countess of Carlisle, shocked his eyes back into focus … and the first thing he saw clearly was the face of Lucy Hay, with the brown eyes, arched brows, and wide mouth so like Isabeau's, her features curved in the exact expression of sympathetic concern he'd seen so often on the face of the Demoiselle de Bonnefont.

Clearly, he must still be delirious.

Another kick inside his stomach doubled him over, and he retched. He felt like he had shards of broken crockery tumbling through him, and he seemed to be gargling a razor. He heaved up nothing but bitter spittle, though tears leaked from his eyes and oozed down his cheeks. It was a bad episode, but not as bad as it had been earlier. When the world stopped spinning he could see that he was still in Aramis's front room, on the floor in front of the fire, where he was huddled in a nest of blankets, now filthy with various bodily fluids. The furniture had all been pushed back and the room was teeming with people, both men and women.

And he was, he realized, quite naked.

"Aramis!" he croaked. His throat was raw as sand. "What the devil…?"

"It's all right, d'Astarac." Aramis knelt beside him—and he *was* holding a drink in his hand, the bastard. "Bazin has been taking care of you, helped by Vidou and Cocodril, whom I sent for. And Madame Durant, who's a midwife, lives just 'round the corner, so I sent for her too, and she brought her daughter, Amélie, and…."

"Jesus in a handcart!" Fontrailles cried, wrapping himself in the slimy blankets. "Why not the nuns from the Carmelite convent?"

"Well, the convent gates are locked at night, d'Astarac, so…."

"*Eeuhh!* What are these *things* on my *stomach?*"

"Those are the leeches Bazin put on to draw out the evil humors. And he said you should drink this decoction, as it will speed the evacuation of your bowels."

"Aramis, the only thing I want evacuated is *this room*. I would be very much obliged if you would get these people *out* of here! Except you, Vidou: stay and help me get cleaned up. And Cocodril! Keep close to the countess and make sure she doesn't leave the premises."

Lady Carlisle looked deeply hurt. "But, Louis—it's all just been a terrible misunderstanding!"

"Madame, don't call me Louis," said the Vicomte de Fontrailles. "And there has not been a *misunderstanding*, there has been a *clarification*. Now, out!" he rasped. "Out! Out! Out!"

Two hours later, as dawn and the sounds of the wakening city filtered in through the shutters, Louis d'Astarac, Lucy Hay, and Aramis sat around the latter's dining table, the hunchback pale but determined, the countess smiling but tense, and the musketeer at ease, as if nothing untoward had happened. Lady Carlisle had been remarkably contrite toward Fontrailles, and had done her best to help him overcome the effects of the poison. In fact, she was so sweet, and so gorgeous, that Fontrailles was nearly ready to forgive her.

Still playing the host, Aramis said, "Can I get you anything, Madame? Or you, d'Astarac? Bazin makes an herbal infusion that I've found to be a marvelous restorative after a night of excess."

Fontrailles snorted. "A night of excess. Is that how you'd describe it, Madame Countess? Or was it just another typical evening's entertainment for you?"

"Oh, Monsieur, that's unjust! I did everything possible to help nurse you back to health!"

"Probably because Aramis threatened not to tell you how to find de Caus if I died. Am I right, Aramis?"

The musketeer smiled but said nothing.

"That's good enough for me," Fontrailles said. "Nonetheless, I'm surprised I did survive. Though we've had only a limited acquaintance, Madame, I don't think you're the sort who leaves anything to chance. Why aren't I dead?"

"Well, is *that* a nice thing to say!" cried the countess, a picture of decorous indignation. "And I thought you were a gentleman."

Aramis cleared his throat. "Really, my dear, d'Astarac has a point—and I feel you should address it."

"Well! I merely ... that is to say...." The countess looked down, her fingers toying with a monogrammed handkerchief. "Well ... when I poisoned monsieur's wine … I used only half the usual dose. I knew I should poison him—he's an agent of the cardinal!—but somehow, I couldn't bring myself to give him a lethal dose."

She blushed to the tips of her ears.

"Incredible!" said Fontrailles. "You're embarrassed because you *didn't* murder me."

With a fiery glare the countess leapt to her feet. "That's quite enough, Monsieur! I am not accustomed to tolerating such insults from anyone!"

"Sit down, *cher amie,*" Aramis said mildly. "We can't very well adjourn the meeting before business has been addressed."

The countess clamped her mouth shut, worked her coral-hued lips for a moment, then wrapped her mantle around her shoulders, sat down, and nodded tightly, once.

"All right, Aramis," said Fontrailles, "the meeting is called to order, and you have the floor."

Aramis smiled pleasantly. "Thank you, d'Astarac. Now, since we've determined that you and Lady Carlisle have a common purpose, let's put the past behind us and consider your mutually profitable future."

"So tell us where we can find Salomon de Caus," Fontrailles said.

Aramis looked put out. "Really, d'Astarac! You take the fun out of everything."

"I had my fun last night. I'd just like to get on with it, if you don't mind."

"Oh, very well." Aramis assumed a declamatory posture. "As you both know, my sojourn in the King's Musketeers is really only a temporary diversion from my eventual distinguished career in the Church. As such, I maintain numerous connections with the various Catholic orders. It was from one of them that I learned that your Monsieur de Caus is confined in a hospital under ecclesiastical administration."

"A hospital?" said the countess. "Which one?"

Fontrailles squawked, "Don't say it, Aramis!"

Aramis said it. "Bicêtre."

"A *thousand* little blue devils! I already knew that, Aramis, and now you've gone and told the Duke of Buckingham's agent!"

"I don't understand. What is this place?" asked Lady Carlisle.

"I suppose you might as well know." Fontrailles grimaced at Aramis, who merely shrugged. "Bicêtre is a prison for the mad. It's a ... *terrible* place, Madame. Even if you were sane when you were put in there, you wouldn't stay that way for long."

The countess looked at Aramis. "Is it really that bad?"

"It's certainly true that very few of the troubled souls committed to Bicêtre were being redeemed," Aramis said. "The institution's practices were badly in need of reform, so it was recently placed under the jurisdiction of a different order."

"Which one?" asked Fontrailles.

"The, uh, Society of Jesus," Aramis said.

"Indeed?" said Fontrailles. "So you have friends among the Jesuits, my dear Aramis?"

"One tries to be polite with everyone, of course."

"Aramis is so *good* at making friends," Lady Carlisle said, "aren't you, darling?"

"Right," said Fontrailles. "Then we'd better have Cocodril in so I can send him for Beaune, Gitane, and Parrott. We need to make plans. I intend to go in to Bicêtre tonight, if possible, and get de Caus out."

"Slow down, Monsieur," said the countess. "I have an interest in this too, you know."

"Oh, you're going with us," Fontrailles said, with one of his alarming smiles. "I'm sure your talents will be very useful—and I have no intention of letting you out of my sight for a moment. Aramis, you're coming along as well."

"Afraid not, old friend," Aramis said. "I am otherwise engaged."

Fontrailles stopped smiling. "Oh, no, you don't. You're not wriggling out on me now."

"But I am, d'Astarac. I have to go on a short trip with certain people, and on no account can I be detained. Not even for you, *mon ami.*"

"Now see here, Aramis...."

"Louis. I've given my word."

Fontrailles glared, then nodded. "I think I see. You're involved with Buckingham and his secret visit, aren't you? That's how you came to know Lady Carlisle, here."

Aramis smiled pleasantly, but he had that swordpoint glint in his eye again. "D'Astarac, old friend," he said, "your brain is a wonder, but your tongue wags far too freely. Discretion, *mon ami*, discretion at all times. Now, call upon me on any other occasion, but tonight I must disappoint you."

"All right, Aramis," Fontrailles said slowly. "This time I won't press it."

Aramis clapped him on the shoulder. "Oww!" Fontrailles howled. "*Peste!* That's right where it hurts!"

"Never fear, d'Astarac. You'll be fine," Aramis said. "And don't worry about the Jesuits. If Lady Carlisle here couldn't kill you, you have nothing to worry about from the Society of Jesus."

Fontrailles rubbed his shoulder, scowled, and said, "Aramis—why, exactly, do you musketeers always have to be so cursed *hearty?*"

The Château de Bicêtre was situated on a hill just outside Paris—but its real location, Louis thought, was on the outskirts of Hell. And by penetrating to the subterranean pits where the most hopelessly insane were confined, they had entered the Inner Circle of the Inferno.

It was dark in the dungeons of Bicêtre: the only light was their own, a glimmer from a dark-lantern they kept carefully shuttered to conceal their presence … and so they wouldn't have to look too closely at their surroundings. Worse than the dark was the stench, an overpowering odor of decay and human degradation that was staggering even to habitués of Paris, the most malodorous city in Europe. But worse, far worse than the stink was the *sound* of the place, the unending chorus of wordless wailing of those suffering agonies of the soul.

Entering Bicêtre had been surprisingly easy. The estate was surrounded by a tall brick wall that served to confine those relatively-mobile madmen who were shackled merely to heavy weights, rather than to a staple in a wall. Picking their way around the outer wall in the darkness they had found an unused postern gate behind the château, which Beaune had unlocked in three quick motions with one of his delicately-curved metal picks. Fontrailles's little group—himself, the countess, Cocodril, Beaune, and Parrott—had ducked through the gate and flitted across a derelict garden to the back wall of the château, where they found another locked door that Beaune swiftly unlocked.

Louis knew that if de Caus were confined to Bicêtre he wouldn't be allowed to wander around like the shuffling wraiths that haunted the upper stories. He'd be chained in solitary confinement—which meant the pits beneath the château.

They'd found their way down into the underground labyrinth by the simple expedient of asking an insomniac inmate they met dragging his chains down a ground-floor hall. He was counting down from thirteen to one, over and over again, and without interrupting himself had answered by pointing toward a heavy door at the end of the corridor. Beaune had unlocked it easily. The big man had modestly hung his head while Fontrailles praised his skills, and Lady Carlisle had said: "We have a joke in England about Bedlam, our own madhouse just outside London. Getting in, we say, is the easy part...." And everyone had smiled.

No one was joking now. Behind the door had been stairs leading down into the pits. They waited now in a small pool of light at the foot of the steps, listening to the weird, heart-rending wails of the inmates, while Parrott, with another lantern, scouted ahead.

A low groan of utmost despair reverberated through the darkness, and the hairs on Louis's neck rose. *"Mille diables,"* Cocodril murmured. "I wish I hadn't come."

"It was your idea," Fontrailles said. "I wanted to leave you with the horses, but you insisted, so Gitane got the job."

"From now on, no more arguments, Monseigneur."

"That would be nice."

The groan came again, louder. Lucy Hay huddled closer to Fontrailles, which gave him an unexpected jet of pleasure, until it occurred to him to wonder if she had a dagger hidden somewhere about her. "The name of this place—Bicêtre," Lady Carlisle said haltingly. "It's strange, even for a French place-name. What does it mean?"

"It's not French," Fontrailles said, "it's English, a corruption of the name of the lord who built this château when the English occupied Paris. The word was originally Vincester."

"Winchester?"

"That's what I said."

"Ah. As our Bedlam was originally Bethlehem."

"A holy name for such an unholy place."

"Not so loud, please, Monseigneur!" hissed Cocodril. "You're stirring them up."

"There's a light," squeaked Beaune. "Parrott's coming back."

A pinprick luminescence swayed toward them through the blackness until it was close enough to reveal the underlit features of Parrott, his face a mask of shock under the dark sprawling birthmark. Fontrailles said, "Well, Mister Parrott? What have you found?"

"I'm lucky to have found *you* again, Sir," Parrott said, passing a hand across his brow. He was clearly shaken by what he'd seen. "The place is a maze, tunnels lined with niches, and in every niche there's a prisoner chained to the wall. Some are men, some women, some you can't tell if they're even *human....*" He faltered, swallowed. "Some are dead ... I think."

"Any way to tell one from another?"

"No, Sir."

"Merdieu!" Fontrailles thumped the floor in frustration, which generated a chorus of moans and wails. "The Jesuits are so cursed *orderly* that I'd expected them to have organized the inmates in some sensible way."

"Like what?" asked the countess.

"I don't know—alphabetical, maybe, or grouped by affliction. They could at least have put up nameplates!"

"Why don't we just ask 'em which one is Salomon de Caus?" said Cocodril.

"Because if they get the idea we're here to take de Caus out, they'll *all* be de Caus," Fontrailles said.

"Let's capture a guard and make him lead us to de Caus," said the countess.

"No—he'd be able to describe us later," Fontrailles said, "and the Jesuits would know who took him."

"Dead men tell no tales," she said.

"Now *see here*, Lady Carlisle," Fontrailles growled, "I'm not having the blood of some poor devil of a guard on my hands just because he was unlucky enough to draw night duty when we came prowling around! We'll have to think of something else."

"Hmmph!" She crossed her arms. "All right, Monsieur Scholar, you're the one with the brains. So, think!"

"Rrrrr!" Fontrailles snarled, shoulders twitching. "I'm starting to sound like these poor lunatics. All right, what do we know?" He uncurled one bent hand. "Aramis learned from the Jesuits that they had Salomon de Caus here in Bicêtre. Why would the subject even come up?"

"Because the Society was so pleased to have found him!" said the countess.

"Right! They've been looking for him, too, because they want to find *The Three Mystic Heirs* so they can suppress it."

"But de Caus wouldn't be quick to tell them what he knew because he was a loyal retainer of the Winter King, enemy to everything the Jesuits stand for."

"And that means ..." Fontrailles trailed off.

"Yes," said the Countess. "They'd put him to the Question."

"Parrott," Fontrailles said, "did you come across a torture chamber?"

"Yes, Sir, I did," said the Englishman, "but I was in no hurry to go in, I can tell you."

"They're not that bad," Beaune piped.

Everyone turned to stare at him. "I just mean," he said, embarrassed, "you get used to it. If you're not the one being tortured, that is."

"Ah," said Fontrailles, having no idea what else he could say. "Very well, Parrott, lead the way. We'll start our search there."

Parrott led them through a labyrinth of noisome tunnels that seemed to extend far beyond the foundations of the modest château above. Each dark-lantern, shutter slightly ajar, emitted a vertical bar of light that illuminated a sliver of their surroundings—but a sliver was more than enough. The inmates were confined in what was essentially an open sewer. Water trickled in through the outer walls, mingled with the prisoners' wastes, and drained sluggishly along furrows in the tunnel floors. They stumbled through the slime as they followed Parrott through the maze, slipping on mold and fruiting fungus, kicking at chittering vermin. Several times Fontrailles swiveled his lantern to glance at the inmates, and then wished he hadn't.

Finally they reached a stone-walled chamber in what Louis reckoned must be the foundation of the squat, square tower at the corner of the château. They opened the shutters of their lanterns for more light and saw a stairway leading up to a door in the castle above. On the floor of the chamber were all the expected instruments of torture: stocks with a boot; a brazier, now cold, flanked by an array of irons; a wheel; and a rack.

On the rack was a man. Or what was left of one.

"Christ Jesus!" Fontrailles said. Something was terribly wrong with the man's shoulders and arms; they were distorted, elongated in a way that made Louis's stomach lurch as if he'd been poisoned all over again. This, he realized, must be how people felt when they first laid eyes on *his* deformity.

"They've racked him. His upper limbs are disjointed," Beaune said, with no more emotion than a wheelwright describing a broken spoke. "He's not dead, though," he continued, untying the man's wrists. "I can put him right again—somewhat—if you like. But don't look, Madame and Monseigneur."

Fontrailles gulped, then nodded. Lady Carlisle turned her head, but Louis set his jaw and watched the whole procedure. At the first horrid wrench the man regained consciousness and screamed, and Lucy Hay gasped and grabbed Louis's arm. The screams continued until Beaune completed his work with a final, sickening pop. He said, "Ah! There, now: he's passed out again."

Fontrailles said, "Cocodril, get up to the top of those stairs and put your ear to that door. Parrott, watch the way we came in. This poor devil made a lot of noise when Beaune, uh, fixed him, and I don't want to be caught by surprise if somebody comes to find out what the racket was."

He realized with pleasure that Lady Carlisle was still holding onto his arm. "Louis," she said softly, and he didn't mind her informality in the least. "If the Jesuits were torturing him it means he wouldn't talk. How are we going to get him to confide in us?"

"I'll have to convince him we're on his side."

"Are you the right person to do that?"

He shrugged his arm out of her grasp. "Yes, Madame, I think I am— despite my appearance," he said stiffly.

"Oh, Louis! That's not what I meant!"

"He's coming around," Beaune chirped.

Fontrailles stepped to the side of the wreck on the table. It blinked at him, eyes swiveling around with terror. "Listen to me, Monsieur," Fontrailles said. The scared eyes widened and spittle leaked from the man's mouth. "We are not here to cause you any more pain," Fontrailles said quietly. "The hurting is over; we're going to take you out of here. But tell me—nod if you have to—are you Salomon de Caus, former royal mechanist to King Frederick of Bohemia?"

The man shut his eyes, but his tongue quivered. He made a noise that sounded like a curse and then clamped his lips together.

Louis closed his own eyes and thought for a moment, trying to recall key phrases from the Rosicrucian works he used to study. He said, gently but clearly, "In the name of Theophrastus, of Trismegistus, of the Mystical Heptarchy, and the Grace of the Most High whom we both serve, I conjure you: *are you Salomon de Caus?*"

The man's eyelids snapped open, and the lines of his face slackened in surprise. Slowly, painfully, he nodded.

"Then," said Fontrailles, "you are saved."

"Or perhaps not," came a shrill voice from above.

Fontrailles spun around, to see a tall man in a black robe at the top of the stairs. Next to him was a soldier, holding a blade to Cocodril's throat, and behind them more soldiers, crowding the doorway.

"And now, heretics, you will all surrender," cried the man in the black robe, "or we will not be so lenient with you as we were with Monsieur de Caus, there."

CHAPTER XIV
THE MAN OF MILKMAQ

The Vicomte de Fontrailles's initial reaction to the Jesuit Surprise was acute irritation with Cocodril. The man was supposed to have been watching the door—how could he be taken unaware by a whole squad of bruisers? Next time he was *definitely* leaving Cocodril with the horses.

Then, as Louis took in the leering, feral face of the black-robed priest at the top of the stairs, it occurred to him to wonder if there would *be* a next time. The Jesuit uttered a short, barking laugh and said, "What's this? Stunned by the realization that your impious incursion has ended in disaster? Typical weak-minded heretics. Now, pay attention: drop your weapons and put your hands on your heads, or your idiot accomplice dies."

Lady Carlisle, Parrott, and Beaune all looked at Fontrailles. Apparently it was up to him. He raised his chin and snapped, "Don't be a fool, Père Whatever-Your-Name-Is. I've been ordered by the Society in Rome to check up on your work here in Paris, and my report, I can tell you, is going to be distinctly unfavorable. Do you realize that you've rendered an important prisoner virtually incapable of telling us what we need to know?"

Père Whatever-His-Name-Was sneered. "Oh, really? If you've come from the General in Rome, Monsieur Crookback, then show me the Fifth-

Tier Esoteric Hand-Gesture of Incontrovertible Authority. What, you don't know it?" Black-Robe's lip curled with contempt. "Just as I thought. Come with me, men." He took a step down the stairs.

"Wait!" Fontrailles cried. He had no idea what he was going to say, but he could see Cocodril's hand creeping toward a knife hilt protruding from his boot-top. He had to keep stalling. "Don't come any closer!" he shouted. "This poor wretch is dying, but not from being tortured. He's got … *the plague!*"

Black-Robe stopped, put his hands on his hips, tilted back his head and laughed long and loud, a shrill braying that evoked wails and moans from the inmates in the nearby tunnels. "Ah, infidel homunculus, you are truly pathetic!" he wheezed. "What are you going to try next, calling out to imaginary confederates who have supposedly sneaked up behind us?"

Actually, that was *exactly* what Louis was planning to try next, but fortunately he was spared any further humiliation as Cocodril made his move. In a sudden explosion of action Cocodril head-butted backwards into the face of the guard holding him, deflected the man's knife from his throat with his left hand, and hip-checked him off the side of the staircase. He drew his own knife from his boot and had it at Black-Robe's throat before the falling guard hit the chamber floor.

"Idiot accomplice, is it?" Cocodril gritted into Black-Robe's ear. "Stay back, bully-boys!" he snarled, wrapping an arm around the Jesuit and twisting, so his prisoner was between him and the armed guards. "Tell them to hold still, priest, or I'll start slicing pieces off you."

"You wouldn't dare," Black-Robe said.

"Wouldn't I?" Cocodril's knife flicked up and down, and blood gouted from the priest's nose. The man screamed and clapped a hand to his face. His nose flapped aside, dangling on a thin strip of cartilage; howling, the priest tried to press it back into place above his lips.

Fontrailles cocked his pistol with a loud *clack* and pointed it toward the soldiers. "Guards! You heard him," he called. "Don't move, or he guts the priest, and I fire." In point of fact, the pistol was neither loaded nor primed, but Louis hoped the guards couldn't tell that from up on the landing.

"Cocodril—back slowly down the stairs with the priest. You guards, there! When he gets away from the stairs, you come down, nice and slow. Behave, and nobody will get hurt."

Parrott was already holding a dagger on the fallen guard while Beaune shackled him. In short order, the other three guards were disarmed and manacled as well.

The priest sat on a stool, crying and spitting blood, while Cocodril stood over him, gaily spinning his knife from hand to hand. "Now, Monseigneur, don't be ashamed to admit that you're glad you brought me along," he said to Fontrailles. "Did you see that move on the stairs? Zut-bam-zut! They never saw it coming."

"And apparently you didn't hear *them* coming," Fontrailles said. "We'll talk about that later. Stand up, priest. What's your name?"

"Jean-Marie Crozat," the priest said thickly. "Ah, my nose, my poor nose." He didn't look much older than Louis, from what he could see of the man's face around the hand holding his nose on. His black Jesuit soutane was soiled by a long crimson stain from the blood that still flowed copiously from his wound.

Fontrailles noticed a half-dozen hand-sized tufts of black hair hanging from a cincture around the priest's waist. "Well, Jean-Marie Crozat, what in God's name is this?" he said. "Some new kind of rosary?"

"They're scalps," the priest said with a touch of defiance. "I took them from the heads of savages in New France. I was there for a year, in the Society's mission, converting the heathens to the true religion. They called me Père Míkmaq." He looked down and spat blood.

"So how did you come to be here, torturing poor madmen?" Fontrailles asked.

"I've said enough," the priest muttered sullenly.

"Beaune," Fontrailles said, "strap this Père Míkmaq to the rack."

"No!" the priest blubbered, spraying Fontrailles with blood. "All right, curse you. What difference can it make? You're all as good as dead anyway."

"No, no," Fontrailles said, "I have the upper hand now, so it's my turn to make the threats. So talk, or suffer nameless horrors. Who's in charge here? I can't believe the Society would give a worm like you that responsibility."

"Frère Kircher is in authority over Bicêtre," said the man of Míkmaq. "The Company assigned me to be his assistant after I was sent back from the New World. They said my methods of converting the savages were overzealous."

"But it seems they found a use for your talents here," said Fontrailles. "Did Kircher tell you to torture this man?"

"No … Frère Kircher wanted me to *frighten* him into talking," the priest said contemptuously. "That never works."

Fontrailles suppressed the obvious retort that it seemed to be working in *this* case, but before he could continue he was interrupted by Beaune. "It's Monsieur de Caus, Monseigneur," the big man said. "He's fading."

Fontrailles stepped back to the rack, where Beaune was mopping the tortured man's brow with a filthy rag. "If he dies now, it's all been for nothing," Lady Carlisle said. She took a closer look at the ruined man, and shook her head. "He's not going to make it, Louis."

Fontrailles turned to Beaune, who said, "I think madame is right. When their color goes and their pulse gets all thready, you know you're losing them."

"Is there anything you can do?" Fontrailles said.

"No, Monseigneur," Beaune said sadly. "They only taught me how to take people apart, not put them back together. We have to get him to a physician."

"All right, then. Beaune, you and Parrott rig up a litter to carry him. As soon as you're ready we'll go out the way we came in."

"Louis," said Lady Carlisle, "can I talk to you for a moment?"

"Of course, Madame," Fontrailles said. "Step over here, by these charming stocks."

Lucy Hay sat down delicately on the bulbous end of a torture boot so she could look him in the eye. "Louis, if de Caus dies without telling us where to find the book, then the priest was right: this *is* a disaster."

"I'm well aware of it, Madame." What Louis was most aware of, as she bent forward to talk with him, was her remarkable cleavage. Wrenching his eyes upward, he said, "What did you have in mind? More torture?"

"No, of course not. Really, I can't think why you have such a low opinion of me. I was thinking of how de Caus responded when you babbled that mystical jargon at him."

"It wasn't just jargon to him, it was the voice of truth. He *believes* in spiritual alchemy," Fontrailles said. "And why not? If a mechanist believes in it, maybe it really works."

The Lady Carlisle smiled, a little wistfully. It was an expression Louis hadn't seen on her before. "Now you sound like my father," she said.

"Hmm." Fontrailles looked at her for a long moment. "Well, there's nothing I can do while he's unconscious. We'll have to hope a physician can bring him around."

"What are you going to do about the priest and the guards?" she asked. "They've had plenty of time to get a good look at all of us."

"We'll gag the guards and leave them shackled to the rack. The priest we'll take with us—I'm sure he knows more than he's told us so far. Now, don't make that face! And don't you dare say 'Dead men tell no tales' again!"

"Well, they *don't*," she pouted.

"It's a risk we'll just have to run."

"We're ready, Monseigneur," Beaune piped.

"Then let's go." Fontrailles picked up his lantern. "Parrott, take the front of the litter. I'll lead, but I want you right behind me, with de Caus close at hand. Don't let me go astray. Cocodril, bring up the rear, but keep your hand around Père Míkmaq's neck. Madame...."

"I'm staying with *you*," Lady Carlisle said decisively.

Louis's heart thumped. *Idiot*, he thought. *But, God's breeches, just look at her. What spirit! Even covered with slime, she practically glows.* "Very well," he said, unable to suppress a brief smile. "Take the other lantern, then."

They plunged once more into the tunnels. They hadn't slogged more than halfway back when the man on the litter suddenly called out. His voice was indistinct, but he seemed to say, "Stop!"

Fontrailles held up his hand to halt the little troop and stepped to de Caus's side. "It's here," the man whispered. "My cell. Almost passed it."

Fontrailles swiveled his lantern to illuminate a miserable hole in the side of the tunnel where empty manacles dangled from a rusty staple embedded in the wall. He turned back to the ruined man. "We're not taking you back to your cell, Monsieur de Caus," he said gently. "We're taking you out. We're going to make you better."

"No," de Caus whispered. "I knew when I was locked in here that I would never leave this place alive. I am dying."

"Hold on, Monsieur," Fontrailles said.

"No," came the whisper, fading. "Too late."

Lady Carlisle elbowed Fontrailles painfully in the hump. "*The book*," she hissed in his ear.

Fontrailles glared at her, then nodded irritably. He turned back to the dying man, tried to put some comfort in his voice. "May the angel Uriel watch over you on your journey to the next life, my friend," he said. "But, Salomon de Caus, in the name of the Monas, there is a secret you must not take to your grave. You must pass it on to the Brotherhood."

"Secret," de Caus whispered. "Brotherhood."

"Brother de Caus, where is the book?" Fontrailles said urgently. "Where is *The Three Mystic Heirs*?"

The mechanist groaned as a spasm shook his broken body. "Book," he said, almost inaudibly. "Bassompierre. Gave it … Bassompierre."

"The marshal? Marshal Bassiompierre?" said Fontrailles.

"Told him … take it brother," de Caus breathed.

"Brother?" Lady Carlisle said. "What brother? De Caus! Brother who?"

"In … England," de Caus said.

And then he died.

A drop of blood splashed on the dead man's cheek.

Fontrailles looked up to see Cocodril and Père Míkmaq, still holding his bleeding nose, leaning over the other side of the litter. "Cocodril…!" Fontrailles said.

"*Imbécile!*" cried Lady Carlisle. "The priest heard everything!"

"Bassompierre," Père Míkmaq said musingly, around his hand. "In England."

"Now we *have* to kill him," Lady Carlisle said.

"We're not killing anybody," Fontrailles said. "Except maybe Cocodril."

"But, Monseigneur…!"

"Save it. Besides, I have a better idea. Beaune," Fontrailles said, "lay poor de Caus here in his niche—and then chain the priest up next to him."

"N-no!" sputtered the Jesuit, spraying blood again. "They might not find me for days! My nose needs immediate medical attention!"

"Beaune will tie a rag around your head so your nose doesn't fall off," Fontrailles said. "Even that's more than you deserve."

"What's that noise?" said Parrott.

They heard distant shouts, and the sound of a door slamming somewhere in the château above. "The alarm's gone up," Fontrailles said. "Somebody spotted something. Are you almost done, Beaune?"

"Finished, Monseigneur."

"Then let's go."

"I'll take the lead, sir," said Parrott, picking up a lantern. "Give me your arm, Madame." And the pair splashed off into the darkness.

"Blood of *Christ!* Not so fast, Parrott!" Fontrailles called, sloshing after them. "My legs aren't that long!"

He followed Parrott's flickering light as best he could, helped along in places by Beaune and Cocodril, but by the time they got back up the stairs to the ground floor Parrott and Lady Carlisle were out of sight. The corridor was swarming with hysterical inmates who shuffled away from Fontrailles and his men, screaming and tugging on their weighted chains. Fontrailles ran, still slipping on slimy soles, toward the back door, which was standing half open. Outside the doorway he slid on the steps and fell heavily, but Beaune and Cocodril picked him up, each with a hand under an arm, and carried him kicking across the dead garden to the open postern. Loud shouts came from the château behind them, but whether from inmates or guards, they weren't sure.

Outside the wall Fontrailles insisted on being put down, and he made it on his own legs to the alley where Gitane was holding the horses. Behind them a bell was tolling in the tower of Bicêtre. "The countess and Parrott!" Fontrailles said, panting. "Have you seen them?"

"No," said Gitane. "Aren't they behind you? Do we wait for them?"

"They were *ahead* of us—so no, we will *not* wait for them." Fontrailles made a fist and shook it, uselessly. "I'm afraid, lads," he said, "that she's done it to me *again.*"

"Bassompierre, you say?" Cardinal Richelieu steepled his fingers. "Now that *is* interesting. He's one of His Majesty's favorites, but often does things that are in no one's interest but his own."

The Cardinal and the Ensign of his Political Squad were in His Eminence's tall dark study, alone except for the colorless, scribbling presence of Le Masle, Richelieu's personal secretary. Fontrailles had stopped at his lodgings just long enough to clean up and dress properly, then gone directly to the Petit-Luxembourg to report. Keeping the night's events to himself would not have been safe. He had told the cardinal everything, leaving out only the participation of Aramis. ...And of the Countess of Carlisle. And the fact that she'd gotten away with Parrott, so the English knew everything he did.

Actually, he'd left out quite a lot.

Trying not to think about the potential consequences of this, Fontrailles said wearily, "What I don't yet understand is the connection between de Caus and Marshal Bassompierre."

The Cardinal shrugged his narrow shoulders. "They may have met in London; both Bassompierre and de Caus have spent a deal of time there. It's not strange that the Rosicrucian should have confided a secret to the *maréchal*; the State has confided secrets to him as well. We just sent him on a diplomatic mission to England—unfortunately for you."

Fontrailles hated to ask, but figured he'd better play along. "Why is that unfortunate for me, Monseigneur?"

"Because now you must follow him, and without delay. Moreover, the

Jesuits may complain to His Majesty about your incursion into Bicêtre, and although they are in bad odor at Court just now because of the Santarelli affair, it's as well to have you leave the city for the nonce. Do you speak English?"

"Yes, Your Eminence. More or less."

"Good. I have just sent Vitray, another of my agents, to London on an urgent mission. If you leave immediately and ride quickly, you may catch him before he sails from Boulogne. Do not take a pony; ride a big person's horse."

Oh, very funny, Louis thought, and almost scowled, before he remembered that he was trying to show only devotion and deference. "I leave within the hour, Your Eminence," he said stoutly.

"But not without this," the cardinal said, extending a hand toward Le Masle. The secretary dotted a period at the end of a sentence and handed a letter to his master. Richelieu signed, sanded, and sealed it, then passed it across the desk to Fontrailles. "This warrant gives you full authority to act in my name—though that will, of course, be of limited use once you are across the Channel," the Cardinal said. "It also introduces you to Boisloré, my man in London, and requires him to assist you wherever possible. If you can, you will return the favor; I have several efforts under way in the English capital, and your wits may serve to help them go more smoothly."

"I will do everything in my power to advance our interests, Your Eminence."

"I am sure you will, Monsieur le Vicomte," said the cardinal. He paused, knit his brow and said, "Your hat, Monsieur—your hat is very … large."

"Broad-brimmed hats are the fashion for cavaliers, as I'm sure Monseigneur knows."

"But *your* hat, Monsieur, is excessive—as are your boots, and your lace. You are conspicuous."

Peste! Vidou warned me this outfit would get me into trouble, Louis thought. "This is my Court attire, Your Eminence," he said. "I dress far more conservatively when on State business." *Or anyway, I will from now on.*

"See to it; our affairs must not be jeopardized by whimsies," the cardinal said sternly. "That book must not fall into the hands of the Duke of Buckingham. If you cannot bring it back to France, you must see that it is destroyed." Richelieu leaned forward, skewering Fontrailles on the point of his gaze. "I rely upon it, Monsieur."

CHAPTER XV
MEN OF ENGLAND AND MEN OF FRANCE

A musketeer and an Englishman walked into a tavern. "Greetings, Messieurs!" called the host. "We don't get many Englishmen in here."

"Peace, Hubert," said the Englishman, smiling. "You tell the same joke every time I pass through Neufchâtel."

"And it's always an honor to serve Your Grace at the Golden Harrow Inn!" Hubert bowed low. "Your usual, Milord Buckingham? I laid in a barrel special."

"Please don't name him quite so loudly, my dear host," said Aramis.

"Monsieur Aramis, you worry too much," said the Duke of Buckingham, "as I've had cause to tell you more than once." He began beating the dust out of his riding clothes with his gloves and then stopped, coughing. "By gad, sir! Your French roads are dusty."

"You prefer the mud of English roads, Milord?" Aramis picked up the tankard that Hubert placed in front of him. "You'll see them again soon enough—perhaps by tomorrow night, if you have a fair wind. If we press on, we can still make Saint-Valéry and get you aboard by nightfall."

"Perhaps so, but I've a mind to spend a few hours here at the Golden

Harrow and catch my breath. You've set a killing pace since we left Paris, and I know you would prefer us to have gone even more swiftly, but you must admit there's no sign of pursuit. We've been on the road a day and a half and we're already nearly across eastern Normandy." The Duke hoisted his own tankard, drained half of it and set it down. "Ah! Besides, it's coming on to storm, and if we continue riding into the wind it'll ruin our hair and clothes."

"Milord," Aramis began. How many times would he have to have this discussion? His Grace the Duke of Buckingham was as stubborn as he was spoiled. Aramis sighed heavily and said, "The cardinal, Milord...."

There was a loud rap on the tavern's front door, and then it swung suddenly inward. Aramis's hand flashed to his hilt and he had his rapier half-drawn before he recognized the newcomers. "Well, well!" he said, slapping the blade home. "What an unexpected pleasure."

"God blind me," said Buckingham, laughing, "if it isn't Her Ladyship the Countess of Carlisle! And is that you, Blakeney? What's that on your face? And what have you done to make your fair hair so dark?"

Sir Percy Blakeney smiled tightly and bowed to the duke. "I was in disguise, may it please Your Grace," he said. "Had a dashed great false birthmark across the left side of my face. Her Ladyship persuaded me to use India ink, and I've had a devil of a time getting it out of my skin."

"Do you say so? What an amusing story that will make once we get back to Court," said the duke. "And what's wrong with that pretty behind of yours, my Lucy? Anything I can help with?"

God's teeth! He probably believes that leer of his is charming, Aramis thought. But he chuckled obligingly, as if the duke had said something witty.

Lady Carlisle grimaced as she rubbed her posterior. "Thanks ever so for the offer, Your Grace, but this is just between me and my saddle. We've ridden like the devil from Paris to catch you, Milord. Fortunately Sir Percy knows your usual route."

"You see, Your Grace?" Aramis said. "If they could catch us, so could the cardinal's men."

"Have done, Aramis, for the love of God," Buckingham said, then turned his smile again on Lady Carlisle. "So, sweet chuck, why such haste?"

The countess lowered her voice. "Because, Milord, we've found out who has *the book*."

"Have you indeed? Then my little excursion to France has been doubly successful! From what Doctor Lambe tells me, that book is a thing I simply must have. Say on, my Lucy, say on!"

She related the final words of Salomon de Caus in the dungeon of Bicêtre. "And Marshal Bassompierre left for London only two days ahead of you, My Lord Duke, traveling by way of Boulogne," she added. "Head north along the coast and we may yet catch him before he leaves France."

"And then what?" said Aramis. "Burgle the baggage of a French royal ambassador in his own country?"

"Such crude methods might not be necessary," interrupted Blakeney. "Bassompierre is said to have a roving eye for the ladies." He nodded toward the countess.

The duke shook his head. "No: Aramis is right, though it pains me to say it. I don't have a ship at Boulogne, and if the marshal sails before we get there, who knows how long it would take to arrange passage? The *Sund* awaits us at Saint-Valéry; she's a quick little sloop, and may even get us to England ahead of Bassompierre. No, I will not go haring off to the Pas-de-Calais.

"And besides," he said, putting an arm around Lady Carlisle's shoulders, "we've ridden hard, and I think the lady and I could both do with a little rest. Eh, darlin'?" The countess forced a smile and looked down in feigned modesty. But she balled her hands into fists.

The dog! It's not three days since she and I risked our necks to enable him to make secret love to Queen Anne, Aramis thought. "Your Grace!" he said. "Might I have a word with Lady Carlisle before you, ah, turn in?"

"Of course, Monsieur—have a word! Have two, or even three!" said Buckingham, all *noblesse oblige*. "Blakeney, tell me more about this amusing disguise of yours."

Aramis led Lucy Hay to a place near the fire and offered her a chair. "Good Lord, no, Aramis," she said. "Ask me to do anything but sit."

Aramis smiled crookedly. "Then we shall stand. You'll be lying down soon enough, it appears." He nodded toward the duke, who was laughing and clinking tankards with Blakeney.

"Since when are you so prudish?" she snarled. "Besides, what would you have me do? Every woman in England is his plaything."

"Indeed? And what does the Earl of Carlisle think about it?"

"He looks the other way. How do you think he got to be an earl?" She closed her eyes for a moment with fatigue, then opened them and sighed. "Is this why you called me aside, so you could berate me? Really, Aramis, I could just slap you."

"My apologies, Madame. I forgot myself," Aramis said coolly. "I wanted to ask about the Vicomte de Fontrailles. If you got safely out of Bicêtre, I assume he did as well. No?"

"I presume so. We left ahead of him."

"What do you mean?"

"I mean Blakeney and I ran ahead and got out before him. But I'm sure he's all right."

"You don't *know?* God's blood! How could you run off and leave him like that?"

"Because otherwise I'd probably be in a French prison," she said, exasperated. "Don't be a half-wit, Aramis! Did you really think you were going to make the two of us into allies? You'd already played him false by planting Blakeney on him."

"I was trying to look out for him!"

She gave a short laugh. "I'll wager Monsieur de Fontrailles won't see it that way."

Plague take me! Aramis thought. *She's right. I've been a fool.*

He felt a hand on his shoulder and turned to see Buckingham. "There are only two rooms in this inn, Aramis," the duke said. "You can share one with Blakeney."

Aramis shook his head. "I regret to say that I cannot stay, Your Grace. I must return to Paris."

"But you said you'd accompany me all the way to the coast!"

"Now that your loyal aides are here I'm sure you can dispense with my services, Milord," Aramis said stiffly. "I find that I have business elsewhere."

"What, Monsieur?" Buckingham said haughtily. "Is this how a nobleman of France discharges his duties?"

"In point of fact, I have assisted Your Grace as a favor to Madame de Chevreuse, whom I esteem, and to disoblige Monsieur le Cardinal, who I count among my enemies," Aramis said. "I am not your man to command, Milord."

For a tense moment they glared at each other, then the duke relaxed, smiled slightly and said, "Then that is my loss and France's gain. If you will go, then go … and fare you well."

Aramis's mouth twitched, but he bowed and said, "Then I will take my leave of Your Grace."

I just hope I can find a fresh horse in this town, Aramis thought, striding toward the stables. *I have a feeling friend d'Astarac is going to need my help, and soon.*

CHAPTER XVI
IN WHICH D'ASTARAC, AS AN AGENT OF INTRIGUE, LOOKS MORE THAN ONCE FOR A ROPE WITH WHICH TO HANG HIMSELF

The Vicomte de Fontrailles had been looking forward to crossing the English Channel from Boulogne to Dover because he'd never been on a real ship before. But once the little Channel lugger began lurching in the rollers that marched down from the North Sea, Fontrailles's face took on the same green hue as the waves. Nausea enveloped him and he began vomiting over the side, almost as if Lady Carlisle had found a long-distance way to poison him anew.

Fontrailles's illness was a source of grim satisfaction to Vitray, Richelieu's other agent, who stood next to him on the rail, occasionally spitting his own bile into the sea. Vitray was seasick too, but having taken ship many times in the service of the cardinal, he wasn't as sick as Fontrailles, which consoled him somewhat. He was a stolid, rather unimaginative publisher from Paris whom Richelieu prized for his dependability rather than his initiative; Fontrailles and Cocodril had caught up with him on the waterfront in Boulogne just as he was about to take ship for England and had attached themselves to his mission.

Cocodril barely noticed his master's distress; a natural sailor, he spent his time aloft in the rigging or whooping in the spray at the bowsprit. The way he clambered up the ratlines and lent the crew a hand with the sails showed he'd spent plenty of time at sea somewhere, and was delighted to be back. Louis mentally cursed Cocodril and his hearty good cheer, when he could spare a moment from the engrossing business of retching his guts out.

Fontrailles was alone at the after rail, staring glumly into the lugger's swirling wake for what felt like the fifty-second consecutive hour and wondering if they'd somehow strayed out of the Channel and were headed across the entire Atlantic Ocean, when there was a sudden thump on the deck at his side and Cocodril's jovial voice cried, "Ahoy, Monseigneur!"

Fontrailles blew out his cheeks like a disgusted farm-horse, carefully grasped the rail with both hands and slowly swiveled his throbbing head toward his grinning manservant. His brain, sloshing about in his skull, gradually realigned its frontal lobes with his face, and his watering eyes brought into focus the features of Cocodril and a second, unfamiliar fellow—who had, sure enough and no mistaking it, a black patch over one eye. Louis groaned.

"Making great time, isn't she, Monseigneur?" Cocodril trilled. "We're almost a third of the way across. Why, from the top of the mast you can already see the cliffs of Dover!"

Fontrailles glared blearily at Cocodril and considered his options, but there seemed to be no practical way to just kill him. "Is that what you came down here to tell me, Cocodril?" he said. "That this torment isn't even half over?"

"By no means, Your Lordship!" said Cocodril. "Had I but known that you were suffering so from the dreaded *mal de mer* I should have been at your side some time ago, lavishing upon you what small succor and solace I could provide! No, Monseigneur, I merely wanted to introduce to you this sterling new acquaintance, whom I fancy can be of inestimable aid to us.

Shall we come back later, when you may be feeling more like yourself?"

"Later I may be dead, so you might as well get on with it now," Fontrailles said. "Who's your new friend?"

The man stepped forward with a thump, and Louis saw that in addition to missing an eye he was absent a leg, which had been replaced below the knee with something that looked like a piece of tapering, spiral bone. He was a grizzled old salt, with hair like gray wire and weathered skin that was almost indistinguishable from the leather of his worn jerkin. He grinned, revealing a grand total of three teeth, tugged at his ragged forelock and said, "Me name's Breedlove, Yer Lordship, Sobriety Breedlove, and it's right pleased t' make yer acquaintance I am."

"Mister Breedlove is an English sailor, Monseigneur, a 'Jack Tar,' in their parlance," Cocodril said.

"I'd never have guessed," Fontrailles muttered.

"An old Sea Dog, I am, forty years on the waves, man and boy—sailed with Drake, I did, against the Dons, when we burned and sank 'em on this very patch of sea," Breedlove said.

"But this is his last crossing, Monseigneur, before he retires from sailing for good—and where do you think he's going?" said Cocodril.

"Oh, please tell me," said Fontrailles.

"To London! Our very destination!"

"A city I knows for'ards and back'ards, Yer Lordship, like I knows the harbor of me home port o' Plymouth," Breedlove said.

"So I thought he could join us as a guide," said Cocodril, "and since he speaks English he could act as our interpreter. Thus demonstrating once again, Monseigneur: I'm always thinking ahead! What do you say?"

"But we don't need an interpreter, Cocodril. I already know English. Listen: 'Ow much eez ze room for one night een zis 'otel? 'Ave you not got a room bettair?'"

"Beggin' your pardon, Yer Lordship," said Breedlove, "but that ain't quite proper English, like. Here's how you'd say it." And raising his voice, he said slowly and with emphasis, *'Don't—tell—me—you—'aven't—got— no—better—room—you—lying—dog.'*

Louis rolled his eyes, which upset his brain's delicate equilibrium and made him clap both hands to his skull to stop it from tolling like a bell. The ship lurched awkwardly as it rose to mount a roller, and he sat down heavily on the deck. "All right, Cocodril. We'll take him on. What can it possibly matter?" he said. "My life is over anyway."

"A wise decision, which Monseigneur will not regret!"

"It couldn't even begin to compare to the things I regret already."

Cocodril knelt down next to Fontrailles with a look of sympathetic deference. "Is there anything else I can do to help Monseigneur in his time of trial?"

"Help me back up to the rail. I feel another bout of nausea coming on," Fontrailles said. "Then see if the ship's carpenter can make me a coffin."

The next day passed in a sort of delirium for Louis d'Astarac. By the time his senses fully returned Dover was already behind them and they were on the road to London, halfway between towns with the ridiculous English names of Canterbury and Chatham. They were on horseback, Vitray and Breedlove in the lead, followed by Cocodril leading Fontrailles's mount—with the viscount belted into the saddle to prevent him falling off if he got dizzy. Cocodril had thought his master would be better off in a carriage, but Vitray was in too great a hurry to reach London and had vetoed the idea. Fontrailles, who hadn't eaten since Boulogne—and he'd lost most of that into the Channel—had just enough energy left to hang on to his horse and work his lungs. To remind himself of why he was subjecting himself to all this, he tried to think of his beloved Isabeau de Bonnefont, but he kept visualizing her with a black patch over one eye.

They rode all night and arrived on the outskirts of London at dawn, the sun rising behind them and revealing the English capital as it gradually appeared from the morning fog like a ship rising out of the sea. London wasn't as big as Paris, which was the largest city in Europe, and its churches and noblemen's townhouses couldn't compare with Paris's cathedrals and hôtels in either size or number. But London had something that Paris did not: a second sister city of sea-vessels, five hundred ships moored in the Thames below London Bridge, their masts like a bare-boughed forest that had somehow sprung up in the center of the city.

By the time they could see this merchant armada they were in the suburb of Southwark and had to slow their headlong ride as the streets grew close and crowded. Once they reached the approach to London Bridge they spent as much time stopped as moving forward, so Sobriety Breedlove began breaking a trail through the press, cursing or wheedling as needed to open a path for the four horses.

They crossed the river on the great bridge and entered the City of London, where Fontrailles, who could find his way around Paris with hardly a thought, was completely lost within minutes. Even Vitray looked nonplused, but Breedlove seemed to know exactly where he was going, navigating the narrow streets like a harbor pilot steering through the shallows.

Fontrailles's first impression of London was of chaos and confusion, though he thought that might be due in part to fatigue and in part to difficulty with the language. Londoners on the whole seemed *louder* than Parisians, and had a disconcerting tendency to look one in the eye even if they were clearly of lower rank. And despite having a much larger river to carry off its wastes, the town stank nearly as badly as Paris.

Just as the September sun was beginning to peek over the steep roofs of London's three-story houses and reach the streets, Breedlove led them into a neat little square and pointed out a tall new townhouse. "This here's the address you told me, Cap'n," he said to Vitray, who nodded.

A handsome white carriage was drawn up before the house's front steps, its matched team of grays stamping impatiently, their bridles held by a liveried groom. He gave the muddy travelers a haughty look as they dismounted nearby, and sniffed as if at an unpleasant odor.

Fontrailles climbed down from his saddle and stretched painfully, then followed Vitray around the carriage to the steps of the townhouse. As they reached the foot of the stairs a brass bell jingled and the front door of the townhouse opened. Fontrailles looked up.

At the top of the stairs stood a golden-haired angel in white.

Fontrailles blinked and looked again, but she was still there: a pale angel with delicate features, lips like rose petals and a glorious halo of golden hair, her heavenly body clothed in shining white satin and lace. This vision inspected Fontrailles and his companions, turned to the man at her side (Louis hadn't noticed him before) and said, in a silvery voice dripping with disdain: "Monsieur Boisloré, there seems to be a troupe of mountebanks on your front steps."

Fontrailles shut his gaping mouth and groped for a reply—after all, he was a Viscount of France, and couldn't let such a remark go unanswered, even from an angelic vision—but Vitray beat him to it, choosing to deal with the insult by ignoring it. In French he said, "Your pardon, Madame and Monsieur, for appearing before you thus unannounced, but we come from Paris on missions of the utmost urgency. I am Antoine Vitray, and based on your description, Madame, you can be no one but the Comtesse de Winter; if so, it is to you that my message is directed."

The golden angel smiled so sweetly that Fontrailles thought he must have misheard her words of a moment before. "Then, Monsieur Vitray, you must come inside without delay," she said with a voice like music, in French as flawless as her English. "Your people can tend your horses, and we will tend to *you.*"

"I am the Vicomte de Fontrailles, Madame and Monsieur," Louis said, a touch stridently, as he didn't want to be dismissed as one of Vitray's "people." He continued, "I, too, am from Paris"—though he didn't care to mention *His Eminence* in the street, they'd know whom he meant—"and I have pressing matters to discuss with Monsieur Boisloré."

Some emotion flickered across the angel's perfect features—amusement? irritation?—before she turned her breathtaking smile on Fontrailles. "Then join us, Monsieur le Vicomte," she said, "and welcome!"

It was strange: the most beautiful creature he'd ever seen had smiled on Louis, and he felt … confused. If Isabeau had smiled at him like that his heart would have leapt into his throat—and if Lady Carlisle had smiled so he'd have melted into his shoes. But when this Comtesse de Winter favored him with a smile like the first warm sun of springtime, it left him somehow untouched. Bizarre.

Vitray, apparently, felt no such qualms: face beet-red, grinning like a simpleton, he bounded up the stairs like a hound to its master, pausing on the landing to bow once more all the way to the ground, sputtering honorifics. Fontrailles shook his head in wonderment, then straightened his wilted collar and followed Vitray into the townhouse.

In Boisloré's salon they repaired the errors of etiquette committed in the street by going through their introductions all over again. Once everyone's social standing had been properly established and refreshments had been served by unobtrusive servants, Vitray withdrew to one corner of the room with the lady. Fontrailles and Boisloré took the opposite corner, and the cardinal's instructions to his agents in London were conveyed in two sets of quiet murmurs. This task completed, with initial questions asked and answered, the four then thoughtfully reconvened in the center of the salon.

Milady de Winter drew a small ivory-handled fan from her sleeve and tapped Boisloré on the arm. "Monsieur," she said, "I hope you have nothing planned for today, because I'm going to need your assistance with some arrangements I have in mind."

Fontrailles drew himself up until his eyes were level with Milady's décolletage and said, "I deeply regret the inconvenience, Milady, but I require Monsieur Boisloré's aid on an urgent matter of my own." He had to act immediately: if he was somehow to search Bassompierre's luggage for *The Three Mystic Heirs*, the best time to do it would be while the ambassador's household was still unsettled from his journey.

Milady smiled sweetly at Fontrailles and said, "Oh, but Monsieur le Vicomte will surely give the preference to a lady."

Fontrailles tilted his head in polite acknowledgment of her request, but said, "Monsieur le Vicomte would be only too delighted, but Monsieur le Cardinal's instructions were explicit, and I am obliged to consider them first." Something about this woman frosted Louis, and he felt no inclination to do her any favors.

Apparently the feeling was mutual, for there was more than a little ice in her voice as she replied, "My instructions from His Eminence are equally explicit—and as an associate of the cardinal with longer standing than you, as a full countess, and as a lady, I claim the precedence."

Fontrailles was outgunned, and could only give in with as much grace as he could muster. He favored her with a deferential bow and said, "In that case, Milady, I am honored to cede you the priority."

"You'll do more than that, Monsieur le Vicomte," she said in a voice of poisoned honey. "It occurs to me that I can use your assistance as well in accomplishing my mission. You *are* fully committed to the service of the cardinal, are you not?"

Cornered. Louis made an appalling face and said, "Of course, Milady. His will is my will." He cleared his throat and said, a little nervously, "What is it we have to do?"

"Oh, nothing much—a little thing, really," Milady said with malicious relish. "You, Monsieur le Vicomte, are going to help me steal the French Queen's diamonds right off the neck of the Prime Minister of England."

CHAPTER XVII
IN THE SOCIETY OF JESUS

Monsieur Aramis liked to think that his religious training placed him a cut above the other King's Musketeers by granting him unique insights into the human heart and mind—including his own. So when he arrived at the gates of Beauvais, hot, dusty, and tired, he didn't stop at the first tavern, but rode through the horse market, past the towering walls of the Cathedral of Saint-Pierre and across the town square before pulling up at a tavern within sight of the Porte Paris. He thought that, once he was rested, he would be more likely to immediately resume his ride to Paris if he had the open road before him rather than the distractions of a town.

The tavern was smoky and had a dangerously low ceiling, but at least its interior was cool, so Aramis chose an empty table and beckoned to the host. He was just lifting a well-earned glass of wine to his lips, with a silent toast to absent friends, when he heard one of them mentioned behind him. "D'Astarac, or Fontrailles," said a voice with a pronounced German accent. "A small man with a hunched back—you could not mistake him."

Aramis finished his sip of wine—which was not bad, as he'd specified a vintage from Champagne rather than the local swill—before turning casually to see who was inquiring about his friend Louis d'Astarac. The host was shaking his head and shrugging apologetically in response to a man past his mid-twenties, just a few years older than Aramis, with mild brown eyes under a pallid, furrowed brow set in a harmless-looking oval face. Though the man was dressed in dusty, nondescript traveling clothes, to Aramis's trained eye there was something ecclesiastical about him.

The stranger saw Aramis looking at him, so the musketeer raised his glass and said, "*Bonjour,* fellow traveler. You look as dusty and dry as I am. Will you join me in a drink?"

"Gladly," said the stranger, "though I must admit I prefer beer to wine."

"Yes, I thought I detected one of our neighbors from the Germanies," the musketeer said. He stood and bowed from the waist. "Monsieur Aramis, of Paris."

"Athanasius Kircher, of Mainz," the German replied, "though I, too, am a Parisian, at least for the time being."

Kircher: yes; Aramis had heard of him. He was a German scholar, the man the Jesuits had placed in charge of the Château de Bicêtre when the Society had assumed control of it. If he was looking for Louis d'Astarac here, a day's ride north of Paris, then his friend had succeeded in escaping Bicêtre ... but not without being recognized, for now the Jesuits were on his trail.

But perhaps, Aramis thought, he could put them off the scent. "Did I hear you asking after a hunchback, a man with the airs of a noble?" he asked.

"Yes, indeed!" said Kircher, a little too eagerly. "Have you seen this man? I ... have a message for him."

"Yesterday morning, in the port at Le Havre."

"*Donner!* He moves fast. That's Richelieu's hand, and no doubt," said Kircher, the creases deepening in his brow. "He'll have taken passage to Portsmouth long before I could catch up to him."

"It must be an important message you bear, Herr Kircher," said Aramis.

"It may be," the German replied warily.

Aramis felt the familiar gravitic tug of intrigue, an attraction he'd already surrendered to more than once in his young life. Would he throw caution aside and plunge in again? It seemed so: already he heard himself lowering his voice and saying, "Our meeting like this, Herr Kircher, is no chance one. I see the hand of Providence in it."

Kircher was suspicious. "How so, Monsieur?"

"I overheard you inquiring after Monsieur d'Astarac, the Vicomte de Fontrailles. I'm in a position to help you, because I know Monsieur de Fontrailles," said Aramis. "Know him very well indeed."

Kircher looked coldly at Aramis, which made the musketeer reconsider his approach: the German might not be quite the gullible naïf he appeared. "And you said you saw him at Le Havre?" said Kircher.

"Yes…" said Aramis. What had Kircher said? Portsmouth? "…Taking ship for England."

"Then, for the moment, he is beyond the reach of either of us."

"But Fontrailles is a servant of Monsieur le Cardinal. He will return to Paris upon completion of his mission, whatever it is. And when he does, I will know it."

"Will you?" said Kircher. "You know him well, you say. Why offer to inform on him?"

"There's no reason *not* to—is there? After all, you merely said you had a message for him," Aramis replied. "Besides, I have hopes that my assistance will earn me a reward."

"The order to which I belong is not a wealthy one, Monsieur Aramis."

That was a howling untruth, but Aramis knew he wasn't supposed to believe it—it was just the opening gambit in a negotiation. He said, "But it's not money I'm after. Though currently a member of the King's Musketeers, I was trained for the priesthood, and am ambitious to return to a career in the Church. I happen to know that the order to which you belong, Herr Kircher, is the Society of Jesus, whose connections are widespread and whose influence is great. I would prove myself useful to your Company, Monsieur," said Aramis, "in hopes that the Company may prove useful to me."

"Now that," said Kircher, "is a language my order understands, from the islands of Japan to the jungles of the New World." He sat back and appraised Aramis for a minute, then seemed to come to a decision. "Well, if the Vicomte de Fontrailles is already on his way to England, I may as well return to Paris and resume my duties there. Your proposal is an interesting one, but it will require further discussion before I can decide if there is real merit to it. Will you ride with me back to Paris, Monsieur Aramis?"

"I would be honored, Herr Kircher. And now, let us drink," Aramis said, raising his glass, "to a mutually profitable association."

"May the Lord so bless us," said Kircher.

CHAPTER XVIII
MILADY AND MILORD

It had never previously occurred to Louis d'Astarac that he might have an insane fear of being confined in a tight, narrow space, probably because this was the first time he'd ever found himself in such a situation. Or maybe it wasn't: he *had* spent a year in childhood locked in Ambroise Paré's iron corselet, which was not all that dissimilar to being folded up and jammed into the tiny cabinet under the rear seat of Milady de Winter's dove-white and perfumed carriage.

On top of being imprisoned, twisted like a contortionist, inside a pitch-black jouncing cushion-topped half-sized coffin until he was ready to gibber and scream, he'd had to listen for the better part of an hour to the nauseating byplay of the Countess of Winter and the Duke of Buckingham as they seduced one another. Milady's painfully blatant double-entendres were topped only by Milord's leering smug-ignorant witticisms, and Fontrailles was grateful when they finally shut up and proceeded to remove each other's clothes. But that all-too-brief interlude was followed, inches from Louis's ear, by the rhythmic thumping, passionate cries, and theatrical moans of some very athletic sexual congress. It seemed to go on and on, so long that Louis began to wonder if, when the signal finally came to do his part, he'd be able to move at all.

When the prearranged triple rap on his coffin door finally sounded he almost missed it, taking it at first for just another drumbeat of ecstasy. But then he realized he'd been given his cue, and he scrabbled at the trap door until he found and flicked open the latch that held it shut.

He wasn't particularly worried that the duke might hear him, given all the noise the carriage was making as it drove over the dirt roads of the London suburbs (not to mention the considerable noise the couple were making themselves), but he was concerned that Buckingham might happen to glance down and see him as he squirmed out of his under-seat niche. So after opening the trap his first move was to slide his head halfway out so he could see where the duke was looking.

Of course, he needn't have worried: Buckingham's full attention was focused on his own pleasure, and he probably wouldn't have noticed if a troop of light cavalry had ridden in one door of the carriage and out the other. His vigorous mounting of Milady was nearing its climax, and the sight of two such gloriously handsome people screwing with reckless abandon might have captured Louis's full attention too, if he hadn't realized that he couldn't feel his legs and might be paralyzed from the waist down.

In momentary terror at the thought of being permanently crippled, Louis fumbled a pair of embroidery scissors out of his sleeve and jabbed them hard into his thigh. And he felt it, thank God! ...So much so that he inadvertently yelped and tried to sit up, cracking his head on the cabinet's doorframe.

He lay for a moment, blinking away stars, then realized from the rising pitch of gasps and moans that the carnal ballet on the seat above him was reaching a crescendo, and he had only seconds to act. He took up the embroidery scissors again and looked desperately about for his objective.

(The cursed embroidery scissors: implements which, Louis was convinced, had been given to him by Milady just to emphasize his humiliation, as they were delicately crafted in the form of a graceful metal heron, with tiny cutting blades formed from its slender beak. Couldn't she have given him some small but sturdy shears, say, or a short, sharp dirk?

Oh, *no*—she had to give him tiny scissors shaped like a *bird*.)

But there was his goal: a wide silk neck-ribbon of deep royal blue, adorned with a dozen astounding matched diamond studs, peeking out from under a discarded doublet less than an arm's-length away. He twisted the upper half of his body out of the cabinet, hooked two fingers into the blue ribbon and dragged it toward him, ignoring the pain that lanced down the length of spine, as well as the gasping and sudden rain of tiny pearlescent droplets from above. The scissors were in his other hand; with two quick snips he detached two of the diamond studs, popped them into a pouch, and slid the ribbon back under the doublet. Then he shoe-horned himself back into the hated niche and latched the door behind him, just as Milord and Milady gave a final dual groan and collapsed heavily to the floor outside his cabinet.

Merdieu! Louis thought. *I didn't even have time to look and see if Milady is a real blonde.*

CHAPTER XIX
PLASH OF CHAMPAGNE

Louis d'Astarac's blurred and overlapping mental images of Isabeau de Bonnefont and Lucy Hay concerned him, and he gave quite a bit of thought to it. And the more he thought about it, the worse it became. His treasured recollections of pleasant Armagnac afternoons spent with Isabeau wandered down strange new paths when he tried to imagine Lady Carlisle in Isabeau's place, reclining in a leafy bower and chatting comfortably and companionably about life, nature, and art. And his oft-visited memory of encountering the Countess of Carlisle stark naked in a notary's bedroom would transform into a fantasy of finding the Demoiselle de Bonnefont in the same situation, and then inviting Louis into the bed.

What was behind this confusion of the two women? Was it their superficial resemblance to each other, or was he just subject to the universal male desire to sleep with every attractive woman he encountered? If so, what did that say about his True Love for Isabeau? He tried to imagine Isabeau strong enough to brave the dungeons of Bicêtre in pursuit of a goal, or capable of poisoning a rival, but he couldn't quite do it. On the other hand, how could he admire Lady Carlisle's character if she was so hardened that she could just about murder a person who'd never done her any harm?

Isabeau had spent all her life in the hills of Armagnac. If she had grown up a creature of the English and French royal courts like Lucy Hay, would she be more urbane and worldly-wise, or just more callous and cynical? And if Lady Carlisle had grown up in a sheltered backwater like Armagnac, would she be a creature of innocence and charming naïveté?

No, somehow that didn't seem likely.

He sighed as his musings reached the same conclusion they always did: in any event, neither woman (nor any other) was going to look at him seriously so long as his back was crooked and his limbs were twisted.

"Hssst!" Cocodril hissed. "If Monseigneur would deign to interrupt his doubtless profound contemplations, he would note that the revered Marshal Bassompierre is now snoring loudly enough to be heard even out here."

Returning, with some relief, to the business at hand, Louis saw that Cocodril was right. Bassompierre's London residence was a house in Leadenhall Street with a small garden behind it. Fontrailles and Cocodril were in this garden, crouching beneath a back window, while inside the house the Marshal of France snored like an ox with asthma.

Slowly, Fontrailles rose until his eyes reached the sill of the window and he could peek into the ambassador's bedchamber. The old roué, lying on his back in bed, face slack with sleep, was visible by the light of a pair of flickering wax tapers. The young woman lying wide awake at his side spotted Fontrailles peering in through the window, sat up and waved gaily.

"Har!" said a voice at Fontrailles's elbow. "She's a pert little package, and no mistake!"

"Breedlove!" Fontrailles said, clutching his chest. "You nearly gave me heart failure! What are you doing here? You're supposed to be standing by the horses so we can make a quick escape."

"I didn't want to miss nothin', Yer Lordship," said Breedlove, his single eye gleaming in the gloom. "I seen an' done near everything in my life, but I ain't never been an intelligencer before. Them horses is fine—I tied 'em up with knots what only a sailor knows."

"And which can be cut by a knife such as every thief carries, so get back there and do as you're told. *Merdieu*! You're still on probation, you know, and can be discharged without cause at any time in the next ninety days."

"Aye-aye, you're the Cap'n. I'll shove off," Breedlove said sulkily. "But if anything exciting happens, sing out, see?"

Watching him stump off, Fontrailles reflected ruefully on the flaws in his hiring practices, then turned to Cocodril and said, "All right, let's go in. But quietly, you understand?"

"I shall be like a feather on a midsummer zephyr, Monseigneur!"

"Yes, I should think that would suffice."

Fontrailles gingerly pulled open the garden door, which his hired young woman had made sure was left unlatched, and stepped into Bassompierre's bedchamber. The candles guttered momentarily as the night breeze found its way into the room, before Cocodril, behind Fontrailles, quietly closed the door. The flickering flames were reflected in the bright eyes of the fresh-faced young woman in the bed, who was sitting up with the sheet covering her breasts, watching them curiously. Cocodril doffed his peaked cap and bowed to her gallantly; she smiled, and sent him a wink.

Fontrailles snapped his fingers silently in front of Cocodril's grinning face and whispered, "Keep your mind on business. We're here to find a book— remember?"

"Of course, Monseigneur. You may rely on me," Cocodril whispered back, still grinning. "But gallantry knows no holiday!"

Fontrailles scowled and made the *cut it* gesture across his throat, and then turned to survey the room. It was a jumble of portmanteaus, crates, and half-unpacked trunks. If they had to search everything they'd be there all night—but fortunately, they knew just where to look. At Fontrailles's suggestion, Boisloré had suborned the marshal's *valet-de-chambre* with a lavish outlay of the cardinal's gold. After a brief negotiation and the transfer of a down payment, the man had described the appearance and location of the box that contained Bassompierre's books, and had agreed to introduce a young courtesan (also on Boisloré's payroll) to the marshal on an evening when he had no other female engagements.

Milady Winter, who had insisted on being briefed on Fontrailles's plans, had found these arrangements entirely too complex. "Why not just murder the man in his bed and then rob him?" she said.

"Assassinate Ambassador Bassompierre?" Fontrailles had sputtered. "I can scarcely even *say* it, let alone do it. And I don't think the cardinal would approve. We're better off burgling Bassompierre's baggage. And at least I can wrap my lips around that, though just barely."

Milady had then offered to lend Fontrailles her favorite pet monkey to perform the actual burglary. "He could do it with ease," she said. "He's quick, quiet, and nimble, and takes direction better than those louts you have assisting you now."

Wishing Milady would just mind her own business, Fontrailles replied, "If your monkey is as good as you say, why didn't you have *him* hide under your carriage seat and steal the diamond studs for you?"

"Oh, I wouldn't trust any really important mission to a *monkey*," she said archly.

"By the way, why did you want only *two* of the diamond studs? Why not take them all?"

"That is Monsieur le Cardinal's business," she replied. "If I were you I would attend to his lesser concerns, such as your own mission. It can be dangerous to get out of one's depth."

What a sweetheart, Louis thought. It was obnoxious to have to defer to this woman, but she outranked him and wasn't about to let him forget it. He swallowed his irritation and said, "I am much obliged to you for your advice, Milady de Winter."

"If you're going to use English honorifics, you should try to get them right, Monsieur. It is just Milady Winter," the blonde beauty said, cold as stone. "Where did you learn your English?"

At least this time he didn't have to do the job with a pair of prissy little embroidery scissors—just a grinning assistant who couldn't stop trading glances with the woman in the Ambassador's bed. "Come on, Cocodril," Fontrailles whispered, tugging at his manservant's sleeve. "It's in this corner. Help me move this trunk."

They lifted the tall wood-and-leather trunk and carefully set it aside. In the shadows behind it was the oaken library box Bassompierre's valet had described. Fontrailles knelt down before it and ran his fingers over the top and sides, but couldn't figure out how to open it in the dark. He whispered to Cocodril, "Go get one of those candles so I can see what I'm doing."

The candles were next to the bed—where the woman was. "On second thought," Fontrailles said, "I'll get it myself. You stay here."

The Special Ambassador of France was still snoring, Fontrailles saw, though he'd definitely shifted position. Graying now and putting on flesh, Bassompierre was still a handsome man who'd had a reputation in his day as one of France's leading rakes. He snuffled, and smiled a little in his sleep ... perhaps, Louis thought, dreaming about the pleasantly plump young woman who warmed the bed at his side. A half-smile on her rosy face, she was still watching everything attentively, like a member of the audience at one of the theaters across the river in Southwark. Fontrailles nodded to her as he picked up one of the candlesticks, and she smiled cheerfully back.

With the box illuminated by the candle the reason he hadn't been able to open it was obvious: the cursed thing was locked. The valet, damn him to all the hells, had mentioned nothing about it. "I wish Beaune were here," Fontrailles muttered.

"What do we do now, Monseigneur?" Cocodril asked.

"We can't break it open in here without risking waking up the marshal," Fontrailles said. "We'll have to carry it out into the garden."

It was heavy, but not so heavy that two men couldn't heft it, even if one was a rather stunted hunchback. Fontrailles took the lead, backing carefully toward the garden door, looking over his shoulder to make sure he didn't trip over anything.

Meanwhile, Cocodril was waggling his eyebrows at the girl in the bed, who pursed her lips into a little kiss, then dipped the bedsheet to flash one rounded breast at him. Cocodril grinned his huge grin and, while still holding his end of the library box, gave the young woman a jaunty half-bow. And Louis watched in horror as Cocodril's scabbard rose up behind him and knocked a half-full Venetian decanter off a table.

Louis thought the decanter shattering as it hit the floor was the loudest sound he'd ever heard—until Cocodril, doused by a jet of Champagne wine, let go of his end of the box, sending it crashing to the ground. The ambassador instantly stopped snoring, sputtered, and said, "Eh? Eh? Whazzat?"

Fontrailles looked wide-eyed at the young woman sitting next to Bassompierre as the man struggled up from the depths of sleep, but she just continued to watch the show delightedly and showed no signs of taking any action. In a panic, Fontrailles scuttled across to the bed, seized the surprised girl's shoulders, turned her toward Bassompierre, and shoved her chest-first into the marshal's face. Bassompierre snorted again, then made a happy sound, threw an arm over the woman and settled back into sleep.

Louis let out a breath he hadn't noticed he'd been holding. The young woman had belatedly gotten the idea and was now crooning a soft lullaby into the ambassador's ear. Fontrailles glared at Cocodril, but his manservant didn't seem the least bit embarrassed. Then he heard a slight creak from the inner door behind him, and turned to see it open just far enough to admit the bulbous head of Bassompierre's valet, his three chins quivering as he nervously gulped.

Fontrailles smiled his appalling smile and crooked a finger toward the man, beckoning him in. The man looked anxiously toward the marshal's bed, but hearing nothing but his master's snores, he sighed, nodded, and entered the bedchamber, shutting the door quietly behind him.

Fontrailles led the fat valet over to the library box, pointed to it, and then mimed inserting and turning a key. The valet just shrugged, which made his chins quiver again, and smiled blandly. Cocodril stepped menacingly behind him and put his hand on his hilt, while Fontrailles pointed at the valet and repeated the throat-cutting gesture. The valet snorted silently, pointed at Fontrailles, and mimed dropping a loop around his neck and suddenly jerking it up taut.

Fontrailles scowled, then made the universal hand-gesture for money. The valet smiled and nodded slowly. Fontrailles drew out his purse and counted ten Spanish *pistoles* into the valet's open hand. When he stopped, the valet curled his lip contemptuously at the coins in his hand and made as if to return them in disgust. Fontrailles held up his own hand to stop him, then counted out ten more *pistoles*. The valet looked satisfied, put the coins quietly into his purse, patted his clothes, and drew a key from an inner pocket with a look of mock surprise. Fontrailles took the key, made sure it fit into the lock, then pointed toward the inner door and dismissed the valet with a wave of his hand.

Once the valet had pussyfooted out of the room and closed the door behind him, Cocodril whispered, "What now, Monseigneur? Do we open it here?"

"No," Fontrailles whispered back. "I still think we're better off taking it into the garden. Let's pick it up again—but this time, don't drop it!"

Cocodril looked hurt, but he kept a tight grip on the box, and they managed to get it out into the middle of the garden and set it down on a marble bench. It opened easily enough with the key, the top creaking back to reveal Bassompierre's personal traveling library. There were almost two dozen books, new and old, large and small—but none of them, Louis quickly determined, were *The Three Mystical Heirs of Christian Rosencreutz*. Louis was searching through them a second time, almost frantically, when he noticed a folded scrap of paper tucked into a copy of Brantôme's *Recueil des Dames*. He pulled it out and read:

I got here first. Stop gaping like a farm boy.

The note wasn't signed. But Louis knew, of course, who'd written it.

CHAPTER XX
THE TREACHERY

The Vicomte de Fontrailles was peeved. It seemed to him that ever since he'd met the Countess of Carlisle he'd been in a continual state of exasperation. He wondered if he would be less irritated if he were repeatedly thwarted by a man rather than a woman. As a nobleman of France he had always taken it as an article of faith that he was every woman's superior, even if he was a stunted *bossu*. In Paris salons he'd heard the idea playfully bandied about that women might, in their own sweet way, be the equal or better of men in some limited areas, but it had never occurred to him to take such ideas seriously. Yet this Lucy Hay seemed to be besting him in a battle of wits, the one quality where he considered himself stronger than most men.

Fontrailles sneezed, and blasphemed horribly. On top of everything else, the cursed English weather was getting to him. They were trudging back to the inn where they'd taken lodgings through a night that was "dark as a Dutchman's heart," as Breedlove put it, breathing atmosphere that seemed equal parts smoky fog and soaking rain. Water dripped from Fontrailles's nose, ran down his neck, and squelched between his toes. If he'd had a dog, he would have kicked it, but he didn't, so he took out his ill humor on his manservant instead.

"Cocodril, you near-as-blazes fouled up the whole burglary with your idiotic gallantries to that girl in Bassompierre's bed," Fontrailles griped. "What is it with you? Are you in the pay of my enemies?"

"Monseigneur wounds me to the heart!" Cocodril pounded his chest theatrically. "How can you doubt my loyalty after all we've been through together? Besides, your enemies don't seem to value Your Lordship at your true worth, as what I've been offered to betray you are pitiful sums unworthy of consideration."

"Oh, very funny, Cocodril—but I suppose I deserve it. Look, I don't really question your loyalty, just your judgment."

"And in an attempt to improve my judgment, Monseigneur, I am studying your methods closely, and hope soon to observe a success from which I can derive a salutary lesson."

"Ouch. Perhaps that's enough on that subject. Breedlove, are we almost there? Maybe we'd get on better if we tried swimming instead of walking."

"'Ere we are, Yer Lordship: *The Cat and Infidel*." Breedlove raised his lantern to show the sign above the door displaying a colorful Turk with a tabby. The old sailor shook like a dog, spraying them both, and said, "It's me for the fire and a mug o' mulled wine!"

"An excellent plan," Fontrailles said, stepping through the door into the smoky warmth of the inn. "Perhaps it's Breedlove's methods we should be studying, Cocodril."

The host hurried up with a letter for the viscount, which he said he'd been asked to deliver to Milord Fontrailles as soon as he came in. Louis saw that it was addressed in the same hand as the note he'd found in Bassompierre's library box, quickly broke the seal and unfolded it. It read:

My Dear Louis,

If you have not already made an attempt to obtain what you are seeking from His Excellency the Ambassador, don't bother: I have the book already. However, I think we can still be of use to one another, and have a proposition for you that I believe you will find attractive.

Meet me as soon as you can, on the farthest barge tied up at Buttolph Wharf.
"Camille"

"Another letter from Monseigneur's ladyfriend?" Cocodril asked lightly, trying to read it sidewise without appearing to do so.

"It is, in fact," Fontrailles replied, folding it again. "And she wants to meet me right away. Breedlove, do you know where Buttolph Wharf is?"

"Like I knows me own fingers! Why, many's the time…."

"That'll do. Please be so kind as to lead us there."

"What? Monseigneur intends to go back out tonight?" Cocodril was aghast.

"Too wet for you, Cocodril?" Fontrailles asked. "Perhaps you'd prefer to stay behind?"

"By no means! I'm simply concerned about Your Lordship's health."

"I'm deeply touched. Believe me, I'm no more interested in going back out into that pissing night than you are, but if there's a chance of salvaging this mission I'm going to take it. *Merdieu!*" He thumped the nearest table. "I am fed up with being fed up, and in no mood to be made a fool of any further! We leave in a quarter of an hour, which should be just enough time to change into some dry clothes. Any questions?" Cocodril and Breedlove looked at Fontrailles with wide eyes and shook their heads. "Good. I didn't think so." Fontrailles drained his mug of hot wine and headed for the stairs to his room.

Somehow it was even darker on Buttolph Wharf than it had been in the narrow streets on the way there. Fontrailles asked in a low voice, "Is that it, that small ship on the end of the dock?"

"Aye, Cap'n—but she's no ship." Breedlove's quiet reply was almost swallowed by the fog. "That there's a spritsail barge, and you'll only see her like in the tidewater rivers of the Channel coast. Shall I board 'er, Yer Lordship?"

"No, I'll go first. But hold the lamp so I can see the plank—I don't fancy a plunge in the Thames tonight." Fontrailles adjusted his lace collar and tried to straighten his hat's plume, but it was sopping wet and refused to do anything but droop sadly over his crooked shoulder. Back in the inn, when he'd pulled an array of dry clothing from his trunk, he'd somehow laid out his best outfit; once he'd realized what he was putting on he rationalized that it would take too long to unpack other clothes, especially after making that speech to his loyal retainers about acting without delay. So even though he was wet through to the skin again, at least his wet clothes were good ones. He straightened his shoulders, insofar as that was possible, and walked carefully over the gangplank onto the boat.

Cocodril and Breedlove followed. There was no mystery about where to go: the barge had only one small cabin toward the stern, and a thin bar of light shone from the crack under its single door. Fontrailles made his way to the cabin and knocked, and a familiar voice said, "Come in."

"Wait outside," Fontrailles said to his men.

"What, in the rain?" said Cocodril.

"Will ye be safe?" said Breedlove.

"I'll be fine. I have my pistol," Fontrailles replied, though he was by no means sure he could rely on the weapon, despite its being wrapped in a swatch of oilcloth to keep out the English damp. But there was no way to check the powder and priming outside the cabin without exposing it to the rain that he feared. *Ah, well. Press on regardless,* he thought, and opened the door.

Lady Carlisle was sitting on a sea-trunk near a small, glowing stove, completely enveloped in a rich woolen cloak, apparently alone in the cabin's single room. *But that doesn't mean she doesn't have help within hailing distance,* Louis thought. He removed his dripping hat and bowed.

Lucy Hay smiled and mimed a curtsy without rising. "Good evening, Monsieur le Vicomte," she said lightly. "You're prompt—I like that in my men."

"I'm not your man just yet, Madame," Fontrailles said, still standing by the door. He looked around the cabin; a lamp burned on a little table, lighting the room fitfully. They did seem to be alone. "You'll forgive me for being somewhat standoffish," he said, "but our previous encounters have made me a little wary."

"Oh, really, Louis—prudence is so very unbecoming in a cavalier. And after all, what do you have to complain of? You want the only known complete copy of *The Three Mystic Heirs,* don't you? Well, I have it … and I'm willing to share it with you." She folded her hands on her lap and smiled again.

She was entirely too delectable. Fontrailles tilted his head skeptically and said, "You want the book for Buckingham and I want it for Richelieu. How can it be shared?"

"Because I didn't go after the book just to turn it over to the duke. I wanted it for myself, because I want to *use* it. And you, I suspect, have the same motive. No?" She arched one slim brow.

This was not what Louis had expected. "Use it?" he said. "How? And why?"

"I'll start with the *why*—if you'll come over here by the stove and dry off." She gestured toward an empty stool near her trunk. "Really, it makes me shiver just to look at you."

Prepare yourself, Louis, he told himself, *here comes a tale of woe.* He walked toward her, made another brief bow, and sat on the stool. It *was* much more pleasant near the stove. "All right, Madame," he said. "I'm listening."

She pulled back the cowl of her cloak and her dark hair tumbled free. "I like a man who listens," she said, eyes smiling. "There are so few of them. As you probably know, I'm a Percy, and was Lucy Percy before I married James Hay. My father is the ninth Earl of Northumberland. He's a wise and learned man, my father; he was an advisor to Queen Elizabeth and a close friend of Sir Walter Raleigh, but he fell from favor under James the First. Have you heard, in your far-off corner of France, of the Gunpowder Plot?"

"A scheme by radical Catholics to blow up Parliament, wasn't it? About twenty years ago, I think."

"Yes, in ought-five. One of my father's cousins was involved, and as this cousin had dined with him the evening before the arrests, my father was implicated. He had nothing to do with the plot, but the Star Chamber sentenced him to imprisonment in the Tower. For fifteen years the only way I could see my father was to visit him in jail."

"But he's no longer there?"

"My husband was an early favorite of King James, and he used his influence with His Majesty to get my father released five years ago. But he's still officially in disgrace, exiled to his estate at Petworth. The new king, Charles, has nothing against him, but," her expression hardened, "*Buckingham* makes certain my father stays out of favor. He's the royal favorite and prime minister, and wants no one near the king whose stature and integrity might enable them to oppose him."

"I think I see," said Fontrailles, intrigued in spite of himself. "So on your father's account you feel you owe Buckingham no favors."

"And on my own account." Her eyes flashed as she lifted her chin slightly. "He used me when he was on his rise to power, abused my trust and … my feelings. And now that he sits nearly on the throne, he uses me still." She clenched both fists, leaned forward and said through her teeth, "*I will see him brought down.*"

Fontrailles sat back, unconsciously recoiling in the face of her intensity. "All right," he said slowly. "I see your point. But how can *The Three Mystic Heirs* help you bring down the duke and restore your father to his rightful place? And what have I got to do with it?"

"I have reason to believe that book contains power against which Buckingham will have no defense! My father has spent a lifetime studying mathematics, astrology, and alchemy; during the old queen's reign they even called him the 'Wizard Earl.' Father studied Bruno's works, and was a patron of Doctor Dee and Thomas Harriot. Even in the Tower he spent his time in esoteric studies and experiments. Ever since he first heard of this book he's wanted it, as it's said to put all the knowledge of the Rosicrucians into usable formulas that unlock the secrets of creation. My father knows more about these things than any man in Europe—and if he believes it, then so do I."

"Why not take the book to him, then? It sounds like he'd know what to do."

"It wouldn't work. No matter how much he's been abused, how unfairly he's been treated, my father would never use the powers of Christian Cabbala to advance himself or harm another. He believes it would be dangerous to use spiritual alchemy for anything but good works. No," she shook her head, "he'd think it his duty to offer the power of the book to the king, who would just turn it over to Buckingham and send my father back into obscurity."

"Hmm. But, from what I understand of the Rosicrucians, Madame," Fontrailles said thoughtfully, "your father is right. The formulas described by Andreaeus are mainly useful for healing and understanding."

"I don't believe it," she said. "and I'm surprised you could be so naïve, Louis. Power is power, no matter how it's used. A scalpel can be used to cure or kill. Buckingham has the power of a kingdom at his command; there's no material way to get at him short of a suicide attack. But I'm convinced that hidden within that book is the power to bring him down! Unfortunately," she sighed, "it's a power I can't unlock. I just don't have the knowledge. I can't even read Latin; my father didn't think it a *proper study* for a woman! I have wits, yes, but I've never been a scholar, unless you count the study of court intrigue."

"And that's where I come in."

"That's where you come in! You're an educated man, a student of the Rosicrucian mysteries, you're clever, and the Good Lord knows, you're stubborn. You can help me use the book to achieve my ends, and you can also use it for your own, though I have no idea what they are."

Lucy Hay, with passion coloring her face and her voice, radiated an appeal that would move almost any man. But the mention of *his ends* brought a sudden bitter taste to Louis's mouth. He stood on his bandy legs and spread his crooked arms. "Have you *really* no idea what I'd use the book for?" he said bitingly. "Are you so disingenuous? *Look* at me, Lady Carlisle."

"But..." She seemed surprised for a moment, then smiled and said, "Well, I *have* seen you, as you may recall, and in the altogether. You're not *that* bad, you know. I've certainly known my share of men who were far uglier on the inside than you are on the outside. Is changing that what you've been risking your life for?"

"What would you know about it?" he said, more bitterly than he liked. "You, one of the most gorgeous women in God's creation. You've never … oh, plague take it anyway." He sat down suddenly. "The woman I love—she turned me down."

"Ah. A woman." Lady Carlisle nodded. "Of course, there would be. And she refused you? Then she's an idiot. Don't spare her another thought."

"Plenty of fish in the sea, eh? Not for me, there isn't," Fontrailles said. "I love her. Besides, if I give up on winning her, where's my motive for helping you? Undertaking to smite the Prime Minister of England with black magic is no casual endeavor."

"Then you'll do it? Oh, Louis! I could just kiss you! …Except that you're in love with someone else."

"Well, I'm not married to her *yet*," Fontrailles said, blushing in spite of himself. "So where is the book? I don't imagine you actually have it here."

"Why not? I know perfectly well you're too scrupulous to take it by force from a lone woman. It's in the trunk I'm sitting on."

"It *is?*" Fontrailles leapt to his feet again. "May … may I see it?"

"Of course, dear boy. Just give me a moment to gather my petticoats."

And less than a minute later he was holding it, in hands that were unashamedly trembling: *The Three Mystical Heirs of Christian Rosencreutz*. It was a heavy book, bound in thick, ridged leather stamped with gilt lettering, damaged where the title had been torn from the spine, and where the hasp of its bronze lock had been forced open. Fontrailles lifted the broken hasp and said, "Was it like this when you got it from Bassompierre's box?"

"Well … no. I'm afraid I did that myself," Lady Carlisle said. "I'd bribed the valet to open the box for me, but apparently I didn't pay him enough for the key to the book."

"That seems to be his usual manner of doing business. Well, I've gone through a lot for this book," Fontrailles said, taking a deep breath. "Let's take a look inside it."

There was a sudden series of sharp thumps from out on the deck, and a noise like a cry choked off. "Devil take it!" Fontrailles said. "Here, hide this, quick."

She took the book. "What are you going to do?"

"Unwrap my pistol and see what's going on," he said.

There was just time enough for Fontrailles to draw out his weapon and check its load and priming before the door to the cabin burst open. It was Cocodril. "Trouble, Monseigneur!" he cried. "Throw me your pistol! Quick!"

Fontrailles tossed it to him underhand. Cocodril caught it easily, flipped the butt into his hand—then spanned the wheellock and pointed the muzzle at his master. "I'm sorry, Your Lordship, but," he smiled and shrugged, "don't move, or I'll have to shoot you."

"Cocodril!" Fontrailles said sharply. "What's this all about? Put down that pistol!"

Cocodril didn't reply, just kept him covered as he moved away from the door.

Into the cabin stepped Milady Winter.

She wore an exquisite white cloak that was treated somehow to repel water so that the rain beaded up on its surface, the droplets shining like thousands of seed pearls, and despite the weather her face and hair looked as fresh as if she'd just stepped from her boudoir. But what riveted Louis's attention was the little gold-chased pistol she held in one elegant and steady hand.

"Treating with the enemy, Monsieur le Vicomte?" Milady said sweetly. "Shame on you. Monsieur le Cardinal will be so disappointed."

"You already got your diamond studs," Fontrailles said. "What do you want here?"

"The cardinal's will, as you so eloquently put it, is my will," she said. "He sent you to London to collect a certain item. I just want to make sure he obtains it."

"I haven't got it yet," Fontrailles said, "but I've persuaded the lady here to help me. If all goes well I should have it by tomorrow night."

"Normally I'd take you at your word, devoted as you are to the cardinal—but I happen to know better." Milady indicated Cocodril with a sideways nod. "What is that you're trying to hide in your skirts, Lady Carlisle? You're not doing a very good job of it. Of course," she added nastily, "you'd do better if you had more experience keeping your knees together."

"That's certainly no subject in which *you're* qualified to give lessons!" Lady Carlisle hissed.

"That's enough!" Milady snapped. "Only a very slight reluctance to attract attention keeps me from shooting you both out of hand. Cocodril, there must be rope around here somewhere. Tie them up, and bring me the book."

"Instantly, Milady! I live to serve!"

"How could you, Cocodril?" Fontrailles said as his former manservant wound tight coils of rope around him. "After all we've been through together!"

"It's true that I owe Monseigneur a modicum of loyalty for his modest salary, but Milady has condescended to remunerate me in a manner much more commensurate with my own estimate of my worth." Cocodril jerked the knots taut. "Also, you may recall that after an unfortunate misunderstanding, Your Lordship rebuked me, not with reasoned discourse, but by shooting off a pistol in my face. That was not an act a man of spirit can easily forget."

"What have you done with Breedlove?" Fontrailles asked, straining surreptitiously against his ropes. No give.

"He's taking a little nap on the deck. Sailors can sleep in all sorts of weather, you know."

"Enough chatter," Milady Winter said from the doorway, where she stood like a statue with her pistol in one hand and Fontrailles's in the other. "Aren't you done yet, Cocodril? The night wanes, and my ship sails for France on the morning tide. Bring me the book."

"Here it is, Milady!"

"Wrap it in that oilcloth and place it carefully outside."

"Louis," Lucy whispered. "I think you'd better do something."

"I agree," Fontrailles said. He tried to twist his hands around to grab at the ropes that bound him, but couldn't quite reach them. "Any suggestions?"

"Done, Milady!" said Cocodril. "What next?"

"Next," Milady said, "you kick over the stove and throw the oil from that lamp onto the coals so the boat catches fire. Then we leave."

"Ah," Cocodril said. "Are you sure?"

Milady swiveled one pistol toward Cocodril and said, in a flat voice, "I'm sure."

"Then your will is my will!" Cocodril said. He darted nimbly to the stove, kicked it over—away from the prisoners, Louis noted with a tiny flicker of relief—then shattered the lamp on the scattered coals. Flames bloomed. With a whoop, Cocodril dashed back to the door and out onto the deck.

Lady Carlisle was closest to the flames. *"Louis!"* she cried.

Fontrailles's arms were bound to his body, but his feet were free. With a guttural growl, he lurched to his feet and charged Milady Winter.

She shot him with his own pistol and he fell at her feet, blood pooling on the deck beneath him.

Milady dropped the discharged pistol contemptuously on his body and, ignoring the shrieking Lucy Hay, stepped out of the cabin and closed the door behind her.

CHAPTER XXI
SIR PERRY BLAKENEY

Fontrailles waited until the cabin door shut behind Milady, then raised his head and shook it to get the blood out of his eyes. He'd fallen hard on his nose when he'd been shot, and it was flowing like a fountain. Lucy screamed; flames crackled; something exploded like a gunshot behind him; Lucy screamed even louder.

Fontrailles got one knee underneath him—*Dieu,* but his chest hurt!—then the other. He pushed his head against the door and slid himself upwards until he was on his feet, drawing a three-foot scarlet smear on the panel and collecting a splinter in his forehead.

He tried to push the door open, twice, but it wouldn't budge—had Milady de Winter barred it on the outside? No, he'd forgotten, it opened *inward.* Coughing out smoke, he shook his head again, mostly to clear it, then hooked a rope-bound elbow behind the wooden door-handle and pivoted.

The door swung inward. Cool air rushed into the cabin and the fire roared its approval. Fontrailles staggered out onto the deck as Lucy shrieked, *"Louis! Don't leave me to burn!"*

He slipped on the rain-slick deck and fell on his face, splattering blood, pain stabbing into his chest so sharply it took his breath away. For a moment all he could see were exploding fireworks. He turned his face up to the rain, and then lurched once more to his feet.

He found Breedlove crumpled in a heap on the deck, in the shadow cast by the mast from the flames rising aft. Louis kicked him and shouted, and prayed he wasn't belaboring a corpse. But after a moment Breedlove sputtered, raised an arm and said, "Belay, Cap'n!"

"Get *up* right *now* and get the *lady* out of that *cabin!*" Fontrailles shouted desperately. He tried to lift Breedlove bodily with the toe of his boot but succeeded only in tipping himself over backward. He slipped again, fell heavily onto his back, and saw more fireworks.

When the world came back into focus Breedlove was stumping out of the smoke with Lady Carlisle thrown over his shoulder like a sailor's duffel. His strange spiral peg leg seemed to give him decent purchase on the slippery deck, but when he reached Fontrailles it went out from under him and he sat down suddenly, though somehow without dropping his burden.

"She's passed out, but I think she hain't dead yet," Breedlove said, then paused to cough. "She's took in a lot of smoke. What happened?"

"Cocodril betrayed us to Milady de Winter."

Breedlove spat. "Hain't surprised. Don't never trust nobody what talks funny like that, says I. Are you all right, Yer Lordship?"

"Just a nosebleed." Fontrailles said. "I got shot, but it didn't take." There were cries from the wharf and a drumbeat of running feet. "The fire's attracted attention. Are they coming to help us?"

"Nay, she's too far gone. Their first thought'll be to keep the fire from spreading to the craft alongsides."

"Then we'd better get onto the wharf before this boat burns to the waterline," Fontrailles said. "Get these ropes off us—the lady first, so she can breathe."

A few minutes later Fontrailles and Breedlove were sitting on a pile of sodden ropes on the wharf, behind a crowd of watermen and townspeople who were watching the barge burn and dowsing any flaming embers that arced away from it. Lady Carlisle was still unconscious, but she was breathing regularly, if shallowly. "What now, Cap'n?" said Breedlove.

"Now we get the lady someplace safe where she can recover, while I figure out what options we still have," Fontrailles said. "We'll take her back to the *Cat and Infidel.*"

"Mightn't we run into that Cocodril?"

"I don't think so. Milady de Winter seemed to be in a hurry to catch a boat to France—and given Cocodril's penchant for treachery, she's unlikely to let him out of her sight. I think we'll be safe at the inn."

At the edge of the crowd they found the crew of a two-man sedan chair who'd just taken home a baronet after a long night's gambling, and then stopped to see the show on the wharf. Fontrailles hired them on the spot. They bundled Lady Carlisle inside, the men hoisted the chair's poles, and the four of them trudged up through the muddy streets toward the inn.

They were nearly there, the sky just beginning to brighten in the east, when Fontrailles heard coughing from within the sedan chair, followed by some most unladylike cursing. He had the porters halt, and opened the door to check on Her Ladyship.

She looked awful, but at least she'd come around. "Louis!" she rasped. "I thought you'd left me to burn."

"No, I just stepped out for a drink and some breakfast. Fortunately, by the time I returned the horde of rats fleeing the sinking ship had borne you out on their backs."

"Bastard. Where are we?"

"Almost to my lodgings. How do you feel?"

"I'm wet through, my hair smells, and I feel like death. Any *other* stupid questions?"

"No, I think I've got it: wet; smelly; dead. Let's get you inside and we'll see what we can do about it."

The Vicomte de Fontrailles had the best room in the *Cat and Infidel,* the only one with its own fireplace. He had Breedlove build a crackling fire, then banished him to the inn's common room with orders to send up mulled wine and some food. Lady Carlisle sat on Fontrailles's bed and gazed grimly into his travel mirror, a silver-plated metal oval with a handle of dark oak. "Louis," she said, "look at this hair. Does this look gray to you?"

"It's ashes," he said. "Uh, I'd offer you some dry clothes, but I don't think I have anything that would fit you."

"Don't worry about it. Just set that chair near the fire." She stood and quickly stripped down to a thin shift of linen, then hung her clothes over the chair near the hearth. "You're staring, Louis," she said. "Pull your eyes back into your head. It's not like you haven't seen it before."

"Maybe so, but I'm not likely to get tired of it," he replied, "…Madame. Begging your pardon."

"Shut up and get your own wet clothes off. At least you have a dry outfit to put on. And no, I'm not going to turn my head."

"That's right—you've seen it too, haven't you?" He started unbuttoning.

She lay back on his bed and spread her hair so it would dry faster. "So why aren't you dead, Louis?" she said. "I saw that bitch shoot you with your own pistol."

"I was lucky. I was stumbling forward at the time so the ball hit me at an angle, and it went into that thick coil of ropes around my chest."

"But I wouldn't think a few ropes would be enough to stop a heavy ball at close range."

"They wouldn't—though I'm impressed that you know it. Here's what finally stopped the ball." He pulled his jerkin over his head to reveal a light mail shirt beneath it.

She sat up, said, "God's teeth!" then began to laugh. He ran his finger over the dented metal rings at a spot two inches below his heart, shuddered, and then painfully pulled the metal shirt off over his head.

"*Jesu Maria*, that hurts. I think the ball cracked a rib," he said.

"But why in God's name were you wearing a mail shirt?" she asked.

"Well, I *was* going to a meeting with *you*, Lady Carlisle. It seemed an elementary precaution."

She laughed gaily and said, "Come here. Let's take a look at that rib. Now, does that hurt?"

"Ouch! Yes, curse it, it damn well does."

"Oh, hold still. If I'm going to bind it up for you, I have to know where the problem is." She put one hand on his shoulder, leaned toward his chest, and ran her fingers over his ribs. He could smell the smoke on her breath.

At that moment the door opened, and a cultured English voice said, "Dear me. You know, when I disport half-naked with a girl in my bedchamber, I always bar the door first."

As Louis stared at the large, fair-haired gentleman in the doorway a volley of emotions ricocheted through him, including (but not limited to) embarrassment, surprise, irritation, confusion, and sexual frustration. "God's wounds, Parrott, what are you doing here?" he cried. "And, uh, what's happened to your birthmark?"

Lady Carlisle stood, looked the intruder in the eye, and said, "Monsieur le Vicomte, allow me to introduce Sir Percy Blakeney, one of Milord Buckingham's most trusted associates." She seemed poised and fully self-possessed, as if she weren't dressed in nothing but a damp linen shift that revealed every detail of her form.

"Don't forget clever. And good-looking," Blakeney said, bowing. "No disrespect meant to you, Monsieur le Vicomte."

"Devil take it, Lucy, you never said Parrott was a blasted fop of an English knight! ...No disrespect meant to you, Sir Percy," Fontrailles said, returning his bow.

"We haven't exactly had time to discuss the matter," Lady Carlisle said, turning to draw her steaming clothes from the chair by the hearth. "I would have gotten around to it."

"Well, I must say, this is most convenient," said Blakeney. "I expected to find only Monsieur de Fontrailles here, but I was looking for both of you, and here the both of you are! Go on with whatever you were doing— don't let me stop you."

"We were getting dressed," Fontrailles said. "We've been out in the rain and had to dry off."

"I've been out in the rain too, don't you know, and if you're done with that chair, I'll just borrow it. I could do with a spot of drying out myself." Blakeney sat down by the hearth, arranging his modish clothing carefully.

"But I say, what is that smell?"

"It's us. We were in a fire," Lady Carlisle said, buttoning. "Why were you looking for us, Percy?"

"No beating around the bush for you, is there, Lucy? When you know what you want, you go right for it." He cocked his head toward Louis.

Fontrailles scowled. "Now see here, you prissy…."

"Stop, Louis. He's just baiting us," Lucy said. She put a hand on Louis's shoulder. It felt good there.

"Ah, well. To business, then," Blakeney said, smiling carelessly. "How goes the search for that book, the what-you-may-call-it?"

"I have no idea what you're talking about," Fontrailles said.

"It's all right, Louis. I said I'd handle it when it came time to explain." She squeezed his shoulder lightly, then removed her hand. "Monsieur de Fontrailles has agreed to come over to our side, Percy, and work on behalf of Milord Buckingham."

Louis inhaled sharply, and then said, "That's right. It seems we're going to be allies, Sir Percy—so we might as well be civil to each other."

Blakeney, still smiling, said, "Well, that's awfully reassuring, I must say. When you dropped out of sight, Lucy, we became concerned. But I see you have everything well in hand." He looked around the room. "Charming place. Did you get the book from Bassompierre? Where is it?"

"We tried, but he didn't have it," she said.

"It … seems it's still in France," Fontrailles extemporized. "It was stolen from Bassompierre before he even left Paris, by someone we know only as the Peregrine."

"Do you tell me?" said Blakeney. "My, you have been busy."

"So we'll have to go back to Paris," Lady Carlisle said. "Right away."

"Well, I'm sorry to disappoint you, but you can't, my dear," Blakeney said. "Buckingham has closed the ports."

"Closed the ports? Why?"

"Something important has gone missing—can't go into details, terribly sorry—so he's embargoed all shipping until the matter comes right."

"But we *must* get to France!" Fontrailles said.

"Not this week." Blakeney shrugged apologetically. "But wait a moment: I have a thought. Day after tomorrow we're sending a Frenchman, a certain d'Artagnan, across on the *Sund* on business having to do with the, er, missing thing. You can go along—provided you stay out of this d'Artagnan's way and don't let him know you're aboard. After all, he's quite likely to run afoul of the cardinal's bullies at some point, and the less he knows, the less he can tell. There!" he said brightly. "I told you I was clever."

"No one ever doubted that, dear Percy," said Lady Carlisle. "But don't sit quite so close to the fire; your lace cuff is smoking."

"Damn me, so it is!" he cried, leaping up. "What a disaster!"

There was a knock at the door. "There's breakfast," said Fontrailles.

"I'll be on my way, then," said Blakeney. "Do hurry up and find this book thing, won't you, Lucy? Court isn't the same without you as its chief ornament. And Milord Duke is becoming rather impatient. There was some wild talk about throwing you in the Tower if you betrayed him on this."

"Don't worry, Percy," she said. "We'll find this Peregrine and get the book for Buckingham."

"I advise you to do so. Because if you can't find him, then as I believe I've demonstrated," Blakeney said, "I can certainly find *you.*"

CHAPTER XXII
PAS DE DEUX WITH SILENT CHORUS

It was supposed to be his night of triumph, one of those moments he lived for, when the machinery of the whole world seemed to turn in response to his genius and reward him with a prize that confirmed his superiority over other men. When the queen had first appeared at the ball without her diamond studs he knew he had won, and another buttress had been added to the edifice of his greatness. Then when Anne of Austria had reappeared with, somehow, twelve diamond studs on her ribbon instead of only ten, his machinery of genius had collapsed and the sweet fruit of victory had turned to bile.

Even in defeat Armand-Jean du Plessis was still Cardinal de Richelieu, the Prime Minister of France, and he had managed to maintain his poise when his king had called him to account in the presence of the queen. But now, almost alone in the chamber of the Hôtel de Ville reserved for him during the ball, he could feel the mocking demons of failure circling him, tempting him into the despair that was his secret sin. The black cloud was rolling over him again: he could feel it, shadowing his mind, dulling his thoughts and drowning his reason.

The room was empty except for a pair of servants in the livery of the City of Paris who were snuffing the candles and gathering the unburnt ends. The City Aldermen had purchased thousands of waxlights for the fête they'd thrown for Their Majesties, a shocking expense that could be defrayed only by recovering the remnants. Usually the cardinal was wary of letting his iron mask slip even in the presence of servants, but this defeat, so sudden, so unexpected, was too much for him. He sank onto an armchair, crumpled slowly forward, covered his face with his hands, and gave himself up to the darkness.

His failures and faults paraded before him in the forms of scornful women; he cringed as they spat at him and sneered their contempt. He tried to master them by herding them into groups, classing them by category of weakness, but they jeered at him, bit their thumbs, and would not stay where they were put. They were his flaws, his own, but they would not obey.

He felt a gentle hand on his shoulder. He knew that hand, and its touch somehow precipitated all his despair into a black bubble that erupted in a single sob. He sighed, exhaling deeply, then spread his fingers and opened his eyes to see the ugly, loving face of his only friend. Father Joseph.

"What afflicts you, my son?" Father Joseph asked gently. "Fear not, for God is with you. As always."

Richelieu sat up straight and looked about him, blinking away his visions. Most of the candles were gone now and the room was darker, but the tapers still burned in the chandelier above, and the two servants were puttering around in the corner, having some difficulty with the mechanism used to lower it. Father Joseph smiled, and the bristles at the corners of his mouth rippled like the quills of a porpentine. "Ah, you grieve over the affair of the studs. That's so, is it not?"

"It was so close, Joseph," Richelieu said, his voice uncharacteristically weak. "But it failed." He clenched his fists on his knees. "*I* failed."

"This is but vanity, my son," Joseph said. "You are the planner, and the plan was good—*you* did not fail. Someone else failed in the execution, and him we will punish, or some opponent succeeded, and him we will co-opt to our own purposes. Is this not your invariable practice? Is this not the root of your greatness? What is failure but a lesson from Our Lord, and an opportunity to learn and grow closer to Him?"

"Perhaps, Joseph," said Richelieu, "but such opportunities as this was do not present themselves every day."

"Do they not, my son?" Joseph's deep-set eyes crinkled around the edges. "Then this is a day to rejoice, not despair."

Richelieu was suddenly alert. "You have news, Joseph."

The Capuchin nodded, his peaked cowl bobbing. "A note—from your crookback intelligencer, the little Fontrailles."

"He has the book!"

"So he claims...."

"Ah! But he does not bring it to us."

"He wishes," Father Joseph said, "to *bargain* with us."

Richelieu smiled. "And that's why you are pleased. I know your mind, Joseph, I know it: you don't like this Fontrailles, and now you think we'll have both the book, and a reason to put him severely in his place."

"If God so wills," Father Joseph said humbly.

"Then come," the Cardinal said, standing suddenly. "This is indeed an opportunity. We have work to do, and plans to make."

He strode toward the door, followed closely by the Capuchin, passing the servants who were still fumbling with the chandelier crank. He noted them absently, for they were a mismatched duo: one so large he strained the seams of his livery, while the other had but one eye and wore a patch. But his attention was focused now on the possibilities of the future; he left the chamber behind and thought no more about them.

CHAPTER XXIII
THE ENTR'ACTE

Fontrailles watched from around the corner of the stable as the young Chevalier d'Artagnan mounted the magnificent horse that had been waiting for him, dug in his spurs and galloped off down the road to Paris. "Well," Fontrailles said, "he's gone, at least."

The Lady Carlisle said, "Thank God for small favors." She drew back the hood of her cloak, shook out her hair, and donned a heron-feathered hat handed her by her maidservant. "I've had enough of lurking in corners and ducking into doorways whenever that Gascon lout should happen to come my way."

"I just hope d'Artagnan hasn't taken the only horse in town," Fontrailles said. "We're going to have to ride like the devil to be sure of arriving in Paris before Milady de Winter."

"Ride, my eye," she sniffed. "We'll find a carriage. I have baggage and a *fille-de-chambre*."

"My dear Lady Carlisle—or I suppose I should address you as Madame de Bois-Tracy, now that we're back in France," Fontrailles said, with some asperity, "this tiny one-inn Channel port is unlikely to boast such a thing as a carriage-stable. I'm afraid our options are limited to ride or walk."

"So you think we should ride. And for speed, you'd probably have me forego the sidesaddle and ride astride. You'd *like* to see me in a pair of breeches, wouldn't you?"

Fontrailles flushed, but said, "As Madame has reminded me, I've seen it before."

"And you're sure you wouldn't like to see it again?" Lady Carlisle glanced around and saw no one but her maidservant. Playfully, she drew her skirt up above her ankle, then her calf. "Is this what you were after, Louis?" she teased, lifting the hem to reveal her knee, then several inches of delectable thigh. Her maidservant, eyes wide, turned her blushing face away while Lucy slowly turned her leg, then dropped her skirt and said, "There! You've had your fun. Now find me a carriage."

Louis, who'd been staring in spite of himself, looked away and grumped out a "Hmmph!" He clapped his hat on his head and said, "I don't think we're going to conjure up a carriage in Saint-Valéry no matter *how* much leg you show."

But he was wrong. In the barn behind the inn they found the carriage in which Lady Carlisle had traveled from Neufchâtel the week before. The innkeeper was in Buckingham's pay and had kept it for her, along with the team. They needed to hire a driver—Sobriety Breedlove, true to his resolution to retire from the sea, had stayed in London—but fortunately the host's strong young son was eager to take the job.

"You knew this was here all the time, didn't you?" Fontrailles said as Lady Carlisle's baggage was loaded onto the carriage's rear platform. "You were making game of me again."

"Oh, stop pretending to be surly, Louis," she said, handing her *maquillage* case up to her maid. "You're riding to Paris in style with two lovely women in a closed carriage, and you couldn't be happier."

It was true. He was grinning like the village idiot. "You know," he said, "sometimes, two women can be one too many."

Lucy Hay laughed aloud. "Shall I have the maid ride outside with the driver? Don't you just wish! Count your blessings, Louis, but do keep your head."

"I'll have to," he said, offering her his hand as she climbed up into the carriage. "We're going to have to use our time while traveling to figure out how to get the book back from Milady de Winter, and in doing so make it look like it came from someone called the Peregrine."

"I'll leave that part to you," she said, arranging her skirts on the seat. "This 'Peregrine' idea was entirely *yours*."

"And a fine idea it seemed at the time," he said, taking the seat opposite her. "It kept our necks out of the noose."

"Oh, Buckingham wouldn't go that far. He'd just clap me in the Tower for a while."

"I doubt if he'd treat me quite so gently," Fontrailles said darkly, then nearly lost his balance and fell off his seat as the carriage lurched forward onto the road.

"Careful, Louis!" Lady Carlisle said. "You wouldn't want to end up on my lap!"

It was a rough ride. The innkeeper's son, encouraged by Fontrailles's promise of a bonus if he made good time, and by a glance under her lashes from Lady Carlisle's maid, set a breakneck pace. They paused to rest the horses at Neufchâtel, and again at Beauvais, but by the time they reached Chantilly the team was ready to drop. The driver himself was reeling with fatigue, and the passengers, bruised and jarred to the bones, also felt in need of a break, so they stopped at the Inn of Grand Saint-Martin to rest while the horses recovered. "We can afford the time," Fontrailles rationalized. "With Milady de Winter's ship delayed by the embargo, we should still reach Paris well ahead of her."

Unfortunately, the best room in the inn was occupied by a wounded cavalier who refused to give it up, even to a countess. "He's a veritable ogre!" the innkeeper complained. "He won't pay his bill, and threatens to blow out the brains of anyone who tries to dispossess him of the room. My best room!" The host shook his fist toward the window on the first floor, from which came an off-key rendition of an off-color cavalrymen's drinking song. "He sends out his man to plunder my kitchens, stealing all my best viands! Thank the good God I have a lock on my cellars."

"It sounds to me like he's found a way into your wine stock as well," Fontrailles said, nodding toward the window.

"The Lord prevent it! Won't Your Excellency do something to rid me of this Monsieur Porthos?"

"Porthos the Musketeer?" Fontrailles said. *"Merdieu.* What's he doing here?"

"Being a one-man plague! Oh, Monseigneur, if you know him, won't you please beg him to have mercy on a poor innkeeper and move to another establishment?"

"Sorry, my man. La Comtesse's business is of the utmost urgency, and we can't afford to get entangled in tradesman's squabbles."

"I won't be in trade much longer if this keeps up," the host grumbled, but he gave them two rooms on the other, quieter side of the inn, and promised that their horses would be well looked after.

It was late afternoon and the town's bells were tolling *nones* when the driver scratched on their doors to rouse them. The horses were ready.

Louis woke slowly, still half-mazed from a dream of Isabeau riding with him in Lady Carlisle's carriage, and he was still bleary when he joined the lady herself in the common room. The innkeeper was bringing them a jug of watered wine when there was a commotion in the stable-yard and a clatter of wheels and hooves. A moment later their young driver burst into the common room. "Madame! Monsieur!" he cried. "They're stealing our horses!"

With a curse, Fontrailles leapt to his feet and dashed out the door, followed closely by Lady Carlisle, but they were too late: a dust-caked white carriage was vanishing out the gate, drawn by their team of freshly fed and rested horses. An exhausted team of matched grays were quivering and blowing in the yard, and as they watched, appalled, one of them dropped to its knees, fell on its side and expired.

"Louis! Did you recognized that carriage?" said Lady Carlisle.

"I should—I spent half a day in London crammed under its seat," he snapped. "It belongs to Milady de Winter! She either brought it with her across the Channel or had one just like it waiting in Calais." Another of the grays, bloody foam at its mouth, collapsed in the dust of the stable yard. "*Peste!* We'll have to find another team, and she's certain now to beat us to Paris."

"That's another one I owe that blonde bitch," Lady Carlisle said. "The debt's rising to a level I'm not comfortable with. Let's find those horses, Louis."

It was dawn of the next day by the time their carriage passed through the gates of Paris. As their horses clopped down broad Rue Saint-Denis, Fontrailles was surprised by the unusual number of coaches and cavaliers coming the other way, some of them weaving drunkenly and belting out snatches of popular songs. "What's this all about?" he said. "It looks like everybody's coming home from an all-night celebration."

"Aldermen's Ball," Lady Carlisle muttered from where she lay slumped in a corner of the cab, face covered by her hat. "God, what a night." She dragged the hat from her face and gazed at him listlessly. "The fête at the Hôtel de Ville for Their Majesties is all Paris was talking about for weeks. How could you not know about it?"

"I suppose I've been thinking about other things," he replied.

At that she smiled and sat up, and he realized, with some wonderment, that she thought he meant he'd been thinking about her. *Women,* he thought. *How can a man even begin to understand them?*

"And what are *you* smiling about?" she said.

"I'm laughing at myself. I learned it from you," he replied.

The streets around the Châtelet were jammed with revelers coming from the Hôtel de Ville, blocking all access to the Pont du Bois, so Fontrailles ordered the driver to turn right along the quay and take them to the Pont Neuf; at least that way they were moving with the crowd rather than against it. Eventually they arrived at the great bridge, already thronged with peddlers, preachers, strolling comedians, and itinerant dentists. When they reached its midpoint they turned left onto the Île de la Cité and into the relative quiet of the Place Dauphine.

Fontrailles had the carriage stop in front of the house where he had lodgings, then hopped out and offered his hand to Lady Carlisle. "My humble abode," he said. "We'll find out what my men have to report, then decide on our next move."

"I need to wash," she said, climbing down stiffly. "And so, for that matter, do you."

"I'm afraid Ensign de Fontrailles will have no time for that, or for anything else," said a stern voice with the ring of authority. "His presence is required elsewhere—immediately."

"My dear Comte de Rochefort!" Fontrailles said, trying to swallow his dismay. There he was, the cardinal's hatchet man, looming twice as large as usual with a face as grim as death. Louis decided to try friendly banter. "You look terrible, Rochefort! Have you been dancing all night at the party? Not that it isn't nice to find someone waiting to greet you when one comes home from travels to a distant land."

"I'm in no mood for inane pleasantries, Fontrailles. The Comtesse de Bois-Tracy, is it not?" Rochefort bowed slightly to Lady Carlisle. "You choose interesting traveling companions, Ensign. The paper mentions only your name, but I dare say it can be stretched to include madame, here."

"What paper would that be, Rochefort?" Fontrailles asked nervously.

"The warrant, Viscount," Rochefort said with relish. "You're under arrest."

CHAPTER XXIV
THE SUMMER-HOUSE

Sobriety Breedlove was frightened, sweating profusely and rolling his eyes helplessly. Which was not to be wondered at, thought Sir Percy Blakeney, as the man was tied to a heavy chair and being threatened with non-elective surgery by a dangerous lunatic.

The dangerous lunatic was Doctor John Lambe, Astrologer-Elect to His Grace the Duke of Buckingham. He was a tall, broad-shouldered, energetic man who was sweating nearly as much as Breedlove, enveloped as he was in a black satin robe embroidered with red and gold symbols of the stars and planets. His stained and scarred hands emerged from pendulous sleeves that tapered nearly to the floor and were perforated with scores of burn-holes, which alone was enough to make Blakeney glad that he'd never taken up the pursuit of alchemy. Lambe was humming tunelessly as he fumbled through a leather case filled with metallic implements, some straight, some curved, some hooked, but all very, very sharp.

The Duke of Buckingham stood behind Breedlove's chair, hands on his hips, regarding his astrologer's preparations with fond amusement. They were in a summer-house on the grounds of his mansion in Chelsea, and no one else was around but a pair of burly guards who waited just outside.

Buckingham leaned forward and said, suddenly, into the prisoner's ear, "I'm told your name is Sobriety Breedlove. Are you a Puritan?"

"M-my parents was, Your G-grace," Breedlove sputtered, without taking his eyes from Doctor Lambe and his case of tools.

"Then I presume they taught you to respect your betters, and to always speak the truth," said the duke.

"Th-that they did, Your Grace," Breedlove said. He swallowed, and added, with a touch of bravado, "They also taught me about loyalty … Your Grace."

"Ah. Excellent. But a man should never *stop* learning, eh?" Buckingham said, polishing his nails against the breast of his gleaming golden doublet. "So the learned doctor here is prepared to teach you some new lessons. Unless you're ready to tell us everything you know about your master's activities here in England."

"Ah, here it is!" said Doctor Lambe, drawing out a long, curved blade that looked like it belonged in a butcher's shop.

"But I don't know nothin', Your Grace!" Breedlove said, staring at the shining steel.

"That's not what my man Blakeney tells me," Buckingham said in a friendly tone. "He says that you went everywhere with Monsieur de Fontrailles and can tell us all about it—who he met, what they did, and what they talked about."

Breedlove clamped his mouth shut, but continued to stare at the blade in Lambe's scarred fingers. The alchemist smiled and said, "Your Grace, there's something I've just been dying to try. You know how I've sometimes read omens for you by reading the entrails of animals?"

"Indeed I do, Doctor. And I've been impressed by your success."

"Well, Milord Duke, if I can do that well with the bowels of a dove or a dog, just *think* what I could do with the entrails of a man!" The doctor's eyes were bright as he waved the blade enthusiastically.

"But I told you, I don't *know* nothin'!" Breedlove cried. He struggled against his bonds and stamped his feet against the floor, trying to push over the heavy chair.

"Blind me, Your Grace, but I believe the man has a false leg!" Doctor Lambe put his tools down on a side table, knelt and rolled up Breedlove's slops. "Jesus, Mary, and Joseph!" he cried. "Milord! Do you see this?"

Buckingham came around from behind the chair and looked curiously at Breedlove's leg. "What is it? Wood carved in a spiral?"

"Wood? Ha-ha-*ha!*" Lambe laughed in genuine glee. "It's a *unicorn's horn,* Milord—a unicorn's horn! On a broken-down sailor's leg!"

"No! No, it ain't!" Breedlove cried, struggling again. "It's just the nose off a narwhale! It came off a fish, I tell ye!"

"Your Grace, we must have this leg," Lambe said. "It's just astounding what one can do with unicorn's horn! Plague cure; poison detection; aphrodisiacs! It's been on here a long time," he said, looking closely, "and the flesh has grown over it, but I can cut it away."

"No! Not me leg!" Breedlove shrieked. "I'll talk! I'll tell everything ye wants to know!"

And in short order, it all came tumbling out: Fontrailles's meetings with Boisloré, the burglary at Bassompierre's, his involvement with Lady Carlisle and Milady Winter.

"The Countess of Winter, eh?" Buckingham said. "Very interesting indeed, by gad."

"Can I have the leg now, Milord Duke?" asked Lambe.

"Of course, Doctor," Buckingham said carelessly. "If he gives you any trouble, take the other one, too." He called in the guards, who lifted the screaming Breedlove, chair and all, and carried him away, followed by the eager Doctor Lambe, humming happily.

Buckingham waited until the shrieks dwindled into the distance before turning to Blakeney. "You'll have to forgive me for that, Percy," said the duke. "I know you don't approve of Doctor Lambe, or his methods."

"What, disapprove of his methods? Surely not. They're so very effective," Blakeney said dryly. "His astrological charts are the best in the kingdom—they always tell Your Grace exactly what you'd most like to hear."

Buckingham frowned. "Percy, you know I don't like it when you take that tone with me. Come, don't be such a wet blanket! They used to call you the Laughing Cavalier."

Blakeney looked away. "Your Grace knows why I don't laugh quite so much these days."

"Yes, Percy, I know—but you can't wallow in grief forever. They used to call you Diogenes, too, did they not? Well, truth-seeker, find me the truth of this book. If what it contains is half as important as Lambe says, it would be a crime if it fell into the hands of the French."

"I don't suppose I can argue with that, Your Grace."

"I should say not! And based on what Master Breedlove tells us, I don't think we'd better trust our dear Lucy to handle it alone. I don't like her connection with this French hunchback—such people give me the fantods. And the involvement of Milady Winter is particularly disturbing, especially since we've determined that it was probably she who made off with the diamond studs."

"Your Grace still hasn't told me the details of how she managed that theft," Blakeney said, with a little smile.

"She ... that is to say ... never you mind," Buckingham said. "Let's just say she's a dangerous woman whom we shouldn't let out of our sight. Percy, I think you'd best go to Paris to keep an eye on Miladies Winter and Carlisle, and to make sure that once the book is found, it comes to me. You'll go incognito."

Blakeney bowed. "As you wish, Your Grace—though this time, I'd rather do without the birthmark."

"I don't think it will be necessary. I'll send Baron Winter as nominal leader and you can blend in with his entourage. His standing as Lady Clarice's sister-in-law will be useful if we need to take official action against her."

"Baron Winter?" Blakeney raised an eyebrow. "Will he be told everything?"

"Of course not. Winter's a good man, quite reliable, but no intriguer." Buckingham clapped Blakeney on the back. "Take good care of him, Percy—I'm going to need him and his marines for the relief of La Rochelle.

Try to keep the fuss to a minimum. But whatever it takes," he said, "bring me that book."

"I shall endeavor to give satisfaction, Milord," Blakeney said, smiling. He bowed gracefully and took his leave, but once outside the summer-house his expression darkened. "This covert agent business is not quite the amusing diversion I'd hoped for," he said to himself, "and the more I see of the noble Buckingham's other aides, the less I like the idea of being one of them. Still, I suppose I must get this book for him—better he should have it than Richelieu. Though if it's as useful as all that," he mused, sampling the perfume of a late-blooming rose, "I shouldn't wonder but that others will be after it, as well."

CHAPTER XXV
ARAMIS

Though it was a sunny day, the room on the first floor of the only inn in Crèvecœur was gloomy, as the drapes had been drawn almost to a close. Three men sat in the austere chamber, from which every worldly comfort had been removed, and talked in low tones.

"So it is agreed, then," said Aramis the musketeer. "The price of my admission into the Society of Jesus will be *The Three Mystic Heirs*—should I be able to lay my hands upon it."

"We have confidence in your resourcefulness and finesse," said Athanasius Kircher.

"As long as you understand," Aramis said, "that I have no intention of allowing my friend d'Astarac to come to harm."

"Heh," said Jean Crozat, known as Père Míkmaq. "So you say. But I know your sort, and you are not a man who will allow another to come between you and something you want."

Aramis stood, hands clenching in unwonted agitation, but before he could reply the sound of hoofbeats came from the yard outside. The musketeer stepped to the window and twitched one drape aside. *"Nom de Diable!"* he cried.

For he had recognized the rider as d'Artagnan.

Kircher said, "What is the meaning of this impious outburst, Brother Aramis?"

"A friend of mine has just ridden up. I thought he was dead!" Aramis said. "What joy! ...But he mustn't find us here discussing heretical books."

Míkmaq said, "You told your man to make sure we weren't disturbed."

"This gentleman is not so easily deterred," said Aramis, "but if you will take my advice on how to handle this, he'll suspect nothing. He knows I've always intended to leave the musketeers and return to the Church. Adopt the false names I gave to Bazin, and pretend to be quizzing me about the thesis I must present to qualify for ordination."

Kircher nodded happily. "Yes, indeed. Most amusing. I shall play the stern taskmaster."

"But I don't know anything about playacting!" said Père Míkmaq. "Bah! This is absurd."

"Just pretend to be a rural curate who knows nothing," Aramis said. "You can manage that, can't you?"

Míkmaq seemed to be on the verge of a sharp reply when Kircher interrupted: "Of course he can. What will you use for your thesis?"

"These notes I was making for a poem," Aramis said, gathering some papers from his writing table.

"A *poem?*" said Míkmaq. But Kircher hushed him: they could hear boots coming up the wooden stairs. There was a brief commotion on the landing outside the room, and then the door opened suddenly.

"*Bonjour,* dear d'Artagnan," said Aramis.

CHAPTER XXVI
THE REVELATIONS OF JOSEPH

The Comte de Rochefort said, "I must ask you for your sword, Monsieur de Fontrailles," in a tone that made it clear he wasn't merely asking.

"Why? You're not afraid I might try to use it on you, are you, Rochefort? Or attempt to poke the cardinal with it?" Louis was trying to keep up a front of careless affability, but he could feel himself starting to sweat. *Under arrest.* This was bad.

"It's just how these things are done, Fontrailles. I've taken many men into custody for His Eminence and seen everything, so I advise you not to try any tricks," Rochefort was stern. "And you can cease looking around for an escape route, Madame. The man behind you with the pistol in his pocket is one of mine."

"I thought he was just happy to see me," Lady Carlisle said. "Now what?"

"Now we all get into this rather road-worn carriage of yours and pay a visit to Father Joseph," Rochefort said. "He's most eager to see you, Fontrailles. You seem to have done something quite treasonous." He gestured, and a man stepped forward whom Fontrailles recognized as the bruiser with the eye-patch who'd previously escorted him to see the

Capuchin. One-eye opened the door of the carriage, took a quick look inside, and nodded to Rochefort, who climbed in and offered his hand to Lady Carlisle. "You first, Madame; then you, Fontrailles."

"What about my maid?" Lady Carlisle said.

"She can ride with the driver, or walk—or jump in the Seine, for all I care," Rochefort said. "You two sit on the front seat, facing me. My man will ride the lead horse."

Fontrailles looked around the Place Dauphine but didn't see anyone who might help, and as their little drama was occurring behind the carriage, none of the passersby appeared to notice what was going on. He glanced at the house and saw a dismayed Vidou peering back at him from an upstairs window. Good; at least someone would know he'd been taken. Rochefort said something in an impatient tone, so Fontrailles sighed and joined him and Lady Carlisle in the carriage. It immediately began to move, turning back toward the Pont Neuf.

"So we're going to see Father Joseph instead of the cardinal?" asked Fontrailles.

"His Eminence is indisposed. I gather he received some rather bad news last night." Rochefort smiled humorlessly. "If you had anything to do with it, Fontrailles, you'll probably be in the Bastille by nightfall."

Lady Carlisle pulled a wooden case from under her seat and began to unlock it with a little key attached to a bracelet on her wrist. Rochefort said, "I hope you don't have a weapon in that box, Madame." He drew a large pistol from under his half-cape and rested it on his knee. "It would be a shame if you tried to do something reckless."

"Don't be ridiculous, Monsieur," the lady said scornfully. "I just want to renew my make-up."

"*Merdieu!*" said Fontrailles. "Is that a double-barreled wheellock, Rochefort?"

"Yes, it is. Over-and-under, with an offset lock on either side," Rochefort replied, with a slight but proud smile.

"What a beauty!"

"It's a Spät, of Munich. Look at the inlay on the pommel."

"Lovely! Though I'd think the barrels are a trifle short for real accuracy."

"If they were longer, the thing would be heavy as a musket."

"You men and your guns!" Lady Carlisle snapped, putting away her mirror. "You're like children! It's revolting."

"We simply admire beauty when we see it," said Rochefort. He was almost charming.

"Beauty, in a gun! Beauty is found in art, or music," the lady said.

Rochefort sneered. "I leave music to the Italians and art to the Dutch. I'd rather have a Spanish sword, a German firearm—or a French lady," he said, remembering to be gallant.

"Well, *I* like art and music," Fontrailles said.

"Oh, shut up, the both of you," Lady Carlisle said in disgust, and they spent the rest of the ride in silence.

The carriage pulled up in front of the forlorn house on Rue Garancière where Fontrailles had met Father Joseph before. Rochefort conducted Louis d'Astarac and Lucy Hay into the dismal rear room that served as the Capuchin's audience chamber; to Louis it seemed the shapeless patches of mildew on the walls had only grown and darkened since his last visit. Almost immediately the inner door opened to admit Father Joseph, clad as ever in his coarse, cowled robe, moving almost soundlessly across the rough floor on his bare, bristled feet. *Enter Spook, stage right,* Louis thought.

Rochefort bowed correctly and said, "The Vicomte de Fontrailles, Monseigneur. And his companion, the Comtesse de Bois-Tracy."

Joseph came around the bare wooden table that, with a couple of chairs, was the room's only furniture, and padded toward them. At his approach Lucy recoiled slightly. "The Comtesse de Bois-Tracy," Joseph whispered. "I have heard of you, Madame." Hands buried in his broad sleeves, he surveyed the countess closely for a moment with unwinking eyes, then turned to Rochefort. "However, that is not her only name, Monsieur le Comte," he said softly. "Madame, here, is also Lucy Hay, née Percy, Countess of Carlisle and the wife of the Earl of Carlisle, one of Buckingham's most trusted aides.

"Indeed?" said Rochefort.

"Absurd! Don't be offensive, Monsieur!" said Lucy.

"Can the truth offend, Madame?" Joseph quietly replied. "Let every man speak truth with his neighbor, says the Bible. I have informants in every Court in Europe—including England, where your description is well known. It is useless to dissemble."

"I am the Comtesse de Bois-Tracy," she said firmly.

Father Joseph shrugged and turned to Fontrailles. "His Eminence is disappointed in you, Monsieur de Fontrailles. You were awarded a mission of great responsibility and have repaid the cardinal's confidence with a sordid attempt at extortion. It was most unwise."

Joseph's protruding eyes stared into Louis's; he blinked and said, "Actually, Monseigneur, I have no idea what you're talking about. I've performed my duty both loyally and capably, tracking the book-we-shall-not-name to London and back to Paris, with the collaboration of Madame de Bois-Tracy here." He swallowed nervously and asked, "What do you mean by extortion?"

Father Joseph's nostrils flared, causing the bristles that lined their interiors to writhe and point toward Fontrailles like black needles—but his voice, when it came, was still a whisper. "There is no point, my son, in continuing a deception that has failed. Do you deny sending a letter to His Eminence stating that you have the item, and wish to negotiate terms for turning it over to him?"

Lady Carlisle stifled a gasp. Fighting down panic, Fontrailles said, "I do deny it! I've sent no letter, and had only just returned to Paris the moment Rochefort detained us, as you can ascertain quite easily, Monseigneur. The letter … the letter must have come from the culprit we've tracked back to Paris from London, a person we know only as the Peregrine." He was sweating, damn it to all the hells, but suppressed the urge to wipe his palms on his breeches.

"A culprit, known only as the Peregrine," Joseph repeated, and shook his head sadly. "This flight of juvenile fancy does you no credit, Monsieur de Fontrailles. A man who studied with the Oratorians should be above such follies. Yes," he nodded, "I have looked into your history—and that of your family. I believe I can even guess why you wanted that heretical work for yourself. There is a woman, I believe, a Huguenot girl named de Bonnefont. You sued for her hand, and she refused you. Isn't that so?"

Louis felt a hot jet of anger cut through his fear. "What of it?" he shot back.

Unperturbed, Joseph shrugged again. "Nothing, my son. But if you sought to impress her by achieving some *coup de main*, your efforts have been wasted. She has married another."

Louis stopped breathing. The room reeled—or maybe it was him. "Married?" he said, mouth dry as dust.

"I thought perhaps you were unaware of the fact," Father Joseph said. "Do you still deny you have the book?"

Louis d'Astarac, unable to speak, nodded, and put a hand to his throbbing temple. Married!

"A pity, *mon fils*," Joseph hissed. "Liars shall have their reward in the lake which burns with fire and brimstone, which is the second death. You and your companion shall be remitted to the Bastille. There you shall be put to the Question and eventually tell us all we want to know."

"You don't dare!" Lucy said, almost shouting. "I am the Countess of Carlisle! I represent the British Crown, and this man is under my protection."

"Not at all, Madame," Joseph said, voice seeming to drop as hers rose. "You are the Comtesse de Bois-Tracy, as you and your companion have both averred, and thus subject to the justice of the Most Christian King of France."

"You overreach yourself, monk," she said haughtily. "You cannot threaten me. My husband is the Earl of Carlisle; my father is the Earl of Northumberland."

"Your husband, alas, is far away," Joseph said, "and your father, of course, is dead." She gasped, and he said, "Did you not know? Rejoice, daughter, for your father is with Christ."

The blood drained from her face. Lower lip trembling, she seemed on the verge of fainting; Louis came alive and led her to a chair, then turned angrily to glare at the Capuchin. Rochefort, he saw, was smiling—the bastard was enjoying this.

A knock resounded from the room's main door. "Ah, the coach from the Bastille must have arrived," Father Joseph said. "Monsieur de Rochefort, would you be so kind as to admit the guards?"

"Of course, Monseigneur," Rochefort said cheerfully. He went to the door, opened it—and then raised his hands and backed into the room. He was followed by a long pistol, then by its wielder: dark-faced Gitane, his one eye gleaming dangerously.

Without a moment's delay Father Joseph padded to the inner door, pulled it open—and stopped, for the frame was filled by the outsized form of Beaune, also holding a pistol, and dressed, like Gitane, in the livery of the Hôtel de Ville.

Joseph turned back into the room. "I presume these are your men, Monsieur de Fontrailles. This is worse than useless; you may escape this house, but then you will be fugitives, hunted by the most efficient police in Christendom. Where can you go?"

"I'm not about to tell *you*, am I?" Fontrailles said. He marched up to Rochefort, who was no longer smiling, and said, "I'll have my sword back, Rochefort. And that fancy pistol of yours."

"You would sink to theft, Fontrailles? I had thought you a gentleman," Rochefort said stiffly.

"I'll leave it outside," Fontrailles said—he really *would* have preferred to keep it, but Rochefort's remark had nicked him on his honor. "It's too noisy a toy to leave with you."

"So we're not to kill them, Monsieur?" Gitane said.

"No, Gi–" Louis stopped himself. If they were going to leave witnesses, he'd better not use names. "No, we won't kill them." He turned to Beaune. "Can you lock them in?"

"I don't have the key, Monsieur," Beaune said, and smiled shyly, "but for these locks, I don't need one. I'll make sure they stay in until someone lets them out."

"Good. Come, Madame. We're going."

"I'm ready," she said, standing. "Which way do we go?"

"The front's the only way out," Gitane said.

"Then out the front we shall go. Keep them covered while he–" Fontrailles nodded toward Beaune "— deals with the doors."

In the outer foyer they found their driver, the son of the Saint-Valéry innkeeper, watched admiringly by Lady Carlisle's maid as he nervously held a knife to the throat of Rochefort's one-eyed bruiser. Fontrailles cocked the double-barreled Spät—*Lovely action,* he thought—pointed it at One-Eye and said to the driver, "I'll take over here. Go get the carriage ready to drive." Relieved, the young man nodded and went out the front door, the maid clinging to his arm.

"Your men," Lady Carlisle said. "How did they…?"

"I left them with orders to keep a close watch on the Spook—I mean, Father Joseph," Fontrailles said. "Also, Vidou saw us being arrested, and may have tipped them off."

"Exactly, Monsieur," Gitane said, as he and Beaune joined them. "We knew that this dog," he said, indicating the other one-eyed man, "was the Capuchin's creature, and they would bring you to this house. Dog-face told us others would be coming soon to take you to the Bastille, so we knew we had to get you out."

"Well done, from first to last," Fontrailles said. "Do we leave in the carriage?"

"I don't think we should talk about it in front of Dog-Face," Beaune said.

"You're right," Gitane said. He regarded Joseph's man sourly for a moment, then clouted him savagely on the head with his heavy pistol. The man dropped like a felled tree.

So much for brotherhood among the one-eyed, Louis thought. "They know the carriage," he said. "They'll follow it."

"Put the driver and my maid in the carriage, wearing our hats," Lady Carlisle said. "Your men can drive it away and abandon it a few streets from here. We can walk."

"You recover quickly," Fontrailles said.

"I'm just trying not to think about … other things."

"All right, that's what we'll do," Fontrailles said. "And fast, before the coach from the Bastille *does* get here."

Moments later he and Lady Carlisle watched the carriage drive off up Rue Garancière toward the Petit-Luxembourg, and then turned and walked in the other direction. As the carriage turned onto Rue Vaugirard at the upper end of the street, a coach entered at the lower: a heavy coach, with bars on the windows and armed men riding on the rear platform. Fontrailles and Lady Carlisle averted their faces as it passed, then hurried off down the street.

"Louis, where are we going?" Lady Carlisle said.

"I don't know," he replied. "But I do know it must have been Milady de Winter who wrote that extortion letter purporting to be from me. She has the book, and she thinks we're dead. We have to get it from her."

"My father really *is* dead," Lady Carlisle said.

And Isabeau de Bonnefont has married Éric de Gimous, Louis thought.

"Tell me, Louis," she said, grabbing his arm and stopping him. "Louis, please," her voice was haggard, "*what are we still doing this for?*"

CHAPTER XXVII
THE WINE OF ARAMIS

It was a market day, and the narrow streets of Paris were crowded with produce wagons from the farmlands that surrounded the ever-hungry capital, as well as all the citizens who made their livings in the city's alleys and avenues: hatters, flower-sellers, itinerant tailors mending clothing on the spot, food-vendors selling meat pies and grilled pigeons, dung-carts collecting nightsoil, and, as Fontrailles and Lady Carlisle passed Saint-Sulpice and neared the gates of the Saint-Germain Fair, an increasing number of beggars and whores.

The Vicomte de Fontrailles, a hatless hunchback dragging a distraught English noblewoman through the crowded streets, felt as obvious as a naked nun on a stage. Locked doors wouldn't hold Rochefort and Father Joseph for long, and then the hounds would be after them. Passersby who saw Fontrailles recoiled with the usual superstitious fear of the deformed, and he knew that, if questioned, they would remember him.

When they reached the Rue de Petit-Bourbon he turned left, and pulled Lady Carlisle behind the posts of a borne so they wouldn't be run down by a passing carriage. "Lucy!" he said, shaking her gently. She was weeping quietly, tears rolling down her cheeks. "Madame! My Lady! Do you think the Cardinal's people know of your connection with Aramis?"

She sniffed, then shook her head and said, "I don't know. I don't think so. But that damned monk knew who I was—and about my father's death! He must have a pact with Satan!"

"I never mentioned Aramis in my reports," Fontrailles said, "and though we were close friends years ago, that was when he went by another name. We'll have to chance it. His house is only a few streets away—we'll go there."

"All right," Lady Carlisle said. "I suppose." She drew a handkerchief from her sleeve and wiped her eyes. "God, I must look awful."

"We'll worry about that later," Fontrailles said. "This way."

They went west along Petit-Bourbon and turned up Rue Férou. The closer they got to Rue Vaugirard the more nervous Louis became, for they were returning to the neighborhood of Richelieu's lair, the looming Petit-Luxembourg. But Aramis's house was on Vaugirard, between Férou and the Rue des Fossoyeurs, so there was no help for it.

When they reached the corner Fontrailles scanned the broad and busy Rue Vaugirard in both directions, but didn't see anyone he knew to be one of Richelieu's agents or guardsmen. "We're nearly there, Lucy," he said. "If we can maintain a casual demeanor and avoid slinking furtively, perhaps no one will notice us."

In fact, no one appeared to pay any attention to them as they walked the last few steps to Aramis's doorway, though Louis's humped back itched as if he were being watched. Fontrailles rapped loudly on the door; then, after a minute, rapped again.

No response.

"Name of the Devil! It didn't occur to me that Aramis might not be at home, or even out of town," Fontrailles said. "If we try to break in, we *will* attract attention. Then it's the Bastille for Louis d'Astarac."

"No need for that," Lady Carlisle said. "As it, um, happens, I have a key."

"Do you really?" Fontrailles looked at her. "Well, well. I didn't realize you and Aramis were such *good* friends."

"Really, Louis—do you think I jump into bed with everyone? Aramis let us use his place as a safe house when Buckingham was in Paris, that's all." She took a purse from her travel-cloak and produced a key, and a few moments later they were inside Aramis's lodgings.

It was dark within; the shutters were closed on all the windows, and the air was stale and smelled of old ashes. Spiders had been at work in the corners. "He's definitely gone," Fontrailles said. "Bazin too. This place has been closed up for days."

"Good. I don't want to see anyone." Lady Carlisle went into the front room and collapsed suddenly onto a divan. "Oh, *Louis!* We've made a terrible mess of things, haven't we?"

"Bah! The situation isn't that bad," Fontrailles said stoutly. "I've seen worse."

"You have?"

"Well ... not really, no. But if we can find a way to get that book from Milady de Winter, we may yet avoid the torture chamber. Look on the bright side: thanks to quick thinking and decisive action, we've found a good place to hide for a while. And if I know my Aramis, his larder is well stocked with good food and better wine."

"Wine?" Lady Carlisle sat up. "Why didn't you say so before, you silly ass? I need an immediate drink. Maybe ten."

"At your service, Madame. If there's one thing hunchbacks are built for, it's uncorking bottles."

When he returned to the dim front room a few minutes later with a bottle and a couple of glasses, he saw that she had removed her travel-cloak and was lying back on the divan, staring at the ceiling. He poured her a glass of Aramis's red wine and she drank it off quickly, then held out the glass for more. "That's not watered, you know," he warned.

"Good," she replied. "More."

He poured her more. This time she sipped it, leaning back against the arm of the divan. He poured one for himself, set the bottle down on a side table and looked around for another chair. She patted the divan next to her, and he sat down obediently. *Like a lapdog,* he thought. *Yes, that's it. She probably regards me as something like a talking pet. Certainly not as a man.*

"My father," she said, staring at the ceiling again, "wasn't a great man, and he was sinfully proud, but he had a good side. They clapped him in the Tower because he was related to one of the Gunpowder Plotters and was friendly to Guy Fawkes, but he was friendly to many people. The great house at Petworth was always full of people from all walks of life. My father wanted to know everything and listened to everybody.

"Emotionally, he was distant—not because he was cold, but because he was easily hurt. Nonetheless, I adored my father. Even so, I wasn't like him. He was a proper gentleman, and I was never … proper. Even when I was a little girl, listening to sermons in church, I knew I wasn't a good person." She shuddered, and turned her head to look at the wall. "Then I was introduced to the world of the Court in London, and found that that's what I wanted: the power; the wealth; the men. And from the very beginning, the men wanted me. I loved that. I first slept with a man when I was eleven years old." She smiled distantly. "And with a woman when I was fourteen. It's all a game, sex at Court. It has rules, and you keep score—and you have to call it *love*. That's the most important rule of all.

"I played the game with relish, making conquests of powerful men, scoring devotion and gifts. My … *fame* … spread, and eventually even my father learned what I'd become. He ordered me to go home, back to the country—but I defied him. I married James Hay, a pretty boy, a minor Scots nobleman fresh out of King James's bed, where he'd briefly been a favorite. I was eighteen years old. The king made my husband Earl of Carlisle, and I … I got to stay at Court, and continue to play my games. And now I was playing at the highest level, with the greatest names in the realm.

"Then George Villiers came on the scene, and the game began to get ugly." Lucy took a long swallow of the dark red wine. "Before him, King James would keep a favorite for a season or two, and then his eye roved onward. But once Villiers caught the king's eye, he made sure he kept it by ruthlessly cutting out anyone else His Majesty might favor. James made him Duke of Buckingham, gave him power—and once he had the power to take what he wanted, Buckingham used it."

She drank, and held out her glass for more. Louis saw that his own glass was empty as well and refilled them both. "For all his intimate attentions to King James," she continued, "Buckingham really preferred women. At first, when he began to cast his eye on me, I was delighted. I knew I'd never make a conquest of the king, but having the royal favorite as a devoted lover would be nearly as good. However, it soon became clear that Buckingham had no intention of *courting* me. By then he had power, and he didn't ask—he commanded."

She drank again, and glared at the ceiling, as if her eyes would bore a hole into it. "Buckingham gave my husband a prestigious new career as a diplomat, and then sent him on long missions overseas. While he was gone—and sometimes, even when he wasn't—I became Buckingham's mistress. Or at least, the chief among them."

This time Louis refilled her glass before he was asked—and his own, as it was somehow empty as well. She drank and said, slurring her words slightly, "I didn't let him see that I'd grown to hate him. It was too dangerous. Buckingham's a cunning devil—he made sure to ingratiate himself with Prince Charles, the heir, so that when James died he continued to be royal favorite with the new king. He became, if anything, more powerful than ever, and ensured that his feet never touched the ground by walking on the necks of men like my father."

She swayed slightly on the divan, blinked back tears. "I wanted to make Buckingham pay, Louis. I wanted to use the Rosicrucian magic to cause the gates of Hell to open up and swallow him. I wanted to restore my father to his rightful place in the realm. I was willing to damn myself to eternal torment if I could do that one good thing. And now it's all been just a sinful waste." She held out her glass again.

"So you fear damnation?" He filled her glass; his, too.

"I've always known I was going to Hell. By now I expect it more than fear it. It's why I know I have to find what joy I can here, while I live." She sat up and looked at him, a wry smile on her lips. "You don't believe in Hell, do you? Or Heaven, for that matter."

"Why would you say that?" he asked uncomfortably.

"I could tell by the way you looked when I talked about it." She smiled openly, her perfect teeth gleaming in the darkness. "I may not be able to read Latin well, or Greek, but I can read men like storefront signs."

He looked away from her, eyes hooded. "This time you're wrong. Of course I believe in Heaven and Hell. The Catholics and Protestants may not agree on much, but to deny the afterlife to either sect is to court the stake." He drank, a long draught.

"Don't worry, Louis—I won't tell. I've got near-heretics in the family, remember? They call my father the 'Wizard Earl'." Her smile vanished as her face fell. "No, *called*. He's dead now. And I'm alone." She stifled a sob.

The great lady suddenly seemed nothing more than a sad little girl. Louis reached out for her, but stopped himself when his hand was still inches from her shaking shoulders. *What am I doing?* He thought. *Must be the wine.* He drew his arm back and said, "Isn't there … isn't there anyone you love?"

She gave a short, bitter laugh. "I don't think the word means the same thing in my world that it does in yours," she said, and drank again. "But you have a girl, don't you, Louis? What was that name the monk said … de Bonchamps?"

"De Bonnefont. Isabeau de Bonnefont," Louis slurred. Talking was becoming more difficult; his tongue was feeling decidedly thick. Maybe if he just spoke carefully she wouldn't notice that the wine was getting to him. He took another drink. "But she married someone else. Joseph said."

"Fuck him, and all his kind," she said, somewhat indistinctly. "Monk bastard."

Her glass was empty again. She held it out. He refilled it, and his own, and noticed that that finished off the third bottle. When had he opened the other two? He couldn't remember. He drank, and said, "I love her, Lucy."

"What does she look like?" she said. And drank.

"Looks a little like you," he said. This was funny, so he laughed. She laughed too. "But she married Éric," he said.

"Then she's a si … silly ass. Fuck her," Lucy said.

"Never did," he said. *And now I never will.*

"Then fuck me," she said softly. "Fuck me, Louis."

She leaned slowly into him, soft and hot, and kissed him on the mouth, her lips wide open. He froze a moment in shock, then returned the kiss, and they collapsed into one another, kissing avidly, tears running down their cheeks.

They kissed, and kissed, breathing each other's breath, wrapping their arms tight around each other, tight ... then they slipped off the divan and fell to the floor.

"It's too small!" she said. This was the funniest thing Louis had ever heard, and he laughed. They both laughed, until they couldn't breathe. They giggled, and groped, and kissed some more, then stood, swaying, and stumbled into Aramis's bedchamber, laughing and leaving a trail of clothes behind them. They batted aside the bed curtain and tumbled onto the mattress, locked in a tangle of limbs.

It was completely dark in the bed, but Louis didn't need his eyes, he felt like he already knew every inch of Lucy's body, had always known it. She was eager for him, almost desperate, and within moments he was inside her, as she wrapped her legs around him with a cry that mingled need and triumph.

They flowed into a rolling rhythm like a mutual pulsebeat, each stroke driving him higher, farther, until it seemed he was two places at once, his body gloriously merged below with Lucy's, while his mind soared up, high into the darkness, above the bed, above the room, above the house, until he could see all across darkening Paris. Making love to Lucy felt *good*, and *right*, and *true* ... and where else was truth to be found in the shadowed, shamble of a city that rolled out before his mind's eye? In the Louvre? Not *there*— only *here*. (*Ohh*, Lucy sighed.) The Petit-Luxembourg? Not *there*—only *here*. (*Yes*, Lucy cried.) In Joseph's shabby house? Never *there*—only *here!* (*Oh, yes!* Lucy gasped.)

And then he knew. "Lucy! *Unh*. He lied!"

"Hhhhh...."

"*Jo*-seph! *Oh*. Your *fa*-ther's. Not. *Dead!*"

"Hahhh...?"

"And *she's. Not. Wed! Ahhh....*"

"*Oh! Oh!* ...Oh, Louis. Louis."

And they cried, and laughed, and kissed.

And slept.

CHAPTER XXVIII
THE REUNION

Gray light was filtering through the curtains surrounding Aramis's big bed. "My aching head," Fontrailles groaned as he rolled over. "Do you feel as bad as I do?"

He was alone.

He pulled the curtain aside and surveyed the bedchamber: no feminine clothing on floor or furniture. He dropped back on the pillows, scowled, and then sighed.

Of course, he thought. *She woke up, saw what she'd been sleeping with, and fled in horror.*

His face twisted into a mask of disgust. *But I'm even uglier inside than outside. I love Isabeau, yet I slept with another woman. I'm a swine.*

A noise intruded from the salon: the front door lock rattled, then the door squeaked on its hinges.

Fontrailles leapt from the bed, looked around wildly. Where were his breeches? Where were his weapons? Where did Aramis keep *his* weapons? At random, he jerked open the door of a handy armoire; a flock of lace-trimmed shirts hanging on the inside of the door fluffed and danced, their sleeves caressing his face.

"See anything you like?"

It was Aramis, in the door of the bedchamber, smiling his crooked smile, curse him. Fontrailles blew all the air from his lungs in relief, then put his hands on his hips and said, "Aramis, what earthly use can one man have for so many shirts?"

"So I don't have to parade around naked, of course. Shall I avert my eyes while you dress?"

"Thank you," Fontrailles said. "It's the least you can do."

"My philosophy of life in a nutshell."

Fontrailles followed last night's trail of clothes back into the salon, donning each piece as he found it, and scandalizing poor Bazin, who was coming in the front door with his master's travel bags. "You know, d'Astarac," Aramis said, following him while looking pointedly at the ceiling, "if I weren't a gentleman bound by the ironclad laws of hospitality, I might ask just what the devil you were doing trespassing in my home while I was away ... and"—he sniffed histrionically—"not alone, either, unless you've taken to wearing ladies' perfume."

"What if I had?" Fontrailles said, pulling on his boots.

"A person who wasn't your friend, as I am, might say it was an improvement."

"It occurs to me, *my friend,* that I have some rather pointed questions for you, too." Fontrailles tied his shirt laces, and then donned his doublet. "When you recommended that I hire Parrott, you knew you were planting an English spy on me, didn't you? What was his real name—Blakeney?"

"Ah. Parrott." Aramis smiled disarmingly. "I just wanted to make sure you had someone with brains beside you, in case...."

"...In case I forgot to use my own? Thank you very much, *mon ami.*"

Aramis sighed. "It seemed like a good idea at the time."

"Didn't it occur to you that he'd betray me the first chance he got?"

"I didn't think he'd go so far as to actually harm you. And he didn't, did he? Curse it, d'Astarac, what do you want from me? I'm perilously close here to apologizing, which you know is against my principles."

"All right, d'Herblay, all right, let it go." Fontrailles looked around for his hat, and then remembered it was gone, ornamenting the head of the carriage driver.

"Ah ... one hates to persist, of course," Aramis said diffidently, "but what *are* you doing here, d'Astarac?"

"Hiding from Father Joseph and the Comte de Rochefort."

"Blood of Christ!" Aramis's diffidence vanished, replaced by taut wariness. Pencil-thin moustaches bristling, he strode to the front door, locked it, then opened the shutters on the window a crack and peered out into the street. "How bad is it?" he said sharply.

"Bad," Fontrailles replied. "The cardinal's reserved a room for me in the Bastille."

"Well, you can't stay here," Aramis said. "Normally I'd be only too happy, but I'm expecting visitors who may come at any time, unannounced—and it wouldn't do for them to find you here."

"I'm really not sure where else to go," Fontrailles said. "They'll be watching my house and searching all the inns. And most of my money was in my bags, which have probably been seized."

"Money!" Aramis said. "Pray don't mention the stuff! I'm hard up against it myself. Let's put your case up to my comrades. The four of us should be able to think of something."

Aramis sent Bazin off to arrange a meeting, which gave the two friends time to share some breakfast, and Louis an opportunity to brood over the pre-dawn disappearance of Lucy Hay. He'd been with her every day for the past week, and now he found that he missed her company badly. He thought about Isabeau, and his midnight certainty that Father Joseph had lied about her marriage. He still loved Isabeau dearly, of course. But he missed Lucy. What did it all mean?

Aramis, toasting bread at the kitchen fire, said over his shoulder, "Did you find that thing you were after in England?"

"The book?" Fontrailles said, suddenly wary. D'Herblay was one of his oldest friends, and knew him better than anyone except Isabeau—but on this subject, he didn't fully trust him. "We, ah, found it never really left Paris. It's in the hands of someone we know only as the Peregrine."

"The Peregrine? What a romantic alias! I could almost adopt it myself," said Aramis. "Where is our dear Lady Carlisle?"

"To tell you the truth, I have no idea," Fontrailles said. "She's wanted by the cardinal, too."

"Is she? Bad luck," Aramis said. "But she has a way of landing on her feet. Cheese or honey?"

Two hours later Aramis's friends were assembled at Athos's house, around the corner in Rue Férou, and there in the parlor the Vicomte de Fontrailles received his first formal introduction to Messieurs Athos, Porthos, and d'Artagnan. All seemed preoccupied, displaying only a shadow of the hearty camaraderie that Fontrailles had come to expect from such high-spirited musketeers. But Aramis seemed to command their respect, and they listened attentively enough as he explained Fontrailles's dilemma.

"If Aramis vouches for you, that's good enough for me," said Athos, a man who exuded a quiet dignity that Louis found somewhat intimidating. "However, while I am always happy to do His Eminence the Cardinal a disservice, I have room in this place only for myself and my man, Grimaud, and I've sworn not to leave until my current financial predicament is resolved."

"Whereas while I have plenty of room," the looming Porthos boomed, "I'm engaged right now in a delicate matter involving a certain great lady and I couldn't risk compromising her with the presence of a guest. As monsieur is a friend of Aramis," Porthos gave his extravagant moustache a significant twist, "I'm sure I need say no more."

"And I think my place is *already* being watched by the cardinal's men," d'Artagnan said. "I wish I knew how to help, Monsieur de Fontrailles, but I'm new to Paris, and am acquainted with very few people here." The young Gascon was the only one of the three who seemed genuinely distressed by Louis's plight.

"Put your faith in Providence, young man," Athos said. "The cardinal's morals are far from exemplary, and I have no doubt but that in your quarrel with him, the right is on your side. God will provide a solution."

Fontrailles scrutinized Athos's expression, but found no trace of irony—the man was sincere.

"Hem." D'Artagnan's manservant, looking apologetic, cleared his throat. *"Hem."*

Athos glared at the lackey, apparently offended by his presumption, but d'Artagnan said, "Yes, Planchet? What is it?"

Planchet stepped shyly forward and said, "Monsieur really has no place even to spend the night?"

"That's right," Fontrailles said, "except for the Bastille, it seems."

"Well, I know it's not what Monsieur is used to, but ..." He looked at d'Artagnan, who nodded. "If I might, I'd suggest the stables at the Hôtel de Tréville, where messieurs keep their horses. I could sneak Monsieur in, and he could sleep on the straw in an empty stall. It's not much, but it's warm—and I doubt His Eminence's men will expect to find Monsieur there."

"D'Artagnan, I fear Planchet needs another thrashing," Athos said. "Such an offer to a gentleman is an insult."

"On the contrary, I accept, with gratitude," Fontrailles said. "If you were the one faced with prison and the rack, Monsieur Athos, you might see the matter differently." Athos raised an eyebrow, but made no reply. Fontrailles continued, "I thank you for your hospitality this morning, and have one more favor to ask of you."

"Of course, if it's within my power," Athos said. "Though if what you need is money, I warn you in advance, there's little to be had between us."

"No, Monsieur Athos, all I ask is a sheet of paper, a pen, and some ink," Fontrailles said. "I need to write a letter."

CHAPTER XXIX
THE HALL OF ENTRAPMENT

While the Church of Saint-Leu would have been the towering central edifice in any town of the provinces, as churches in Paris went it was no more than medium-sized. Fontrailles arrived there early, well before the start of the Sunday service, and took up a position standing behind a column on the gospel-side, a location from which he'd be able to survey the entire congregation without being obvious about it.

As the pews began to fill, Fontrailles tugged a few stray pieces of straw from his hair, souvenirs of his night in the stables, and fought to control his anxiety. Would Milady de Winter show up? A great deal depended on this.

Milady had thought Fontrailles dead, burned to death in Lady Carlisle's barge on the Thames, which was presumably why she had borrowed his name when she'd attempted an incognito sale of *The Three Mystic Heirs* to the cardinal. Getting hold of that book was the only hope Louis had of avoiding death or imprisonment at the hands of Richelieu's many agents—so he had sent a note to Milady's house in the Place Royale announcing that not only was he still alive, he was still acting for His Eminence in the matter of the Book. Furthermore, he wrote, the cardinal was aware that she had been behind the offer to sell it to him, but Richelieu was disposed to be broad-minded about the matter, and had empowered Fontrailles to offer Milady a thousand Spanish *pistoles* for *The Three Mystic Heirs*. He proposed to meet her Sunday morning at the Church of Saint-Leu, a place public enough to ensure a good-faith transaction, but where they could nonetheless effect a discreet exchange.

Fontrailles had brought with him a bulging purse heavy with coin. It was mostly filled with copper *deniers*, topped by a few golden *pistoles*, but he hoped that Milady wouldn't stop in church to count the money.

To get the double handful of coins he'd had to sell his oversized sword, holding out just a few crowns for living expenses and a new, less ostentatious hat. He was gambling that if Milady de Winter thought the cardinal knew she had the book, she'd grab at an offer to sell it, knowing that if she refused, His Eminence was in a position to simply take it from her. It wasn't a foolproof plan, but given the circumstances, it wasn't bad, either.

The pews were nearly full, the choir had already started singing, and Louis d'Astarac was seriously considering going into a panic when the Comtesse de Winter finally made her entrance. With her striking beauty, icy hauteur, and splendid gem-studded attire she caused quite a stir; the Church of Saint-Leu wasn't a fashionable place of worship for the *Grands* of the Court, and Milady, followed by a maidservant and a young black boy bearing a red velvet cushion, attracted a wave of sidelong attention.

What drew Louis's eyes was the velvet pouch adorned with Milady's coat of arms that was carried by her pretty maidservant. For it was a book bag.

Milady kept her eyes straight ahead as she walked up the aisle, not deigning to acknowledge the curious and admiring stares of the congregation. She stopped near the front at one of the best pews, though it was already partly full. As those seated there shuffled deferentially toward the outside, the gaudily-dressed black boy preceded Milady into the pew and carefully placed his cushion where his mistress would kneel for her devotions. The maidservant followed the countess, sat down beside her at a respectful distance, and opened the velvet bag.

She drew out a small leather-bound missal and handed it to Milady.

Fontrailles couldn't tell from where he was standing whether the embroidered velvet pouch was now empty—but he assumed it was not, and that *The Three Mystic Heirs* was within it. The book bag provided the perfect camouflage for bringing a heretical Rosicrucian tome into a Catholic church.

The service began. Milady, whose expression showed only rapt devotion to the Word of the Lord, looked up from her missal and, without moving her head, slowly surveyed the Church from one side to the other. When her gaze reached Fontrailles, standing in the shadows behind his pillar, her eyes stopped and locked with his own. He gave her a discreet nod, which she acknowledged with slow blink and a slight, satisfied smile. Then she returned her attention to the mass. The transaction, of course, would have to take place once the service was over.

Though still anxious about the impending exchange, Louis was nonetheless immensely relieved that it seemed the deal was on. Once he had *The Three Mystic Heirs* in his possession, he could copy out the sections that might enable him to cure his deformity, then negotiate trading it to the cardinal in return for having all charges against him—and Lady Carlisle—dropped. He might even find himself restored to His Eminence's favor; he was quite certain that possession of the Book meant more to the cardinal than revenge on a temporarily-renegade agent, especially one who'd proven himself resourceful.

As the mass progressed through its familiar course, Fontrailles considered the congregation of Saint-Leu on this Sunday morning: some obviously devout, some seemingly bored, most merely patient and semi-attentive. Of the devout, he wondered, which came here from love of God, and which from fear of hellfire? In France attending mass was a strict social obligation of all who professed Catholicism. But if there were no stigma attached to forgoing public devotion, how many of these worshipers would choose to stay home? What did they really believe?

What did *he* really believe? Lady Carlisle had accused him of doubting the existence of Heaven and Hell ... and in fact, she'd been right. He didn't know what really happened to the soul after death, but to his mind the Church's depiction of paradise and perdition seemed designed more for the purposes of men than God, men whose overriding purpose was to control other men. If God was real, then surely obedience to Him should come from love, not fear.

Was God real? He had to be, or faith itself was senseless. But Louis's skeptical mind had never fully trusted reliance on faith; in fact, he'd always instinctively recoiled from it, even when he was a student in the seminary. Louis, stunted and deformed from childhood, felt that he had only his intellect to fall back on—despite the fact that Saint Augustine called intellectual curiosity a disease that tempted men to try to learn secrets of nature that were beyond their understanding, and which "man should not wish to learn." But if that was so, why had God given men brains with which to think? If faith was the highest virtue to which humanity could aspire, why bother to think at all? Why not just believe?

During a pause in the sermon a noise from among the worshipers, a low heartfelt moan, attracted the guarded attention of nearly everyone in the congregation, Milady de Winter included. Louis followed her glance and saw that the mournful sound had escaped from a middle-aged woman in a black taffeta hood sitting across the aisle on the other side of the nave. She was gazing, her heart in her eyes, at a big man standing off to the side, a cavalier tricked-out in showy martial attire. He seemed quite unaware of the woman in the black hood, despite her increasingly desperate signals.

It was Porthos. But, Louis thought, not even a big bullock like him could be as oblivious as he seemed to be: the musketeer must be playing some kind of cruel romantic game with the lady in black. He noticed that Porthos was making amorous signs of his own—and when he saw that they seemed to be directed at the Comtesse de Winter, he grew alarmed. He had no idea what Porthos was up to, but he was afraid the giant would blunder into his own carefully contrived rendezvous and ruin it.

He looked at Milady de Winter to see if she was taking Porthos's signals amiss, but she seemed to be paying him no attention. Instead, Louis saw her glance quickly toward his own side of the nave, but several pews, or pillars, back. Suddenly suspicious, he looked along the pews for anyone he recognized, then stepped back into the dim bay behind the columns and peered along them toward the entrance of the church.

Two pillars away, prowling quietly toward him in the gloom, was Cocodril.

When he saw that Fontrailles had spotted him, Cocodril stepped out of the shadows and saluted his former master with an ironic smile, his big teeth gleaming in the dim light. Fontrailles ground his own teeth. Some sort of double-dealing was in the wind, and it was clear he wasn't going to get his hands on *The Three Mystic Heirs* this day. He had fallen into some kind of trap, and he had to find a way out of it.

With mass going on Fontrailles couldn't very well retreat toward the altar, so the only way out of the church was past Cocodril. Louis assumed that whatever the rogue had had in mind required stealth and he wouldn't dare risk a disturbance, so he simply marched straight at his former manservant, attempting to stare him down as he approached. Cocodril bowed politely as he passed, still grinning, and fell in behind him, well within arm's reach.

Great, Louis thought. *Now what?* He was a wanted man and could no more risk a disturbance than Cocodril. In a few moments they'd be out in the street, where the scoundrel might somehow find an opportunity to attack him, if that's what he intended. Having sold his sword, Fontrailles wasn't even armed; Cocodril likewise lacked a sword, as only gentlemen were entitled to wear them in city streets, but Louis could see he had his long, razor-sharp knife in a sheath at his belt.

They emerged onto Rue Saint-Denis, the major north-south artery of Paris's Right Bank, crowded even on a Sunday morning with churchgoers. A half-dozen carriages were lined up in front of the church awaiting the exit of the wealthiest worshipers; Milady de Winter's elegant white rig was conspicuous among them.

Fontrailles instinctively turned left, toward the older, denser quarters of the city, like a hare heading for a thicket. This sent him along the line of carriages, of which Milady's was the last. A glance over his shoulder showed him the grinning Cocodril close behind him, but looking beyond him and beckoning subtly. Louis looked ahead and saw Milady's waiting coachman nod in reply to Cocodril's gesture. He uncrossed his arms and moved to block Fontrailles's retreat.

Fontrailles glanced back at Cocodril, whose hand was already on the hilt of his knife and whose intentions were written clearly on his face. *He's going to knife me right here in the street, pick me up when I collapse, and shove me in the carriage with the help of the coachman,* Louis thought, *probably with some loud remark about my "taking suddenly ill." I've got to get* out *of here.*

He was passing the last carriage before Milady's when he suddenly ducked behind the horses and under the driver's seat, just ahead of the front wheels. It was risking a kick from the rear horse's iron-shod hooves, but before the animal realized what was happening Fontrailles had scuttled safely through and was out into the center of the street, followed by the startled shouts of the carriage's driver.

Louis knew that Cocodril was too big to follow him behind the now-riled horse and would have to go around, but he'd gained no more than a few moments by his maneuver. He looked left: a mill-wagon dusted with flour, a fish-cart, a pot-pedlar, a drover pulling on a bellowing donkey—no help. He looked right, and wished he'd looked that way first: a heavy carriage drawn by six straining horses was bearing down on him at speed, the driver waving his whip and shouting at him to get out of the way, as he clearly had no intention of stopping.

Though Fontrailles's bandy legs meant that his typical gait was closer to a waddle than a stride, in his sleep he often dreamed of running smoothly and effortlessly across the countryside, clearing obstacles in great aerial leaps, landing on his toes and taking nimbly to the air again with perfect athletic mastery. For Louis, the next few seconds took on something of the quality of one of those dreams. With the heavy horses, suddenly magnified to become the largest things in the universe, thundering down on him, all fear drained out of him, time seemed to slow, and he simply bounded forward in an impossibly long leap.

As the horses plunged past something clipped him on the right shoulder and he spun clockwise to face the speeding carriage—which bore, he noted absently, the arms of the mighty Prince de Condé. Louis coolly took a half step back so that the wheels of the carriage passed in front of him, missing him by the width of a thumb but blowing off his new hat. As the rear wheel passed he noticed that the servant-step on the back of the carriage was unoccupied, so with seemingly all the time in the world he reached out, grabbed the vertical rail on the rear corner of the cab and swung smoothly aboard, planting his feet on the platform. Casually gripping the opposite rail with his other hand, he noticed they were passing Milady's carriage, and he saw Cocodril staring open-mouthed at him before disappearing in the princely carriage's cloud of dust. Louis almost waved.

Then the carriage hit a bump with a bone-jarring thud, nearly knocking Fontrailles from his perch, and the world abruptly returned to its normal condition of noisy, confusing chaos. Fontrailles shifted his hands to get a better grip on the rails, coughed in the spraying dust, shook his hair out of his eyes, and realized that his right shoulder hurt like hell. He was rapidly losing strength in that arm; was something broken? If his grip weakened he could fall off, risking serious injury. How far could the driver hurtle down Rue Saint-Denis at this breakneck pace without committing wholesale murder?

In fact, they were almost to the Grand Châtelet before the driver reined in to keep from massacring the worshipers streaming out of the church of Saint-Jacques-la-Boucherie. As the carriage slowed to a stop, Fontrailles slid gratefully off the rear platform and into the street. He staggered out of the traffic and leaned against the corner of a shop, trying to catch his breath. His right arm from shoulder to wrist was cramping up; he tried to rotate it and was rewarded with a stabbing pain from the front of his shoulder between the joint and his neck. He felt the area gingerly with the fingers of his left hand and decided his right collarbone was fractured; it must have happened when he'd been struck by the Condé carriage's lead horse.

Fontrailles was no stranger to pain; he was irritated far more by the idea of losing the use of one arm. Devil take it! As if he didn't have enough trouble already! He grimaced and looked around. Where to go now?

He was completely filthy from sweat, dust, and horse-spit, and felt somehow that he wouldn't be able to think straight until he washed his face. But water cost money in overcrowded Paris, and he wasn't about to pay a water-seller when he was only steps from the Seine.

He considered: his most direct route to the river was Rue Saint-Leufroy, which tunneled straight through the grim medieval fortress of the Châtelet, prisons on one side, the city morgue on the other. Louis shuddered, and decided to take Rue Pierre-à-Poisson around the citadel's west side, even though this meant going through the fish market and (even worse) across the Vallée de Misère, past the abattoirs where butchers worked around the clock slaughtering the thousands of animals needed every day to supply the great city with fresh meat.

He went anyway. As he passed the slaughterhouses, the cries of dying livestock and the metallic reek of fresh blood reminded Fontrailles of the threat of Cocodril and his sharp, slender knife. *He knows I'm friendly with the musketeers, and might find me if I return to Tréville's stables,* he thought. *Curse the rogue! What a fool I was to think I could master such a man just because I'm of noble blood.* Clutching his right arm to immobilize it, he made his way across the butcher's plaza to the stone-paved quay and carefully descended the narrow stairway to the riverbank. *Water,* he thought. *Water on my face, and I'll be able to think again.*

At the bottom of the stairs the world spun around him for a moment and he stumbled, then steadied himself and started across the dried mud toward the brown swirling Seine. Without warning, a hand clamped onto his right shoulder and stopped him short. He cried out in surprise and pain, and twisted to see Cocodril grinning down at him with a hundred teeth, each one gleaming like the blade he held in his other hand.

"How nice to see you again, Monsieur de Fontrailles!" Cocodril said. "I have something I've saved just for you."

And his knife-hand stabbed forward like a striking snake.

Continued in **The Three Monks of Tears** *(The Rose Knight's Crucifixion #2)*

By Lawrence Ellsworth

AUTHOR'S NOTE

The author had a grand time writing this novel, and has dozens of fascinating historical notes that he would love to share with its readers … but this book is long enough as is. For those who are interested, historical notes and many other fine features can be found at the author's website, **swashbucklingadventures.com**.

The early adventures of the first Sir Percy Blakeney are chronicled in two novels by his creator, Baroness Emmuska Orczy: *The Laughing Cavalier* (1914) and *The First Sir Percy* (1921).

OTHER BOOKS YOU MAY ENJOY

The Three Musketeers
The First Book of the Musketeers Cycle
By Alexandre Dumas
Translated by Lawrence Ellsworth

The Red Sphinx
The Second Book of the Musketeers Cycle
By Alexandre Dumas
Translated by Lawrence Ellsworth

The Big Book of Swashbuckling Adventure
Edited and Introduced by Lawrence Ellsworth

The above all published by
Pegasus Books of New York and London

Printed in Great Britain
by Amazon

79343782R00139